HEADS I WIN;
TAILS YOU LOSE

by

Lynne Fox

AN M-Y BOOKS PAPERBACK

© Copyright 2019
Lynne Fox

The right of **Lynne Fox** to be identified as the author of
This work has been asserted by him in accordance with the
Copyright, Designs and Patents Act 1988

A CIP catalogue record for this title is
available from the British Library

ISBN (Print): 978-1-911124-92-4
ISBN (epub): 978-1-911124-93-1

For my parents and my son, Elliott

ACKNOWLEDGEMENTS

Thanks to the team at Cornerstones Literary Consultancy whose guidance and advice helped me hone a promising draft into something so much better. To my readers, Pauline Newstead, Susan Hubbard and Anna Henderson for being prepared to give up their time to keep me on track. To John Fisher for pushing me to actually finish something for once and for his enduring patience and faith in my abilities. I cannot thank you enough. Also to my brother, Dr John Sadd, for his practical support and encouragement.

My love and appreciation to you all.

Lynne Fox

CHAPTER 1

'Vengeance is mine, I will repay, saith the Lord.'

Well, I tried to let the Lord choose the time but I do feel I've waited long enough. It isn't as if I haven't given Him enough time; it's been *seventeen years!* For someone so omnipotent, I would have thought that was more than enough but apparently not.

As a child I believed that Divine Intervention would balance the books if I just prayed long enough and hard enough. I went to church twice *every* Sunday for years; my head bowed, my knees dimpled with patterns from the heavily embroidered hassocks, the words of my prayers so familiar that I could feel their form in my mouth like soothing sweets but as time passed the words only seared like bitter lemons.

So, I no longer ape the contrite humility of the congregation, passively waiting for celestial intervention; instead, I've taken matters into my own hands. After all, there's only so much disillusionment a girl can take.

I was nine when our family tragedy happened; too young then to actively pursue revenge. It was a difficult pill for me to swallow but swallow it I did and I learnt to play the long game.

The 'long game' is something DCI Munroe has little time for. All those years ago, when he was merely a Detective Sergeant, it was clear, even to my young eyes, that he was a man driven by his need to succeed; to gain results and quickly.

As he had walked the path to our front door, the darkening sky had unburdened itself of a summer squall so that he stood in the centre of our lounge, slowly dripping into the carpet. I watched, fascinated, as a thin stream of water ran down from the hair plastered to his forehead and onto his nose before gathering, a glistening orb, suspended at the tip. I silently counted the seconds until it dropped.

Tall, almost six foot and painfully thin, Munroe had exceptionally wide shoulders, his torso tapering to a narrow waist and hips giving the impression of an inverted triangle delicately balancing on its point yet this seeming fragility belied an overpowering presence. The scent of pipe tobacco, exaggerated by the damp that had infused his clothes and person, reminded me of decaying leaf mould, as though he'd just wriggled out from under some lichen-covered stone.

My family shrank under his scrutiny, pressed back into their seats; Mother alternately twisting her handkerchief or dabbing theatrically at her eyes; Father varying between expressions of incredulity at what Munroe was saying and querying looks of doubt in my brother, Matt's direction. Matt, blank-faced, simply looked stunned and I? I was ignored; a thing of no consequence, barely acknowledged.

Since then, Munroe has never been far from my consciousness. Through the ensuing years of schooling, on to my degree course and then to my current employment at a Further Education college, the desire for revenge has never left me.

During the early years I could do little more than scrutinise the local police website and local papers, cutting out or making notes of any references to DS Munroe; all such snippets kept in a box on top and at the very back of my wardrobe. Yet time, as it passes, brings with it new opportunities, new solutions.

I grew up and as I grew DS Munroe moved up the ranks, eventually becoming a DCI and moving to where we both now live. Endover is a leafy suburb approximately fifteen miles from central London that boasts a police HQ covering three counties. Although the residential areas have slowly increased, expanding outwards, the town centre has remained relatively compact so it's not unusual to encounter people you know or, at least, recognise when out and about. Lawns, flowerbeds and several benches adorn the walking precincts tempting shoppers to stop and linger on warm summer days; a theme taken up by the cafes and pubs encouraging al fresco dining.

The police HQ is situated on the outskirts of town, flanked on one side by a sports stadium and on the other by a man-made lake that provides some of the gentler water sports, along with fishing and wildlife reserve. I wonder if Munroe pays these benefits any attention at all.

I moved in autumn to the staccato of crisp leaves disintegrating under my feet as I trudged up the path to my rented apartment, carrying my few belongings. I became settled during early morning mists that lingered, hanging in heavy droplets on boughs denuded of leaves. I watched Munroe and his family in their new home during the first few months of winter as we all hunkered down against the biting winds and I bided my time.

Almost two years have now passed since Munroe and I moved so why, you may ask, have I not completed my task? I've wondered that myself, but it really isn't that easy. If I were the Almighty I could have just cremated him with a massive lightning strike, wiped my hands and had a cup of tea – job done – but, for a mere mortal, things are somewhat more complex.

I've read lots of things about how other people have done it; poisoning, a car accident, pushed under a train, shot, stabbed, strangled, suffocated – Man's ingenuity when faced with disposing of another is amazing but as I reviewed the options and played out likely scenarios in my head, I came to realise that I didn't want him dead; I want him to suffer – years of suffering and to achieve that will require a degree of subtlety.

It's cold in the park this lunch time. I tuck my coat tighter around my legs to fend off the spiteful wind. I guess it is a bit silly spending my lunch break here on such a day, the library would have been cosier, but I need the isolation, I need to think, to focus and I'm always so easily distracted. Like now, I can't take my eyes off a snail that's making its laborious way along the ground at my feet, its tell-tale trail of slime glistening in the cold sunlight, repulsively beautiful. I raise my foot, hover my shiny new boot above it, tantalisingly close. The snail, oblivious, continues on its way until I bring my foot down with clinical precision, smashing its shell into myriad pieces, leaving the snail naked and writhing in the wreckage of its home. I can't help smiling at the analogy it represents.

I settle back on the bench, pulling up my collar a little further, sinking down into the folds of the cashmere scarf that had been a grabbed-for afterthought as I'd hurried from the college. I like this area of the park, even on a day like today. It isn't used very much, probably because it seems to form a dead end and it isn't as manicured as the main areas but it's well away from the playground so always affords some quiet; a cherished interlude from the hubbub of college life.

The whole area is bordered by a mixture of deciduous and evergreen trees and autumn is once again painting the canvas with her vibrant colours. Rhododendrons and azaleas have been allowed to run rampant, smothering smaller plants yet I know that under their foliage a mass of crocuses and snowdrops are waiting in the cold earth, ready to assert them come spring.

Lost in my daydreaming, something nudges my subconscious making me stiffen slightly, all my senses on full alert. I glance about me but nothing seems to have changed and then I notice the smell, sickly, cloying with an underlay of stale urine. I turn to my right to look behind me when a hand grips my left shoulder. Turning instinctively toward it I'm startled by a dirty, sore-rimmed mouth inches from my own.

I cringe, bringing my hands up to my nose, desperately trying to block out the stench of stale cigarette smoke and alcohol. 'Get off me!' I twist my body violently away, wrenching free from the nicotine-stained talons that are digging into my shoulder. The tramp makes another grab at me. His long nails catch on my scarf and for one terrifying second I fear he's going to use it to strangle me. With a strength I wasn't aware I possess I grab hold of my scarf and wrench it free. He stumbles as I yank it from his grip and grabs for the back of the bench to steady himself. I don't wait around but dart forward, my bag flying open behind me and I don't slow down until I reach the main entrance to the park.

Supporting myself on one of the brick pillars that form elaborate gate posts, heaving air into my lungs, I can see the tramp hasn't followed me. I can't believe I managed to run so fast, especially in my new, knee-high boots with the three inch heels. I glance down. The toes are badly scuffed and one heel seems a little loose, damaged by my sprint. The bastard! I only bought them last week!

I look up and glare in the tramp's direction. He's arguing with someone. I can't make out whom, as the tramp's shielding my view, but his anger is unmistakable; arms flailing, body pitching forward, his raised voice a guttural slur, the words indistinct at this distance. He raises his arm, I think to strike but no, it's a futile defensive move. He slumps to the ground and I see one of my students, Barry Mason, standing over him.

Barry remains for a second or two, apparently transfixed by the body of the tramp lying at his feet then seems to pull himself together, throwing the rock he's holding deep into the overgrown herbaceous border that forms a backdrop to the bench.

He turns his gloved hands palm up, inspects them and then, brushing them off, turns and looks in my direction. I cower behind the brick pillar, unsure whether he's noticed me but his gaze seems distracted. He gives a shrug of resignation and turns, walking behind the bench and disappears into the foliage.

I remain where I am for a minute, maybe longer, expecting Barry to reappear but he doesn't. I'm puzzled. There must be another way out of the park behind the overgrown border that I'm unaware of.

So many questions are hurtling around my mind. Why did Barry assault the tramp? How long had he been there? Did he see the tramp accost me? Does he know the tramp? I wonder if I should go back, see if the tramp is alright. If I were a good citizen I should get on my mobile and inform the police, call for an ambulance. I look down again at my ruined, expensive boots.

I glance at my watch, almost two o'clock and I'm due to teach at two thirty. I sling my bag over my shoulder and, without a backward glance, hobble on my wonky heel back to the college.

CHAPTER 2

I spend a lot of time thinking because I'm naturally logical and methodical and I like to plan; a belt, braces and piece of string person. I know this is irrational as no-one can plan for *every* eventuality but, nonetheless, I have to try because it's all part of the game I set myself; the challenge; my reason to exist.

I cast my mind back over the years and visualise myself sitting on the stairs, my arms hugging my knees, folding in upon myself for comfort. I can just see my parents in our lounge, framed by the edge of the door and the wall; like a tableau of idyllic married life. They'd been drinking, they often did, and as always with them the booze raised voices and loosened tongues. It was then I discovered that I was a Mistake; an error of judgement; something to be marginalised and preferably ignored.

I didn't understand it at the time; I was only six, so I went to Matt, my big brother. He looked at me kind of funny and turned his head away, then suddenly swung round, grabbing me and throwing me onto his bed, tickling and telling me I was so gorgeous he wanted to eat me! I giggled and squirmed and shrieked and the moment passed but its undertone, the sense of something wrong, of an unjustified unkindness, lodged deep in my subconscious. Like a festering boil it swelled as the years passed until I discovered the means to lance it. The game I play is my scalpel and I now wield it with ruthless precision.

I pour myself a large glass of Chenin Blanc and curl up on the sofa with my album memories of Matt. Closing my eyes I recall the afternoon I'd found the album.

A young girl, my world had irrevocably changed; my brother had recently died so, as a way of keeping him with me, I decide I will make an album of Matt's life. I traipse round the usual book stores but lack of enough cash and the seeming sterility of new books soon has me making my way to my favourite bookstore; the second hand bookshop at the top of the hill.

Once a dwelling house of some standing, the former home of a local dignitary, its front two rooms are now filled floor to ceiling with shelves crammed so tightly it's often difficult to extract the items you want.

Using my shoulder for leverage, I push against the resistance of the entrance door's strong spring and stumble down the step into the shop, the jangling of the brass bell discordantly announcing my arrival. As the door wrenches itself free of my grasp it slams back into its frame, dislodging a shower of fine dust that floats gracefully in the sunlight before settling on every surface within reach, including me.

I stand for a second, breathing in the muskiness of aged paper, sensing the inherent dampness of the building brush against my warm skin and absorbing the fecund silence of millions of words caught between covers, waiting to be released once more into human consciousness.

I pass swiftly through the front rooms on my familiar route out into the back garden where, in summer, a round metal table and chairs and a couple of wooden benches allow customers to sit and browse for as long as they please. The garden rises quite steeply via a crazy-paved path to an outbuilding, little more than a glorified shed, but it holds treasures that have entranced me since Matt had first brought me here on my eighth birthday to choose my gift. It was only fitting that I should end my search here.

The outbuilding houses a miscellany of items that have mostly seen better days; dejected looking works with worn covers, dog-eared pages sometimes defaced with comments by previous readers but it was this that, to Matt's amusement, I loved.

Browsing through these old, discarded tomes, I find thoughts scribbled in the margins, corners of pages turned down to mark points of interest, sometimes phrases underlined or highlighted and I feel I have a window into other minds; I observe without being observed. It's a good feeling.

It's the album's cover that catches my eye; worn leather, the charcoal-brown of singed toast etched with a filigree of fine lines, like tiny veins. Under the caress of my fingers it feels warm, a living thing. I lift it to my nose and inhale the dust of years, its animal and human scent. Inside are black pages made of an absorbent substance, reminding me of blotting paper but more substantial; here and there photograph corner tabs remain glued to the pages, with occasional annotations in white ink, written in a beautiful copper-plate hand; sad reminders of someone else's treasured memories.

'Y'know, you could use a bit of Dubbin on that cover; real leather it is, high quality once. Just needs a bit of TLC to stop it cracking any further.'

The bookseller, his skin as crazed as the cover of the album, leans in toward me, his fingers gently brushing the album surface as he speaks.

'How much is it?'

He takes it from my hands and turns to the inside back cover.

'Five pounds.'

Carefully, I count out the coins from my purse.

'Oh, I've only got four.'

My voice breaks in disappointment as I hold out my hand, the coins displayed as evidence. He looks at my outstretched palm, its contents shining in a shaft of light from the open door and reaching out, scrapes the coins toward him with yellowed nails; a chicken scratching in the dirt.

'That'll do, young lady.'

I turn, hugging the album to my chest and step out into the winter sunshine. As I round the corner, out of sight of the second hand book shop and its owner, I pop into the sweet shop and spend my salvaged pound.

I've been adding photos and cuttings to the album since my brother's death. Matt, fifteen years old, holding me as a baby, looking for all the world more like a proud father than my sibling; Matt pushing me on the garden swing; Matt helping me balance on my first bike; Matt teaching me tennis; Matt always there; where my parents should have been and then …. No more photos, just newspaper cuttings with sensational headlines; grainy images that blur the chiselled line of his jaw and dull the startling blue of his eyes as though he was already drifting away from me, fading into that "long goodnight" from which there is no return.

I pour myself another glass of Chenin Blanc as I take some stir fry out of the fridge; it will go nicely with the piece of fresh salmon I bought on the way home. I find preparing food a relaxing, therapeutic activity, it acts as a balm to my over-active mind which at the moment is fixated upon Barry. I keep musing about how events can completely alter one's perception of people.

For instance, Barry stands just over six feet; he has a shock of black, permanently tousled hair and the deepest, darkest eyes fringed with lashes that girls spend hours trying to achieve with layers of mascara. His skin has darkened to an attractive bronze by all the hours he spends outside and he has a lean, toned body that attracts all the college females, both staff and students, something to which I'm not immune myself.

Barry has been in my class for the past six months. Learning about art history is not his main subject, he's actually on the Small Animal and Wildlife Course but under the ethos of our Principal, Paul Whitlow, all students are compelled to take a subject outside their main area of interest. The Principal apparently believes this will turn them into more 'rounded' members of society. Complete rot of course but who am I to argue.

Just why Barry chose art history became apparent one afternoon when he asked if I could give him some additional help.

Being new at the college I was keen to make a good impression and my desire to please over-rid my better judgement. As Barry and I sat in the empty classroom, his text book open on the desk before us, Barry moved his chair closer to mine and leant so close that his face was only inches away from my own. His breath smelt of sweet peppermint and his aftershave had a heady, musky base that elicited a slight fluttering of response deep in my belly.

'You know, you have the most beautiful eyes.'

I look up into Barry's face and calmly appraise him. 'Thank you, Barry but you really shouldn't say things like that. Now, what were you having difficulty with?' I prodded the book.

'Keeping my eyes off you, what else?'

'I think you'd better stop, Barry, before you embarrass yourself.'

'I'm not embarrassed. Are you?'

I pushed my chair back and stood, trying to assume some authority, which isn't easy when you stand a diminutive five feet three. 'Out, Barry,' I said walking past him and opening the door.

He obediently rose from his chair and made toward me, 'See you tomorrow,' his smile both inviting and seductive.

I wasn't surprised that Barry fancied me, most men do, especially as I look younger than my twenty-six years, but I was quite confident that I had the measure of him – just a cocky little oik trying it on – until now that is.

The morning after my lunchtime encounter with the tramp I arrive early for my class to find the room abuzz with excited chatter. This is a small group of only ten students and all but one are in a conclave of animated conversation.

'So, what's got everybody's interest this morning?'

The group reluctantly break formation and take their seats.

'Haven't you heard the news?' Terri Westacott leans forward on her desk, her long hair pooling on the surface in front of her, a shimmering cascade of barley yellow.

'What news is that, Terri?'

'The murder in Melsham Park.'

'What?' The surprise spills the exclamation from my lips and my eyes dart over to where Barry Mason is sitting. Immediately, I switch my gaze back to Terri but not before I catch a flicker of concern flit across Barry's face.

Barry sits silent, his chair tipped onto its hind legs, but I sense his attention is focused in my direction.

'I bet it's that tramp that's been hanging about the college grounds.' This time it's Stephen Blake who takes up the tale.

I swallow hard. 'And what makes you think that, Stephen?'

'Cos he's not there this morning and he's been hanging around for a couple of weeks now. Haven't you seen him?'

I vaguely recall seeing a shadowy figure lurking near the woods that form the right hand boundary of the college grounds but I hadn't associated it with the tramp that had so frightened me. 'I think it's a bit early to be surmising as to who it is but I'm sure we'll all find out in time, once the police have completed their enquiries. Now, can we get down to some work please?'

There's a resigned shuffling of bodies as books are tossed heavily onto desks.

I find it difficult to keep the lesson on track as my mind is racing. It seems I may have a murderer sitting in my class who may or may not know that I was a witness to his act. Cautiously, I observe Barry during the lesson. He seems unruffled by the earlier exchange but that could just be bravado.

A murder investigation will undoubtedly be instigated which will surely involve DCI Munroe. If the body in the park is that of the tramp, then I have a hold over Barry that could prove useful but I need to take time and think things through. Munroe has a daughter, Lily, on whom he dotes and she's about Barry's age. Maybe, if I can get the two together … a DCI's daughter and a murderer. I can feel a slight smirk develop as the idea gels but first I need to find out more about Barry.

I can't deny that the end of session bell is a relief and in my haste to leave I drop some of the papers I'm collecting up. As I bend to retrieve them a large pair of Nike trainers clamp down on top of them. Barry bends down to my level and looks straight into my eyes, a searching, penetrating stare. 'I'll help you with those.' He gathers up the papers and hands them to me, holding on to them just a fraction longer than is necessary so that I have to practically tug them out of his hand. 'Seems like it would be a good idea to stop going to the park for a while, yeah?'

'Thank you for your advice, Barry. I'll bear it in mind.'

I can't think he'd be quite so cocky if he does know what I'd witnessed.

At home that evening, I review events. Let's face it, I don't know yet if the body in the park is that of the tramp, for all I know he may have only been stunned from the blow and I didn't go and find out, did I? In any case, why would Barry want to kill him? Admittedly they appeared to be having an argument but that, in itself, is hardly a reason to kill.

◆

Everyone has an Achilles heel; locate it and you have the means to manipulate.

I realise now how little I know about any of my students; they've simply been voids that I try to fill with the requirements of the curriculum. I need to rectify this especially where Barry is concerned.

Mulling things over, I'd bet my salary that the body in the park *is* that of the tramp, it's too much of a coincidence not to be but I can't accept that Barry's attack upon the tramp was simply a random act; perhaps there's something in Barry's background that precipitated such violence. If I'm to manipulate him I need to understand what makes him tick. Just attempting to blackmail him with my knowledge of his crime may not be enough. I need to know which buttons to press.

Barry's personnel file at the college seems the most logical place to start but I know the Principal's secretary, Janet Stevenson, guards all such information with the tenacity of a bulldog so it's not a simple case of merely asking to view the file, she'll undoubtedly demand a detailed explanation of why. Somehow, she must be distracted and removed from the office.

Walking from the college car park the following day I notice some lads hanging about the bicycle sheds and have a 'light bulb' moment. Going straight to Janet's office I inflect genuine concern into my voice.

'Janet, did you come on your bike this morning?' I know that she did, she always does.

'Yes, why?'

'Well, I don't want to worry you but I think some lads are doing something to your bike.'

'What! The little shits!' Thrusting back her chair Janet moves with surprising speed considering her immense bulk, such that I have to press myself against the wall to avoid being knocked over as she storms out the door.

Quickly, I open the cabinet drawer. Janet is meticulous in her filing and labelling so locating Barry's file only takes a few seconds. I scan its contents; the most interesting entry being that against Next of Kin where is entered 'Foster Parents'. I quickly scribble a note of their address and Barry's current address and mobile number. There's no time for anything else, I can hear Janet puffing back down the corridor and hastily make my exit before she returns.

I'm fortunate that today is my slack day for teaching and I've the whole of the afternoon free. I spend some time in a quiet corner of the college library with my laptop, devising a brief questionnaire and flyer.

Returning home I study my wardrobe. As a child I always enjoyed dressing up, pretending to be someone else, creating an imaginary world over which I had control. Now, as an adult, I find the skills I practised back then pay dividends. I eventually choose a smart business suit and low heels. The blonde wig and specs complete the picture. Inclining my head in greeting I admire my reflection. It always astonishes me how so little can create such a transformation.

Barry's address is on the outskirts of town, a little way out in the countryside. I hate this kind of rural driving, finding that I'm holding my breath every time I negotiate a blind bend. I just know that at some point

I'm going to encounter a tractor taking up the whole road and will have to back up for miles.

I don't know what I expect to find but it isn't the rough looking smallholding in front of me. I can see a few goats, hens and a couple of pigs milling about a large enclosure. The house is a two up, two down farm cottage but without the proverbial roses around the door, chocolate box image. Glancing up, the roof tiles are moss covered and in places, clumps of grasses poke their heads above the guttering. Heavy rains must cascade over the side, my assumption evidenced by a three feet wide shadow of damp running down the wall to the left of the front door.

The windows, small paned and sash, are blind with grime; it must be like looking out through cataracts, images clouded and indistinct. Wreathed in an air of neglect the cottage strikes me as a shelter of necessity rather than a home. Just looking at it makes me feel depressed.

I coast past in my car a couple of times; there doesn't seem to be anyone about and the lane is equally deserted; the house standing beside the one straight piece of road in an otherwise tortuous and narrow country lane. What shall I do? I can't keep driving backwards and forwards like this, it's ridiculous; oh, but all that muck! I grit my teeth and on the third pass I will myself to turn in at the gate. The car tyres squelch in the cloying mud. For god's sake, I only had this cleaned yesterday!

Pulling up as close to the front door as I'm able in an attempt to walk as short a distance as possible I open the car door and gingerly start to step out when the sound of bird song is shattered by vicious snarls and barks. Two Doberman hurtle toward me from around the side of the building. Christ! I throw myself back into the car as a waft of rancid, warm breath caresses my face just as I slam the door. Jumping up, teeth bared and slobbering on the glass, their attack instinct borders on insanity.

Oh God, where are my keys? I duck down and rummage in the footwell. I can't see or feel them anywhere and then I realise, I must have dropped them outside. The dogs are still frantically jumping up and clawing at the door. I'd like to smash their heads in.

The cottage door opens and a man in his mid-fifties, swarthy and solid-framed, steps out, carrying hunks of raw meat. 'Hitler! Goering!' He slings the meat over towards the shed and the two dogs vanish as swiftly as they'd arrived.

As he saunters over my skin creeps as though a thousand tiny insects are running over me. He leans down, one hand supporting himself on the roof of my car and motions me to lower the window. I give the briefest shake of my head as I stare wide-eyed into his unrelenting gaze. He dips slightly, reaching down and comes up dangling my keys at the glass. 'If you want to drive out of here, you'd better open the window, luv.' His mouth creases into a sarcastic smirk as his gravelly voice vibrates through the car.

Reluctantly I lower the window a couple of inches and put my hand up for the keys. The man dangles them just beyond my reach, his hand carrying the smell of dead meat, bringing bile up into my throat. 'Not until you tell me why you're here.'

I make a huge effort to swallow and give what I desperately hope is an appealing and conciliatory smile. 'Is this where Barry lives?'

'Who wants to know?'

'I'm from West Park College. He has this address on his personnel file.'

'Then I should think it's a fair bet that this is where he lives, wouldn't you, luv?'

My hackles rise at his sarcasm but I bite my lip.

The man lets out an exasperated sigh, 'Look, luv, this isn't getting us anywhere. Why don't you just step out of the car? I'm not going to hurt you, I promise. The dogs won't bother you while I'm here and *my* bark is definitely worse than my bite.' His face creases into a grin that is mirrored in the crinkles of his eyes; a deceptive yet enticing transformation. He takes a couple of steps back from my car door and holds out his hands in a beckoning stance.

My mind is racing. I can't drive off as he still has my keys and, in any case, to leave having learnt nothing would make the whole escapade futile. Taking a deep breath I treat him to my most winning smile and, opening the door, gingerly step out, trying my best to avoid the mud. In very gentlemanly fashion he takes my hand to steady me as I attempt to negotiate a large puddle just beside the car's front wheels. 'Sorry,' he says, 'forgot my cloak.' His grin widens. Smart arse! I'd like to wipe that smirk off his face.

Inside the cottage the kitchen initially seems surprisingly clean and cheerful yet a quick scan reveals that this is merely surface gloss. The tea towel hanging on the cooker could do with a good wash and the dishcloth on the draining board is so grey it should have been condemned to the waste bin weeks ago. The floor is grimed and the tiled splash back to the cooker is speckled with grease spatters. That and a blackened pan on the top of the stove suggest that fry-ups are the main culinary skill of this household.

The man motions me to a chair at the table where I sit and remove my laptop from its case, setting it on the table in business-like manner.

'Tea?' He has the kettle in his hand and I note that he makes his way quite slowly across the kitchen to the sink taking in my appearance as he moves. I can tell he approves of what he sees.

'That would be lovely, thank you. Perhaps I might explain why I'm here.'

'Sounds like a good idea.'

'As I mentioned, I'm from West Park College and Barry has been nominated for an award – he's one of our brightest students – and I'm gathering some information on him ready for an article should he win. I'm visiting all the nominees. I wonder if you could tell me a little about Barry's background.'

I shuffle a little on my seat, placing my fingers lightly on the keyboard in readiness to type his response.

'No.'

I'm not adept at dealing with such rudeness. I press my lips into a tight line trying to control the urge to snap back.

'Well, perhaps you wouldn't mind, at least, telling me how you came to know him and how he came to lodge with you.'

'Why don't you ask Barry?'

'I just said; he's been nominated for an award. We don't want him or any of the other candidates to know just yet. It would spoil the surprise and possibly raise false hopes.'

The man sighs, his exasperation evident.

'Look, luv, I may be a bit rough round the edges but I'm not chewing on a piece of straw. I don't know why you want to know these things about Barry but you're not going to get any of it off me so I think you'd better just drink your tea and leave.'

For the briefest moment our eyes lock, assessing each other's determination. Deciding the brute won't be swayed I choose to change tack. Slowly folding down my laptop screen I smile sweetly.

'I'm sorry you don't feel able to answer my questions but I'd very much appreciate it if you didn't tell Barry about my visit. This is the first year the college have given out this award and we'd like to keep it quiet until we're much nearer making a final decision.'

'I'll think about it.' He moves to rinse his mug in the sink, 'Bloody hell, stay there, I've got an escapee.'

As he races outside I make a very risky split-second decision. I'm *not* going to endure the indignity of all this simply to leave empty-handed. Swiftly I make my way upstairs; opening the first door on the small landing I find I've hit the jackpot. I recognise immediately Barry's leather jacket hanging over the back of a chair; the phoenix motif drawn on the back had caused quite a stir the first time he'd worn it to college.

There's a single bed pressed up against one wall looking as if its occupant has just rolled out, a chest of drawers, a single wardrobe and a table he's obviously using as a writing desk. The floor is mainly exposed boards with a rug by the bed. The one window looks out over the front garden from where I can see the man trying to shepherd one of the pigs back into the enclosure.

Hurriedly, I open the drawers, careful to replace the clothing as I find it. Under a pile of shirts my fingers touch something shiny, a photograph. A woman and boy, presumably Barry and his mother; Barry would have been about five years old. The woman is pretty in a fragile way but there's a sadness and fear in her eyes that belies the smile on her lips. I carefully replace it. There seems to be little else of interest or use to me until my eye is drawn to the book open on the table. I know I'm not one for wildlife and animals but the illustrations in the book are quite exquisite.

Despite the risk of remaining too long, I find myself turning the pages, enthralled by the artistry. Flicking to the front of the book I see a handwritten inscription: 'For Barry Howden, happy memories. John Simpson.' Simpson is the name of the author/illustrator but who's Barry Howden? I turn to the back cover where there's a brief profile informing me that John Simpson lives in Sheffield.

Glancing out the window I see the pig is back in its enclosure, but Jesus, where's he gone? The man's nowhere to be seen. I lean on the window cill trying to get a better view, my nose pressed up against the glass, momentarily forgetting caution in my desire to locate him. Where the hell is he? I turn and race out of the room, vaulting down the stairs and just manage to be sitting at the table finishing my tea when he re-enters. I stand immediately. 'Well, I don't want to take up any more of your time. Thank you for the tea. May I have my car keys please?'

He places them in my hand. 'I'll walk you back to your car so you don't have to worry about the dogs.'

Trying to get the car into reverse I manage to crunch the gears. 'There's a whole box of them in there somewhere, luv!' He's grinning from ear to ear, laughing at my discomfort; a slight I won't forget.

Once out on the lane I press my foot down on the accelerator, anger making me reckless as I take the blind bends at ridiculous speeds but I won't let this one little setback throw me off course.

By the time I arrive home I've calmed down enough to be able to assess the small amount of information I've garnered. I've discovered the oddity of the name in the book on his desk, 'Barry Howden' as opposed to Barry Mason but all that tells me is that he might have changed his name. The annoying thing is, I didn't get time to note down his foster parents name from his personnel file and I can't recall what I read – damn! Even so, it doesn't tell me why; alternatively, it might not even be him! I'm also wondering why he should choose to leave his foster parents to live in such conditions; perhaps it's to gain hands-on experience in animal husbandry. Maybe I'll chat with Ben, Barry's tutor on the Small Animal and Wildlife course, see if he can provide some insight.

Next morning at college I learn that while I was off, police officers were there talking with students, trying to find out more about the tramp and why he might have been hanging about the college.

I'm heading towards the staff room when Janet, the Principal's secretary, corners me. A disproportionately large woman, her hips and buttocks are so oversized they seem to lower her centre of gravity so that when she walks she sways from side to side like a Silverback gorilla. I find myself pressed against the wall as she leans in towards me, eyes narrowed into a penetrating stare. I flinch and turn my head to one side attempting to avoid her garlic-tinged breath.

'The police want to speak with you; asked for you specifically.' The sneer in her tone is unmistakable and my hand itches to slap her face.

'Really? In what connection?'

'That tramp who's been hanging about the college; they've been talking to everyone.'

'I don't know what they think I can tell them.'

'That's what I wondered but they definitely asked for *you*.'

I keep my voice steady and smile pleasantly, 'I expect they just want to tick me off their list if they're speaking to everyone.'

'Mmm, possibly, thought I'd better just let you know though, so you can get your story straight.'

'Story? Why should you think I need a story?'

'Well, you're the one in the park most lunch times, although, as I told the police, I can't think why, especially in this cold weather. That's somewhere else he went, apparently, so I guess that makes you more interesting than the rest of us. There's no need to look at me like that; I was only trying to help with their enquiries. That isn't a problem, is it?'

'No, why should it be? Are they here now? Perhaps I ought to speak with them, clear this up.'

Janet gives a shrug and turns away. 'I expect they'll get in touch with you when they're ready,' she smirks, 'I gave them your address.'

Gritting my teeth, I watch Janet's bulk receding down the corridor. I could spit venom.

CHAPTER 3

At eighteen I was no longer an uncoordinated tomboy but had, to the dismay of my mother, morphed into an object of male admiration and desire; a change that I was eager to exploit.

My mother was beside herself with a mixture of disgust and envy.

'Do you *have* to sleep with *all* of them?'

Her raised octave reverberated around the kitchen, bouncing off the metal saucepans hanging from their hooks like a badly tuned set of hand bells. Flapping the tea towel toward my face she used such force it cracked like a whip.

I smiled sweetly.

'No, Mother, I don't have to.'

My most useful conquest materialised whilst I was studying for my degree with the Open University. I'd chosen not to move away, mostly so that I could stay in close proximity to Munroe but also so that I could remain at home.

'But *why?*' my mother wailed, her red-painted lips a livid gash across her face, her features contorted in a paroxysm of frustration.

My father, raising his head from the Financial Times he was reading, said,

'Because she doesn't want to support herself; it's easier and cheaper living at home, isn't it?'

Smiling, I walked up to his chair, placed my arm around his neck and leaning close, purred,

'And because I love you both *so* much.'

My father merely shrugged and returned to his paper.

The boyfriends I bedded were not, as my mother supposed, simply random choices; they were, in fact, chosen with the utmost care; the main criteria being their association with the local police force, whether a member of the ranks, a civilian employee or just someone related in some way.

Of course, not all proved useful but, at the age of twenty and two years into my degree course, I struck lucky.

Mick, four years older than me, was a delightful specimen; blonde, tanned with an engaging smile and easy manner. Obviously comfortable in his own skin he moved with assurance and confidence that I found particularly seductive.

I met him at a police gala day; it was held every year to raise funds for the families of officers injured or killed in the line of duty and I'd made a point of attending since I was fourteen. Mick was explaining to some locals the level of fitness required to be a member of the police force, demonstrating the Dynamic Strength and Endurance or Bleep Test which requires candidates to run to and fro along a fifteen metre track arriving at each end line in time with a series of audio bleeps. He suggested some of those watching give it a try only to shrug his indifference as the onlookers drifted away. I, however, remained.

'I'll give it a go.'

I grinned as I stepped forward.

'That's nice of you but you don't have to pity me, really.'

'I'm not pitying you; at least let me have a go at the Bleep Test, it looks fun. I'm good at running; school's athletic champion two years in a row.'

Mick eyed me up and down and made his decision.

'OK then, gorgeous, you show the lads how to do it. Ready?'

'Yeah!'

I knew I could do it. I'd stolen the practice CD from a previous boyfriend's flat simply because it amused me to give it a try. I can even run it backwards!

'Fancy a coffee?' Mick asked, impressed by my performance, 'it can be your prize for showing more guts than any of these lads.'

'Yeah, that'd be good.'

As we walked toward the refreshment tent I casually enquired,

'How long have you been in the police?'

'Since I was eighteen; I really want to get into CID.'

'Is that difficult?'

'Positions don't come up that often but I might be in luck. One of our DI's has agreed to give me a try; it's a great opportunity.'

'That's brilliant. Congratulations.'

This was the kind of close contact I'd been hoping for and made the ensuing four year relationship with Mick worthwhile. Through him I gleaned snippets of information about Munroe and his family, slowly building up my picture of his work and home life. Nothing particularly earth shattering, you understand; Mick wasn't about to jeopardise his career through idle gossip and I had to be careful to avoid any unwanted probing into my reasons by asking too many questions. Yet it was the little things that helped build up the picture; hearing about Munroe's wedding anniversary and his pleasure at how well his daughter was doing at school, his occasional bad tempers when cases weren't progressing as well as he wanted; innocuous in itself but all useful.

I'd known for some time that Munroe had a daughter; I'd seen them together at a few of the police gala days and picked up her name when he'd called out to her. I'd been following her on Facebook ever since; not that there was usually much of interest until, four years into my relationship with Mick, she was posting whining complaints about the family's impending move to Endover.

Mick confirmed Munroe's promotion and relocation one evening just as we'd started a second bottle of wine and, feeling sorry for himself that, according to him, one of the top detectives was leaving, he'd reached the maudlin stage. His usefulness at an end, I'd dumped him the following week and started to make arrangements for my own move. Mother could hardly disguise her delight.

◆

My encounter with the tramp has left me with a mission to replace my damaged boots. Fortunately Saturday morning turns out to be another of Britain's glorious winter gifts; a clear blue sky with a sun so bright it sparkles off the wet leaves that are burnished to a golden glow. Glistening puddles dot the pavement like jewelled stepping stones as I make my way into the city centre.

I make a beeline for the shop where I bought the original pair but, 'Sorry, we no longer have them in your size,' is a response I did *not* want to hear. 'No, there's nothing else here I'd like to try on, thank you,' and so I begin the laborious task of trudging around every shoe shop I can think of. It's so difficult to settle on anything else when I'd found the pair that I particularly liked. My anger at the tramp increases with each unsuccessful shop visit until, 'Yes, yes, yes, these will do! More expensive than the others but actually, yes, I think I prefer them.'

Sitting in a window seat in Costas, sipping my coffee and enjoying an enormous slice of coffee and walnut cake, I'm feeling quite mellow, at peace with the world when, across the street, I see DCI Munroe. The repugnance and anger of my childhood has matured into a more considered appraisal so that nowadays I'm able to view him with the cool detachment of predator and prey.

He's some distance away but even so is unmistakable. I recognise his walk, a kind of loping gait with his head thrust slightly forward so that one almost expects him to break into a trot. His head is turned slightly to his left and he appears to be in conversation but is blocking my view of the person beside him. However, just at that moment they stop and turn to look into the window of the local cycle shop and I can see who his companion is even though they have their backs to me; it's his daughter, Lily.

Swiftly, I gulp down the last of my coffee, wrap the uneaten portion of cake into a paper napkin and, grabbing my shopping, hurry out of the café and make my way across the divide until I'm on their side of the road, but several yards behind, a place where I can observe but remain unnoticed.

As I follow behind along the High Street, staying back but close enough to overhear most of their conversation, Lily's exasperation is palpable.

'Look, Dad, I want to just pop into the library. I've been told they've some leaflets on evening classes being held locally. I want to see if they've got anything I'd be interested in. Why don't you go over to Dougie's café and I'll see you there in a few minutes.'

Munroe doesn't look too pleased at this suggestion but turns away and heads in the opposite direction. I seize the opportunity and follow Lily into the library foyer where a large table is laid out with piles of various leaflets. As I start flicking through, I deliberately catch my sleeve, knocking a pile onto the floor between us.

'Oh hell! Trust me.'

Lily turns at my exclamation and as I bend down to start scooping them up she kindly joins me.

'Thank you,' I smile, 'I'm so damn clumsy.'

'It happens.'

'Yeah, but why does it always happen to *me*?'

Lily grins warmly as we try to rearrange the mess I've made of the display.

'Loads to choose from,' I remark.

'Yeah, can't really make up my mind. I thought I might go for the watercolour painting; a friend did it last year and reckoned the tutor was brilliant, made it really fun.'

I casually pick up the relevant leaflet and give it a quick read.

'Mmm, maybe; I think I'll take this one home and a couple more and give it some thought. Enrolment's Tuesday, isn't it?'

'Yeah, so you've got time to decide.'

I notice Lily puts the art leaflet into her handbag.

'Bye.'

'Bye and thanks for helping me pick up.'

'No sweat.' and she was gone.

As I make my way home I play the encounter over in my mind. It's the first time I've actually spoken with Lily. She strikes me as a naturally kind and helpful person, a little guileless perhaps but that should make her easier to manipulate. She's definitely attractive; I can only hope that Barry will feel the same.

◆

Tuesday evening comes round surprisingly soon and at six o'clock I'm standing in the college foyer, keeping watch for Lily. Fortunately, the foyer is crammed with posters and leaflets so I'm able to look busy rather than just aimlessly loitering.

It's 6.45 before Lily arrives. She's wearing a bright red tailored coat, the collar turned up against the chill wind, making a striking backdrop to her hair, strands of which lay coiled like copper wires across her shoulders, having escaped from where they had been tucked inside. She strides purposefully across the foyer and into the enrolment hall, her head held high, an unaffected elegance in her movement accentuated by her tall, slim build. Envy almost undoes me as I follow in her wake. I've always yearned to be taller, it's an asset that seems to exude a commanding authority which is difficult to achieve when you constantly have to look up to people.

I hold back until Lily joins the short queue for enrolling in the art class, letting a couple of people join the line before me. As Lily completes her application form and turns to leave I deliberately catch her eye.

'Hi. So you did decide on the watercolour course.'

Lily takes a second to register who I am.

'Oh hi, yeah; my friend almost bullied me into it so it better be as much fun as she reckons or I'll kill her!'

'Too right; I'm hoping I haven't made a mistake but the other things all seemed pretty heavy.'

'Yeah, that's what I thought.'

Lily looks at her watch,

'I must be off. See you at class in January.'

'Absolutely, see you there. Bye.' I watch as Lily moves through the glass doors and out into the December night. I realise how much she reminds me of Addie, Matt's girlfriend. She has the same unguarded openness of the innocent. Not the best asset for survival.

◆

Today at college has been somewhat irksome, my afternoon class more interested in the latest football results than learning about Byzantine art so, despite getting home early, I'm not in the best of moods when there's a gentle tap at my door. I know who it is; Mrs Lewis, my neighbour from across the hall. Widowed a few years ago, she's a tiny, fragile sparrow of a woman, constantly in need of reassurance. To take the edge off my annoyance I take a quick swig of the Cabernet Sauvignon I've just opened and go to the door, my smile plastered on with such determination it feels more like rigor mortis.

Despite being small myself I'm quite a bit taller than Mrs Lewis who resembles a prematurely aged seven year old, so as I open the door I automatically look down to her level and am startled to see she's flanked by two broad bodies. Raising my eyes I know immediately that these are police officers even though they're not in uniform. Something about their demeanour singles them out; that self-assured arrogance of people in authority.

The young one on the left I don't know but the other is as familiar as my own reflection.

'Hello my dear, these gentlemen are police officers, I was just coming in the front door myself when they arrived so I said I'd show them to your apartment. One always likes to help the police when one can.' She beams up at both men in turn.

The one on her left coughs quietly, 'Thank you for your assistance, Mrs Lewis; we can take it from here. Miss Thompson, may we come in?'

I really don't want them in my apartment, invading my privacy and contaminating my personal space.

'What's this about officer?'

'Perhaps we could just come in for a moment?' the other one interrupts, pushes at the door and whispers 'We don't want to give the neighbours a floor show, do we?' He smiles slightly and glances towards Mrs Lewis.

'Very well.' I reluctantly stand back and hold open the door.

'Thank you again, Mrs Lewis.' The young one, as he enters, gently closes the door in Mrs Lewis' disappointed face.

I lead the way into my lounge and deliberately stand with my back to the window through which the bright afternoon winter sun is shining, making it difficult for the officers to see my face clearly.

'Is it bad news?' I conjure a slight, tearful tremble in my voice.

'No, nothing like that, we just need to ask you a few questions. Please don't be alarmed.'

I walk slowly from the back of the sofa and sit facing the officers, making a small gesture with my hand, indicating for them to sit on the seats opposite. 'I'm sorry,' I manage to produce a weak smile, 'it's just I haven't had any dealings with the police before so I just assumed...'

'Perfectly understandable.' The young officer leans forward in a friendly manner, his forearms resting on his knees.

The older man is still standing. He has an air of bored efficiency as though he has done this sort of thing so many times before, which I suppose he probably has.

'Miss Thompson, I'm Detective Chief Inspector Munroe and this is Detective Constable Wilson. We're hoping you can help us with our enquiries.'

'Enquiries? Into what?'

DC Wilson holds out a small plastic bag. He's tall, clean-shaven with highly polished shoes and an air of newness about him, like he'd just been taken down from a shelf in Harrods. 'Is this your pen, Miss?'

I take the bag and turn it over in my hands. 'Yes, it is or rather it's my propelling pencil. I didn't know I'd lost it. Where did you find it?'

'Would you tell us where you were Tuesday lunch-time last week, around one o'clock?'

'Why?'

'Please, just answer the question, Miss, it will be quicker for all of us.' The Chief Inspector, still standing, saunters by where I'm sitting on the sofa, so close that his coat brushes my arm and I can smell a faint whiff of pipe tobacco. The image it recalls is so vivid, for a second it takes my breath away. Oblivious to my discomfort, he continues past me to stand looking out of the window.

'Such a long time ago but … lunchtime … I would probably have been in the park. I am most lunch times.'

Chief Inspector Munroe continues. 'Did you see anything unusual when you were there?'

'What do you mean by unusual?'

'Anyone loitering about or acting suspiciously?'

'No, I don't think so; it was very quiet. Why do you ask?' DC Wilson answers.

'A man was found dead in the park last week.'

'Really? How dreadful. I didn't know.'

DCI Munroe turns from the window toward me, a look of scepticism on his face.

'I'm surprised you haven't heard; we've been making enquiries at the college where I understand you work.'

'Oh that, I thought that was about the tramp who's been seen near the college grounds.'

'Have you seen him?' Wilson asks.

'I recall once seeing a man at a distance but I would never recognise him again. Is that the man found dead in the park?'

My question is ignored.

'So, you go to the park at lunch times most days, even in this cold weather; that seems rather extreme.' Munroe smiles sarcastically.

'I suppose it is, a bit,' I concede, 'I just like the fresh air and the quiet; college life can be extremely hectic and noisy.'

'Perhaps you should have chosen a different vocation.'

I smile sweetly.

'You don't seem particularly happy in your work either, Inspector; perhaps you should consider a change of vocation too.'

Munroe observes me coldly, his face a stone mask.

Wilson shoots a look at us both and coughs uncomfortably, wanting to move matters on.

Munroe holds out his hand.

'OK, Miss Thompson, that'll be all for now. Could we have the pencil back please?'

'Oh, I thought you were returning it. It's very important to me; it's solid gold and a gift from someone close.'

'It's a pity you didn't take better care of it then.' I catch my breath at Munroe's sarcasm and will myself not to retort.

''I'm afraid we have to keep it for now,' Wilson says in a placatory tone, 'it's evidence.'

'Evidence! Of what?'

DCI Munroe sounds almost self-congratulatory.

'It was found near the victim's body and the post mortem indicates the time of death would be around the time you frequently spend your lunch breaks at the same spot.'

'But you can't possibly think I had anything to do with that man's death, surely?'

'All lines of investigation are open at the moment,' Munroe informs me. 'We haven't ruled anything out as yet.'

His statement seems like a thinly veiled threat. I need some clarification.

'May I ask how you knew the pencil was mine and that I was in the park that particular day?'

'You were seen.'

'What?'

'You sound alarmed.' Chief Inspector Munroe is studying me closely.

I force steadiness into my voice. 'Not alarmed Chief Inspector; simply surprised. I hadn't noticed anyone else about. It was such a chilly day, the place seemed deserted.' I'm so concerned it was Barry; I have to ask, 'Who saw me?'

'A woman walking her dog; she noticed you standing at the brick pillars examining your boots. Why was that?'

Relief washes over me. 'Oh, yes, I remember; I'd only bought the boots recently, they were really quite expensive but one of the heels had come loose. I've had to buy another pair but, my pencil, how did you know it was mine?'

DC Wilson's tone is quietly conversational. 'The woman recognised you; her daughter attends the college. What with that and the initials engraved in the top of your pencil, it was easy to locate you. Of course, the moment we're able to return it we will.'

'Thank you officer, I would appreciate that.' I give the young man a friendly smile.

Up close, Chief Inspector Munroe shows signs of the wear and tear of the last seventeen years. His face has lost the youthful smoothness I remember – those are not laughter lines but the etchings of strain.

As I show the two officers out Munroe hesitates a fraction, staring hard into my face as if trying to answer some query in his mind but he dismisses it and walks back to their car.

I'm certain he hasn't recognised me. A girl changes a lot on her way to womanhood; I'm now twenty-six and bear little resemblance to the gawky nine year old he'd previously encountered.

My name would mean nothing to him either. I wasn't called Amelia Thompson back then. I had to keep the same initials – my gold propelling pencil, my final gift from Matt, dictated that. I'd changed my name when I began my Open University course, as by then there was no pretence. My change of name was an act of acknowledgement of my parents' lack of feeling toward me and defiance at the carefully constructed illusion they presented to the world.

Closing the door, I wander back into the lounge and reflect on the interview. I'd thought the police would turn up at some point after Janet's spiteful intervention but dropping my pencil is an unforeseen complication. They said they regarded it as evidence but they can't prove I lost it on the day the man died; it could have been any of the lunch times, any week. No, they're just clutching at straws.

CHAPTER 4

It's on the local news. I nearly don't hear it as I'm in the kitchen preparing dinner.

'The police have today announced that the body of the man found in Melsham Park two weeks ago is that of Edward Howden.'

I almost miss catching the savoury pancake I'd just tossed ceiling-ward. *Howden!* Wasn't that the name in the front of the book in Barry's room? I'm sure it was. I wander through into the lounge, pancake pan in hand, and stand transfixed before the TV.

'Originally from Sheffield, he was convicted of the involuntary manslaughter of his wife

due to his alcohol addiction. Howden served three years in prison before being released on condition he attended a rehabilitation programme.'

A photograph is splashed across the screen. My God, I would never have recognised him. The tramp was a parody of the man in the photo. I shudder at what an addiction to alcohol can do as I reach for the glass I'd left on the coffee table and take another sip.

The screen switches to outside Endover Police Station and there he is, Detective Chief Inspector Munroe, preening before the cameras.

'Unfortunately, it seems Howden didn't continue his attendance at the rehabilitation clinic and all contact with him was lost until his body was discovered in our local park.'
'Is it correct, Chief Inspector, that Howden has been seen loitering near West Park College?'
'Yes, that's correct. Our investigations are ongoing in that respect and we're currently attempting to locate his next-of-kin.'
'Any leads as to his assailant?'
'We're following up several lines of enquiry and would ask anyone who may have seen him

*in and around the local area to get in touch
with us.'*
'Thank you, Chief Inspector.'

I press the 'Off' button, deliberately forcing the news out of my mind to concentrate on preparing my meal. If I don't stay focused I'll end up with half of my pancakes on the kitchen floor.

Thinking things through after I've eaten, I ponder the likely scenario that Barry's real surname is Howden and if the Edward Howden on the news is a relation, then it's not surprising that Barry would want to change his name. I recall the entry in his personnel file stating foster parents as his next of kin and it seems a fair assumption that Mason is their name that he has taken. Could Edward Howden be Barry's father? If so, it might explain the assault; God knows, he'd have reason enough.

I think back to the inscription in the book. It wasn't your usual book-signing; it seemed far more personal than that. Intriguing; I wonder if its author, John Simpson, can shed any light.

I spend a couple of hours on the internet. John Simpson has a website and is quite well known in the Sheffield area for his books on local wildlife but particularly for his hand-drawn illustrations which are quite exceptional. Although now in his late sixties he gives talks at local venues once a month, the next being in two weeks' time in the main library in Sheffield. It appears the talks are open to the general public – a 'just turn up' affair. I decide there and then to book some annual leave.

A couple of weeks later I'm on the road to Sheffield and am fortunate that the travelling goes smoothly so that I'm settled in a hotel close to the town centre in time to freshen up and have something to eat before attending Mr Simpson's talk.

John Simpson is a dapper little man, dressed in a slightly dishevelled suit and waistcoat; he reminds me of Charlie Chaplin. His talk is engaging and, displayed larger than life on the screen by an overhead projector, his drawings are awe-inspiring in their detail. He richly deserves the applause he receives.

As people drift away I hang back, selecting one of the books he has on display. Rummaging in my purse, 'Ah, I thought I had the correct money.'

I smile as I hand over the notes and congratulate him on a very enjoyable evening.

'You're most welcome, my dear.' He has a lovely twinkle in his eye as he peers over the top of his half specs. Obviously such a trusting soul, so easy to deceive; it's like dealing with a child.

'I recently saw another of your books, written some time ago I believe. One of my students was showing it to me. He says he knows you.'

'Really? What's his name?'

'Barry Mason.' I say his surname without thinking.

'Barry Mason? Mmm, can't say I recall. Does he live in Sheffield?'

'No, at least, not any more.'

''So he lived in Sheffield at one time, then? Still, can't say I remember the name but then, my memory isn't what it used to be, I'm afraid.'

Mr Simpson emits a quiet sigh of acceptance.

'There was an inscription in the book, I remember. I asked Barry about it but he just shrugged; you know how uncommunicative these young lads can be sometimes.'

'Oh indeed, yes. Can you remember what it said?'

'Yes, that's why I queried it with Barry. It said "For Barry *Howden*. Happy memories, John Simpson."

'Barry Howden! Now that name I do remember. I didn't realise he'd changed his name although, under the circumstances, I can understand why; such a terrible tragedy.'

'I'm sorry, you've lost me; what tragedy was that?'

'It was in all the papers; caused quite a stir in the local community. Barry would have been about nine, I guess; terrible thing for a young lad to witness. It must have been about three years that they lived next door. He was a bright lad and things were fine unless his father was home. Long distance lorry driver I believe. Couldn't handle the drink but couldn't leave it alone either. The papers said Barry had hit his dad over the head with a poker and knocked him out, trying to defend his mother and then called the police but whatever the truth, the poor kid must have been terrified.'

I can sense Mr Simpson's genuine dismay at the turn of events and smile reassuringly as he gazes into the middle distance, lost in his thoughts.

'I think it was best they moved him away although I did miss him but better that he should have a fresh start. So, you teach him, do you?'

'Only a secondary subject; his main interest is the Small Animal and Wildlife course. I believe he wants to get into conservation work eventually.'

'That really pleases me,' Mr Simpson beams, his delight evident, 'I'm sure that lad will go far. Please, wish him well for me. You've made my day, young lady.' He glances down at his watch, 'Look at the time, I must be off; lovely to meet you.'

'And you.'

I watch Mr Simpson as he leaves the library, the spring in his step causing me to smile as I muse on the fact that lies are not always bad. How very interesting our conversation was; so, given enough provocation, Barry *is* capable of violence, even at the tender age of nine; it seems that tendency is still with him.

I debate whether to just leave it here; I don't think there's any doubt that Edward Howden is Barry's father and, after what I've heard on the news report and from

Mr Simpson, I'm not surprised Barry assaulted his dad. I suppose I could do some internet research on the British Library's newspaper collection site. It might be interesting to learn the details of the trial but I doubt it will throw up anything more useful than I already have. No, on balance, it's more important to concentrate on moving things forward than back history.

Back at the hotel I pop into the bar for a bedtime brandy. It's quite pleasant in here, a lot of dark oak panelling and deep crimson seats; a kind of settled, old world feel about it, yet I feel restless, a bit bored with my own company; I need a few hours distraction.

It's very quiet although not that late. There's a middle aged couple in the corner looking as though they both wished they were with someone else and a couple of reps leaning over their laptops, obviously trying to update in readiness for meetings the next day.

I settle back into my comfy seat and briefly close my eyes, savouring the taste of the brandy on my tongue.

'May I join you?'

A slight exclamation of surprise escapes me as I open my eyes.

'I'm sorry; I didn't mean to startle you.'

A handsome man is standing directly in front of me, nursing a glass of red wine.

'No, it's OK. I'm afraid I've had rather a long day.'

He makes a small nod of his head and starts to turn away.

'But please, do join me, some company would be nice.'

His smile widens as he draws up a chair, 'Can I get you another drink?' he indicates my glass.

'Please, it's brandy.'

I watch him as he strolls to the bar. Almost six feet tall with a toned athletic build he cuts an attractive figure. He's smartly dressed in an expensive looking business suit, although he's removed the tie as a small concession to an evening of relaxation. This is a man for whom appearance is paramount and who obviously appreciates quality. He hands me my brandy. 'Are you on holiday?'

'No, not really, just doing a bit of research into my family tree. It seems I once had some ancestors in this area but I've hit a bit of a dead end. I take it you're here on business?'

'The suit is a bit of a giveaway, isn't it?' His smile is quite lovely. I can tell he's a veritable charmer but what the hell, as long as I'm aware it doesn't matter; I can play the seduction game as well as anyone else.

I glance at his beautifully manicured hands and note the absence of a wedding ring; not that that means anything.

Do I mind if he's married? No, not really. It's not up to me to be his moral conscience.

'Will you be here tomorrow evening?' he leans forward across the table.

I sense his unspoken desire and turn my head slightly to one side, looking coyly up at him, a smile of acceptance on my lips. 'I can be.'

'Will you allow me to buy you dinner, then?'

'That would be lovely, thank you.'

'The pleasure will be all mine, I assure you. I can't think of a better way to end the working week than wining and dining with a beautiful young lady.'

I smile, accepting his flattery in the light-hearted manner in which it's intended. 'You said you're here on business; may I ask what you do?'

'I'm a partner in an architectural practice based in London but we've projects all over the country.'

Swiftly, he moves the conversation back to focus on me.

'So, you're tracing your family tree; have you found any notorious or famous ancestors yet?'

I give a light chuckle, 'No, nothing so interesting I'm afraid. I'm beginning to think we've been a decidedly dull lot down the generations!'

He smiles, leaning back in his chair, so obviously comfortable in his own skin. He seems faintly familiar; something about him is chipping at the edge of my mind. Perhaps he reminds me of Mick, my policeman boyfriend; similar build and self-assurance which are probably what makes me find him extremely seductive.

'My name is Amelia, by the way.' I inflect a slight rebuke into my tone that he hasn't already enquired but he glides over it, not the least perturbed.

'Peter, Peter Everard,' he inclines his head slightly, his fingers lightly touching his breast bone, as if bowing.

I can't help but smile and ignoring his flippancy ask,

'So, you're here working. Do you live far away?'

'Coventry; we have a small satellite office there.'

'I've never been but I understand it's a lovely city. Have you always lived there?'

'No, I grew up in Dorset.'

'Really, whereabouts?'

I keep silent as to my own childhood connections with the area.

'Near Dorchester but we moved when I was about sixteen.'

Peter looks at his watch.

'I didn't realise it was quite so late and I, for one, need my beauty sleep; got an early start in the morning.' He makes a poor attempt at stifling a yawn. 'May I walk you to your room?'

Why do I feel that he's deliberately avoiding any further questions?

'Of course.'

As we walk along the hotel corridor he rests his hand gently on the small of my back. His touch is feather light yet it seems to go through me like an electric charge and it takes all my willpower to stop at a chaste goodnight kiss.

He touches my cheek, 'I did mean what I said earlier, you are very beautiful you know.'

I smile my acknowledgement of his compliment and unlock my bedroom door.

Standing before the full-length mirror I appraise my image. What an asset my beauty has proved to be over the years. I turn this way and that, admiring the curves of my well-proportioned breasts and hips. There's nothing voluptuous or brazenly sexy about me but I've perfected an elegant femininity of movement and posture that suggests an inherent sensuality that men seem to find compelling. I allow myself a surreptitious smile; will men never learn not to judge a book by its cover?

I prepare for bed knowing that I really do need to get some sleep but the coincidence of the closeness of our childhood homes coupled with the strange impression of familiarity and my sixth sense that he was deliberately avoiding personal detail, causes me a disturbed night.

Next morning is crisp and clear, encouraging me to put my doubts to one side for a while; instead I might as well turn this trip into a mini holiday and tour some of Sheffield's art galleries.

By the time I return to the hotel my feet are aching and my senses are in overload from the many and varied works of art I've been contemplating. I take a lovely long soak in the bath and apply tasteful yet understated makeup. I wish I'd packed something a bit more elegant to wear but at least I have with me the obligatory 'little black dress' so that will have to do.

When I enter the hotel bar Peter is already there, in conversation with the bartender. His smile of welcome is sincere, tinged it seems with a slight feeling of relief which gives me an unexpected thrill as he places a proprietorial hand on my shoulder. 'Amelia, what would you like to drink?'

There's a group of four men sitting round a table to the left of us and I notice their glances of appreciation in my direction. I see Peter notices it too and subtly places himself in their line of vision, staking his claim to me; men are so territorial!

I allow myself to be shepherded to a table in the corner and take a sip of Pinot Noir.

'I've booked a table in the restaurant for eight; I hope that's OK with you?'

'That's fine.'

Peter is handsome; I can appreciate that more now that I'm not as tired as I was the previous evening. His eyes are a dappled hazel with flecks of gold. He has slight stubble that is expertly shaped emphasising his jaw line, definitely the work of a Turkish barber and full, sensuous lips that readily smile. I find my gaze fixed on their movement as he makes small talk, heightening my anticipation for the rest of the evening.

'How has your research been going? Have you traced any more of your ancestors?'

I snap out of my reverie, take an enormous swallow of wine and force myself into the present, 'Not well, really. Hit a bit of a wall I'm afraid so I used it as an excuse to indulge my interest in art.' By way of explanation I add, 'I teach art history so I've spent the day traipsing round art galleries.'

'I consider that an excellent use of your time,' approval is evident in his tone, 'when I'm in London I often spend my lunch-hours in the art galleries or museums.'

'Which is your favourite?'

'Oh, I think the National Gallery, so many different styles under the one roof.'

'Yes, I agree but for me it's got to be the National Portrait Gallery. I can spend hours just gazing, trying to get a sense of the person behind the paint.'

'Ah, a soul searcher; I can see I shall need to be careful what I say.'

I allow myself a slight smile; indeed you should, around me.

'Excuse me, sir, madam, your table is ready.' The waiter stands politely back and motions us to follow, directing us to a table in the far corner. The restaurant curtains are drawn against the dark December night, the subdued lighting enhanced by candles on each table, giving the illusion of intimacy. There are enough diners to create a comfortable atmosphere, their conversations merely affording a pleasant backdrop of murmurings to our own small talk.

We concentrate on the formalities of wine and food choosing and sit back, our eyes meeting as we contemplate each other. A one night stand would suit me fine but I'd like to know a little more about this man before I take him into my bed. That slight feeling of familiarity is still there.

'Do you have any brothers or sisters?'

Peter looks slightly uncomfortable; I can't imagine why.

'No, no I don't. Do you?'

Shall I admit that I had a brother once? No, I'm not in the habit of sharing Matt with anyone.

'No, like you, I'm a one and only.'

'That doesn't surprise me, you're quite unique.'

Peter raises his glass in salutation as I smile my delight at his compliment.

'Where did you move to?'

Peter looks confused so I explain,

'You said you moved from Dorset when you were about sixteen.'

'Oh, yes, so I did. Nearer to London, better work prospects for my father. How about you, have you moved around much?'

'Like your father, I've only ever moved for work reasons.'

We linger over our meal, conversation minimal but much conveyed by suggestive looks and body language so that, by the time the meal is over, anticipation and sexual desire between us is palpable.

Peter lifts up our second bottle of wine to the light.

'All gone I'm afraid. Would you like a brandy or some coffee?'

I remove my shoe under the table and run my stockinged foot up his calf.

'Actually, I think I'd like to go somewhere quiet.'

Peter's smile is confident, assured; he thinks he's in control. No matter. I can be gracious provided the end result is of my choosing. He stands and offers me his arm as we leave the restaurant.

Entering my hotel room, he pushes me against the wall as the door closes behind us and kisses me hard with an urgency that won't admit delay. His fingers find the zip at the back of my dress and expertly pull it down, peeling the straps from my shoulders. My dress slides to the floor as he bends his head down to kiss my breasts. I place my arms around his neck as he lifts and carries me toward the bed. Kicking off his shoes, he kneels over me, removing his jacket and shirt, tossing them onto the floor as I reach for the zip of his trousers.

I close my eyes and give myself up to animal instinct, the physical sensation so satisfying I have no need of emotional attachment.

Later, under the covers, Peter makes love to me again; slower, gentler and almost reverential. Drifting into sleep I muse as to which I prefer.

Next morning we order breakfast to the room, he pours the coffee and handing me a cup he leans forward and places a tender kiss on my forehead. 'I have to leave today.' It's a statement said in a tone that doesn't allow any discussion so I simply nod my acceptance with a slight downturn of my mouth, implying my disappointment. It does no harm to dissemble.

I watch him leave, a tinge of disappointment spoiling the pleasure of the previous night, it would have been nice to have lingered a little longer but I am, above all else, a pragmatist. I must get back to see what progress the police have made regarding Edward Howden's death and Peter would only be a distraction I can ill afford.

CHAPTER 5

Sitting in the deep leather armchair, its winged sides making me feel like a horse with oversized blinkers, I gaze unwaveringly at the man opposite as the silence between us deepens.

He plays this game at each of our sessions, waiting patiently for me to speak, to unburden; as if to my confessor.

Barnaby has been my therapist for the past eight months. I'd discovered him quite by chance one summer morning when I'd been following Munroe's daughter as she left home for work. Most of my classes at college don't start until nine thirty so I had plenty of time to discover her favoured route.

On this particular morning she'd stopped off in the local mini-supermarket to buy a bottle of water. Following her in, I'd busied myself reading their noticeboard which was where I'd first seen Barnaby's details. He was offering a free 'taster' counselling session and I thought, 'Why not? Could be fun,' so I'd noted his number.

I'd forgotten all about it for more than a week when one evening, sorting through my handbag, I came across my note. I rang and made my first appointment.

I hadn't meant to continue; I just thought I'd see what a counselling session was like but I got such a buzz from that first encounter that I was eager to continue the game.

I come once a month. Sometimes I say little, simply sit and soak up the calming atmosphere. Other times I drop little nuggets of information. It's good practise because I have to remember what I've said in the past. I know Barnaby takes notes so I have to be careful. It's so easy to trip up. The challenge is to sound credible; the best lies are always those that hold a grain of truth.

Barnaby isn't the most rewarding of adversaries in this game of verbal chess; his need to help people makes him somewhat gullible. Although he keeps his expressions bland, non-judgemental, he can't disguise the genuine concern that emanates from his pale, grey eyes. I wonder if his parents had a premonition he'd grow up to be a counsellor so I'd looked up the meaning of his somewhat unusual name; son of consolation, of exhortation and comfort. Amusingly, he tries to practise all three so I pretend he helps. I don't like to disappoint him.

The room is stuffy, carrying the slight odour of previous clients mixed with the scent of the oil burner and pot-pourri. Barnaby never opens the window, which is permanently shrouded with dark, heavy curtains, keeping the world at bay. I wonder what it must be like for him to step outside after a day working in this primordial soup of half-light, listening to the despair of the lost and lonely.

'I hate Christmas.' My voice breaks the deadlock between us.

'Would you like to tell me why?'

I settle back a little further in the leather chair and mull over my options.

'No hurry, take your time.' Barnaby's tone is gentle persuasion.

'Because Christmas died with Matt.' There, a simple statement of fact but facts are not always the whole truth, are they?

'Go on.'

'Matt died in December that year so the Christmas tree was already on order and couldn't be cancelled. I didn't realise that at the time; I was still a child, only nine. Such things didn't occur to me.

I remember sitting on the stairs Christmas Eve Day, excitedly watching as the men negotiated the tree's enormous bulk through the hall and into the lounge, placing it forward in the bay window so that there was still room to get behind it to sit on the window seats.

I knew I wouldn't be allowed to help decorate the tree, I never have. Mother always insisted on decorating it herself when we were in bed. It was her surprise, a sort of family tradition. Each year it would be adorned differently and our tree presents would be different too, sort of themed I suppose you'd call it, but none of that mattered to me. I was simply so thrilled. We were going to have Christmas after all and this time it really would be for me. I really thought it meant I mattered.'

I allow a long silence.

'So, what happened?'

'The tree happened.'

Barnaby raises a querying eyebrow.

'I couldn't wait until breakfast so I sneaked downstairs early while my parents were still in bed. It was ghastly. Instead of brightly coloured baubles and sparkling tinsel mother had wreathed the tree in long, black silken ribbons, like it was weeping rivulets of black tears.

I couldn't grasp what I was seeing, it was such a shock. I remember I reached out to touch one of the ribbons, hoping it wasn't real, that my eyes were playing tricks on me and then, her voice, shrieking. "Don't you *dare* touch that!" I remember my hand sprang back as her angry shout tore through me and I automatically stepped back; I tripped, falling heavily on my bottom. I really hurt myself. I remember I was crying with pain but she just left me there. I can hear her now, the hissed bitterness clipping each word, cold as ice crystals. "Why couldn't it have been you? I could have lived with that." I knew then how much she hated me.'

I choke back a sob and fumble in my pocket for a tissue. Barnaby sits impassively observing. I sometimes wonder what I pay him for.

'What did you do?'

'I crawled behind the tree and clambered up onto the window seat, hidden from view.'

'And?'

'And nothing, I simply sat there all Christmas Day. I don't think my parents even missed me. It was always Matt.'

'Were you jealous of your brother?'

'No, no I wasn't. Do you find that strange?'

Barnaby does his usual trick of answering me with another question, 'Do you?'

'It wasn't his fault my parents didn't love me.'

'Even so, most children would have felt resentment, envy.'

I ponder that for a while, allowing the silence to build so that it adds emphasis to my words. 'But I wasn't *most children;* I was special and my relationship with Matt was special; we had a unique bond.'

'Did Matt feel that too?'

'Of course he did. We were everything to each other, everything.'

Barnaby seems to be considering his response, weighing up whether he dares voice his thoughts and eventually decides to take the risk.

'Matt was seventeen years older, do you not think that he might have viewed the relationship a little differently?'

I purse my lips and stare coldly at Barnaby; how dare he presume? I practically spit my reply, 'No, I do not.'

He shifts uncomfortably in his seat and makes a display of looking at his watch, the signal that my session is over. His caring does not impinge on his business acumen. Attempting to make amends he tries to be conciliatory. 'It's good that you open up a little, Amelia. It will help you move forward.'

'Yes, I know.' Turning toward the door I say, in a business-like tone, 'I'll see you next month, then.'

Barnaby seems reluctant. What a timid mouse he is and I'd barely sharpened my claws. 'Indeed, see you then.'

Returning to my car I wonder whether I ought to join an amateur dramatic group, they'd probably welcome a talent like mine.

◆

Unfortunately, if you wish to live in the presence of others, Christmas is impossible to avoid.

In a week, college will close for the Christmas and New Year break but before then we have to endure a 'festive get-together' with the students; an initiative devised by the Principal, organised and run by the staff and loathed by students and staff alike.

Standing by the drinks table I pour myself a glass of orange juice and, surreptitiously turning my back on the room, take a small bottle of vodka from my handbag and slip a healthy dose into the orange. I need something to get me through this ordeal of forced jollity whilst looking out for Barry. I haven't seen him since my trip to Sheffield and am wondering if the police investigation is unnerving him at all.

I've left my car at home and booked a taxi for ten but already I fear that's later than I can endure.

The room is filling up. I crane my neck looking for Barry but bodies are blocking my view. I've just decided I'll have to start circulating when I notice him leaning against the far wall, drinking a can of coke and looking decidedly bored.

I make my way toward him, deliberately avoiding eye contact with anyone else as I don't want to miss this opportunity. As he watches me I feel his eyes undressing me. I flash him my most brilliant smile. 'Hello, Barry, good to see you here.'

He merely nods his acknowledgement.

'I was in Sheffield recently,' I begin conversationally, 'attending a talk by one of their local celebrities, a wildlife enthusiast, John Simpson. Have you heard of him?'

Barry's attempt to mask the recognition in his eyes by a non-committal shrug of his shoulders isn't lost on me.

'I bought one of his books. You'd probably find it interesting; it might even help with your course; I'll lend it to you if you'd like.'

Barry looks almost embarrassed by my offer but gives the briefest nod of acceptance.

'What got you interested in animals and wildlife, Barry?'

'D'know, just was.' If Barry shrugs his shoulders at me once more I'll slap him.

'Going by the people attending his talk, I got the impression Mr Simpson's been a great inspiration to a number of young people, he seemed a very pleasant man and so enthusiastic.'

I'm sure I perceive a slight tinge of sadness in Barry's eyes but it's gone in an instant.

'Barry, hi.' The female voice cuts across the general hubbub and we turn simultaneously in its direction. A bottle blonde is waving her hand above the crowd, beckoning Barry over. He looks slightly annoyed but as he turns to leave, bends his head down to my level and whispers,

'You look really tasty in that dress.'

Reaching the girl he leans in close, supporting his weight with a hand on the wall above her head then whispers something in her ear and as they turn to leave they both look back at me, Barry with an unmistakable leer and the girl smirking from ear to ear.

I'm so absorbed watching them leave I don't notice Ben, Barry's tutor on the Small Animal and Wildlife course, has sidled up beside me. 'They make a good couple, don't they?' Ben's tone is light-hearted and amused.

'I don't know. Who is she?'

'That's Jess Saunders, second year student on the Secretarial course.'

'Are they an item?'

'Well, in a manner of speaking, they're certainly a pair!' Ben notes my bemused expression. 'Jess Saunders is what is unkindly called "the college bike." She bestows her favours quite freely if the college bitch brigade is to be believed. As for our Barry, well, good looking bloke that he is, he's a prime target for someone like Jess.'

'Do you think it'll last?'

'No, she'll get bored with him before long. He's too steady. Jess is more inclined to walk on the wild side,' Ben gives a rueful smile, 'although having said that, Barry can be a bit of a dark horse. I sometimes think there's a side to him …'

Ben's comment is cut short by Muriel Perkins beckoning him over.

Despite Ben's assurance I can't risk this; although Jess Saunders may be little more than an irritating inconvenience she's a complication I can do without. I need Barry to be free of any romantic attachments for I need him to form a relationship with DCI Munroe's daughter, Lily. If I can bring this about, I will have planted a canker that will fester, corrupt and eventually destroy Munroe's idyllic family.

A murderer as his daughter's lover – how sublime!

When he arrives my taxi driver is determinedly in Christmas mood; tinsel hanging from the inside door handles, Rudolf nodding away on the dashboard and the radio spewing out festive songs; God, how I hate this time of year.

Clambering out, my heel catches on a piece of uneven pavement and I stumble, grabbing onto the taxi door to steady myself. 'Good party was it, luv?'

I glare at the driver, sullenly thrusting the fare into his hand.

'And a merry Christmas to you too, luv!'

As I turn away I hear him mutter, 'Miserable bitch.' but I don't care, I just want to get into my apartment and shut the door on all of it but even as I put my key in the lock of the communal front door I realise the impossibility of shutting it out altogether. The hallway is festooned with streamers and a small Christmas tree with an obligatory Guiding Star on the top twinkles sarcastically at me.

'Amelia, there you are; what do you think?' Mrs Lewis waves her hand to encompass the display, 'Paula in the top flat helped me decorate. Doesn't it look lovely?'

'Yes, it's very pretty. I'm sorry, Mrs Lewis but I'm dreadfully tired; I really must get to bed.'

'Of course my dear, you young things work so hard. Perhaps we can have a little celebratory drink on Christmas Eve; I've made some mince pies.'

I smile non-committally and make my escape into the warm, unadorned plainness of my home. I wander through into the kitchen, slinging my bag onto the sofa as I pass and pull my favourite mug down from the shelf, the words "coffee, chocolate, men, some things are better rich" emblazoned on the front. My sentiments exactly but for now I'll have to make do with just the coffee and then I remember, Ben gave me a Christmas gift the other day. Very sweet of him but he's really not my type. I feel slightly ashamed that I didn't accept it more graciously; if he *really* knew me … I hug the thought; the sense of hidden power is so pleasurable.

Returning to the lounge I see the parcel lying forlornly on the table where I'd tossed it; might as well open it now. Tearing at the paper I'm delighted to find it's a box of luxury Belgian chocolates.

Flicking through the TV channels I eventually give up in disgust as there's nothing worth watching. I can feel my mood slipping down towards the abyss; probably the result of too much wine and not enough food coupled with the strong coffee I've just drunk and the rich chocolates. I feel slightly sick and my head has that muffled woolliness that is usually a precursor to a headache. I know I need to snap myself out of this moroseness but at times there's something vaguely comforting in wallowing in one's misery.

I find my mind turning toward Munroe, sure that if he hadn't come into our lives I would even now be sharing Christmas with my brother. Matt would never have let me down at such a time.

I'd walked past Munroe's home last week, early one evening just as it was getting dark. White lights had been entwined through the branches of the poplar that stands sentinel inside his entrance gates and strings of coloured bulbs edged the downstairs windows. I could see his wife and Lily in the kitchen, happily chatting away as they sat at the table wrapping presents.

Yes, he will go home to the embrace of his family having caused the destruction of mine. If he hadn't insisted on pursuing his ridiculous assumptions Matt wouldn't have felt the loss of Addie so acutely and would still be here. I wonder how many other families Munroe has decimated during his career. Well, Detective Chief Inspector Munroe, I plan to decimate yours.

The shrill ringing of my mobile startles me. I fumble around, for a moment unable to locate it in the subdued light. Strange, it's come up Number Withheld. I don't usually answer unknown callers but in my partially stupefied state I automatically accept the call. 'Hello?'

'Amelia?'

'Who am I speaking to?'

'It's Peter. How are you?'

For a split second I almost say 'Peter who?' before it registers. I feel my body tense as I struggle to control my annoyance at his intrusion. 'I'm fine and you?'

'Absolutely; look, Amelia, I'm going to be in London over Christmas and I wondered, well, I know it's something of an imposition but I wondered, if you're not booked up with family or anything, if you'd like to spend Christmas and Boxing Day with me.'

I can hear his breath down the phone as the silence lengthens while my mind frantically tries to assimilate what he's said.

'Oh, look, it's OK, Amelia, don't worry, I shouldn't have asked.'

'No, no, it isn't that, it's just such a surprise that's all.' Instantly on my guard my mind is striving to recall our conversations in Sheffield. 'It's just I didn't think you knew where I lived.'

'Well, I don't actually,' he sounds sheepish and slightly embarrassed, 'I just assumed, because we spoke about liking to visit the London art galleries, that you wouldn't live too far away from the City, or am I completely wrong?'

'No, no, you're not.' My caution is fighting with the potential opportunity that's presenting itself.

'Look, Amelia, I'm just going to come straight to the point; would you like to spend Christmas with me at my hotel?'

I realise I've no time to prevaricate; I must make a decision now, immediately. The prospect of food, wine and sex with a handsome and likeable man contrasts favourably with what otherwise lies before me, namely another Christmas alone.

'I'd love to, Peter.'

'That's wonderful. I'll text you my hotel details. Come over about twelve on Christmas Day, I'll book a table in the restaurant. They assure me they put on a fabulous spread.'

Sleep doesn't come easily. I feel apprehensive as I assess how little I know about Peter. I'm just becoming drowsy when another disturbing thought crosses my mind. I don't recall giving him my phone number. I try to remember our conversations in the Sheffield hotel but I'm certain I didn't. I'm probably just being paranoid. There may be a simple explanation and anyway, he's invited me to a hotel so that's safe enough. The prospect of not being alone on Christmas Day for the first time in years is not something I'm prepared to throw away on a vague feeling of uneasiness.

I must admit that Peter's invitation has put me in the mellowest of moods, so much so that I even graciously accept Mrs Lewis' invitation for Christmas Eve drinks and mince pies. The delight she shows is pathetic; she must be so lonely to gain such pleasure from so little. The thought of getting old makes me shudder.

Christmas morning is quite grey and dismal but I'm determined to make the most of things. I treat myself to a special breakfast of smoked salmon and scrambled eggs before dressing smartly casual and packing my last minute items

Arriving at the hotel I'm relieved to find Peter waiting in the lounge for me. 'Amelia, I'm *so* glad you could come. Here, let me take your case.' He guides me to the elevator, 'Let's get you settled in and then we'll have some coffee.'

'This is such a lovely surprise. When did you know you'd be in London over Christmas?'

'Only very recently; it's a work issue that, unfortunately, has to be dealt with between Christmas and New Year but nothing to spoil today and tomorrow.'

Having unpacked and hung the items that mattered we return to the hotel lounge for coffee. I can't take my eyes from the enormous Christmas tree in the corner;

decorated in white and silver its adornments form a striking contrast to the rich, deep green of its boughs; its wonderful pine scent inexorably pulling my mind back to the last Christmas my parents ever held, before Matt's suicide spoilt everything. It was so selfish of him.

'Amelia, are you alright? You seem miles away.'

I force myself back to the present.

'Yes, I'm fine; just relaxing and absorbing the atmosphere. This is such a treat, Peter.'

'For me too; I never expected to be spending this Christmas with such a beautiful companion.'

Despite the cosiness of our surroundings and the easy flow of conversation, I'm still uncomfortable that Peter was able to contact me when I can't recall giving him my number. I can't let it rest as I know my concern will mar my enjoyment.

'It's such a nuisance, Peter, but I seem to have lost your phone number.'

'It'll be on the text message I sent you.'

'No, that came up Number Withheld.'

'Oh, I'm sorry, I'm always doing that.' He begins rummaging through his pockets, retrieves his mobile and gives me the number. Whilst entering it into my own phone I continue, 'I was a bit surprised you had my number, I just can't recall giving it to you.'

He looks a little embarrassed and actually blushes slightly. 'Ah, yes. I'm afraid I have a confession to make.

That night in Sheffield, when you were in the bathroom, I took the liberty of looking at your phone. You'd left it by the bedside.'

'Why didn't you just ask me?' I can hear the irritated affront in my voice.

'Because I wasn't sure you'd give it to me and, at that time, I wasn't sure I wanted to keep in touch. I guess you could say I was keeping my options open. Look, Amelia, I'm so sorry, it was very wrong of me.'

'Yes, it was.' I'm furious, how *dare* he invade my privacy in this way.

Peter shifts uncomfortably in his seat, head downcast and when he looks up at me again he resembles a contrite puppy.

I could put an end to this now, go home in a huff but I can't deny I'm enjoying myself and now that he's so obviously in the wrong he's likely to try even harder to please me. Maybe I'll just play this for a bit longer. What harm can it do?

Hopefully, Peter meekly asks, 'Am I forgiven?'

'It seems so.'

Relief floods his face and his smile broadens, 'I'd really love to continue seeing you; I can't believe I ever doubted that I would. When do you start back at work?'

'Not for another couple of weeks.'

'Look, I've got this work issue to sort out but that should be finished by New Year. Could we get together again then, see the New Year in; assuming you don't have any other plans, of course, family to see?'

'No, no plans, no family either; don't you have any relations to catch up with?'

'Afraid not, my parents emigrated to Australia when I was fifteen but it wasn't for me, too hot! So, once I'd finished my education I came back and got a job in dear old England. People think I'm mad but I love it here, cold grey weather and all. I go back a couple of times a year but much prefer to be here at this time – a barbeque on the beach is not my idea of Christmas. So, what would you like to do for New Year?'

I consider for a while, 'There's a lovely coaching inn near me, why don't I see if I can get us booked in for the celebrations?'

'Sounds good to me.'

'OK, I'll send you a text when I've booked.'

I lean across the table, give Peter a light kiss on his cheek.

The rest of the day is an idyllic dream of good food, wine and company and for the first time in years I don't find the whole concept of Christmas nauseating.

We spend Boxing Day in relaxed fashion; a late breakfast, stroll in the park and a brief look into Harrods and Selfridges before dinner once again in the hotel.

Making our farewells the following morning Peter heads off for the underground. I had told him that I'd be making my way home but, on impulse, I decide to stay on in London for the day to indulge in a shopping spree.

Heading back to Kings Cross, I'm so thrilled with my purchases I decide to treat myself to a coffee in the St Pancras Renaissance Hotel whilst I'm waiting for my train.

Relaxing in the main lounge area I suddenly realise that I need to ring the Inn if we're to have any hope of booking for New Year's Night.

'Good morning, I wonder if you have any vacancies for New Year's Night for two people.'

'I'm sorry, madam, all our rooms are taken. We tend to get booked up very early for this time of year.'

'Yes, I suppose so. I should have realised.'

'We can fit you in for the evening meal, if that would suit you.'

I quickly consider.

'Yes, why not; say 8pm?'

I give my name and contact number and immediately ring Peter to let him know the situation but his phone appears to be switched off. Never mind, I'll try again when I get home. He'll need to know so that he can either book into another London hotel or return to Coventry that night.

'Can I get you anything, madam?'

'Yes, a black coffee please.' I sit back in a comfortable armchair and people watch. It's quite busy; from where I'm positioned I can see into a small bar area where business-types are gathering for lunch-time drinks and snacks.

The waitress brings me my coffee, standing partly in front of me so I only catch the briefest glimpse, 'Peter?' A man is walking swiftly, almost running from the bar, heading for the exit. I put down my cup and stand but before I can move forward or call out again, he's out the main doors and gone.

Back at the bar area the bartender is deep in conversation with a manager, pointing in the direction of the main doors, neither looking particularly pleased.

The waitress returns to replenish my cup.

'What was all that about?' I indicate toward the bar.

'I believe someone left without paying his bill.'

'Oh dear, how awful.'

The waitress is philosophical, 'It happens.'

'Not very often, I hope.'

'No,' she smiles, 'not very often.'

I'm probably being ridiculous but I can't get the episode out of my mind. All the way home on the train it keeps rewinding as if it's on a permanent replay. He was *so* like Peter; I could have sworn it was him. I'm just being silly but it'll be a good story to relate over New Year's dinner.

During the following week I try Peter's mobile several times but can't seem to get any connection, then suddenly, I get through although he doesn't pick up. I feel I've little alternative than to leave a voice message.

'Hi, Peter, I've booked us dinner at the Inn for eight on New Year's Night but wasn't able to arrange accommodation as they're fully booked. Hope this is OK with you and you can make alternative arrangements. Please let me know. Amelia.'

Next day Peter rings but I'm driving and can't pick up so he leaves a voice message.

'Amelia, got your message; disappointing but no worries. I'll travel back to Coventry that night; there shouldn't be too much traffic about if I leave it until the early hours. We can still have a lovely long evening together. See you at the Inn about seven thirty. Can't wait.'

I listen to the message once I've parked the car. Thank goodness for that, I was beginning to think I'd never hear from him again and if nothing else I was looking forward to the prospect of dinner and a party atmosphere.

I pop into the Mall for some new perfume and, feeling peckish, stop off in the coffee bar on the top floor. Idly gazing down onto the lower level I spot Barry looking in a jeweller's window. Don't tell me Barry's relationship with Jess Saunders is more serious than Ben supposed. I could strangle the bitch.

Hastily, I gulp the remains of my coffee and hurry down to the lower level. By the time I get to the jeweller's, Barry is already inside talking with the assistant. I try to see what it is they're looking at but Barry's blocking my view. Whatever it is, he obviously agrees the purchase as the assistant is boxing the item and putting it into a small carrier bag.

As Barry leaves I turn my back to look into the clothes shop window and watch his reflection as he heads for the Mall exit.

Damn! If that gift is for Jess then she's more of a threat than I imagined. What a bloody nuisance; I shall have to deal with her sooner than I thought.

◆

I've ordered a taxi to take me to the Inn so I can relax and drink as much as I want. It's a pity that we can't stay the night but maybe it's just as well. I don't want Peter hanging around when I've got more important things to concentrate on. He's been a pleasant interlude but that's all he's going to be.

Ready early as always I decide to spend a few moments with my memories of Matt. Although furnished, my flat is pretty sparse when it comes to storage so I keep his album in the bottom of the built-in wardrobe. I'd prefer to have it in my bedside drawer unit but the album just won't fit.

Perching on the end of the bed I slowly turn the pages. I adore browsing the photos of Matt and I as children; we were so close, I felt there was a kind of telepathy between us but as I progress through the pages such photos become less frequent. There are more of Matt on his own; one's that I'd sneaked from my mother's family album. Even after all these years, although I still enjoy looking at these photos of him, it rankles that I'm not in any of them; that I wasn't allowed by our parents to share in his achievements; yet another form of their neglect and disdain.

Casting my mind back, I gaze into the middle distance. They always made me call them "Mother" and "Father", even from a very early age; such an effective way to keep me at arms-length; a barely tolerated visitor rather than a member of the family.

I glance back down at the album. There's one of Matt receiving his degree, Matt holding up a tennis trophy, Matt raising a glass of beer to the camera and then, Matt with Addie, his girlfriend. It's the only photo I have of them both and that only because it's impossible to cut Addie out without ruining an excellent shot of Matt.

I'm completely lost in my thoughts, losing all track of time when I'm startled by the doorbell.

'Oh Christ, that'll be my taxi.' Hastily, I put the album back into the wardrobe and, grabbing my coat and handbag, hurry to the door.

When I arrive at the coaching inn Peter is already in the bar, nursing a pint of bitter.

'Amelia, you look wonderful!'

Walking over to me, he wraps a protective arm around my waist and placing an affectionate kiss on my cheek asks,

'Shall we have champagne with the meal tonight?'

'Oh please, that would be superb.'

We're allocated a table to the side of a roaring log fire; the oak panelling and low-beamed ceiling of the restaurant forming a cocoon against the dark wintry night. We're just beginning dessert when I remember,

'Oh, I meant to tell you, something really weird happened the day you left after Christmas to go to your job.'

Peter smiles indulgently and leans forward a little over the table, 'You have my full attention, Amelia.'

'I decided I deserved a treat so after you left I spent time in London shopping and then I went into the St Pancras Renaissance Hotel for coffee whilst I was waiting for my train.'

Peter's smile seems to have faded as he asks,

'About what time was this?'

'What does that matter? Please, just listen, this will make you laugh. I was sitting having coffee in the main lounge when a man hurried out who looked exactly like you!'

Did I detect a slight flicker of alarm in Peter's eyes? If I did, he recovers very quickly.

'Like me?'

'Yes, I could have sworn it was you but that's not the funniest part. Apparently, the man left without paying his bar bill – did a runner in fact!' I giggle as I take a sip of champagne, 'So I do hope it wasn't you.'

'Amelia, how could you even think such a thing of me?' he looks stern but then his face creases into a grin, 'No, it definitely wasn't me. I was working south of the river all week.'

'Well, that's a relief. You must have a doppelganger.'

'They do say everyone has one,' Peter raises his glass and toasts, 'to my doppelganger.'

'To your doppelganger, whoever and wherever he may be.'

The hotel manager claps his hands for attention.

'OK everyone, it's nearly midnight.'

By the time everyone in the restaurant have risen to their feet and linked arms in a raucous rendition of Auld Lang Syne, no-one is aware that the weather conditions have greatly deteriorated.

It's as Peter and I drift through to the lounge for coffee that the seriousness of the situation becomes apparent. Pulling back one of the heavy brocade curtains we peer out at a landscape transformed from that we encountered on the way in. Mounds of snow have built up on the cars and by the hedgerows; the wind is blowing huge, swirling snowflakes so dense it's practically a white-out.

Peter's concern hardly needs voicing. It's obvious that it would be foolhardy to drive all the way to Coventry tonight. Hesitantly he asks.

'Do you live far from here?'

'No, only a couple of miles; I intended to get a taxi back but I think I'll have a very long wait for one now.'

'I definitely won't try to drive all the way to Coventry in this, it would be madness; it's possible that under the circumstances, the hotel might let me crash out in their lounge but that doesn't seem a particularly comfortable way to end a lovely evening. If it's only a couple of miles to your place I reckon I can drive that safely; would you let me doss at yours, just for tonight?'

I can't really think of a good reason to refuse. I probably will have a very long wait for a taxi if one comes at all and I don't fancy spending the night trying to sleep in a chair. In any case, I think I'll feel safer with Peter driving than a stranger as I'm somewhat intoxicated having drunk most of the champagne.

It'll only be for one night; I intend to end our relationship in the morning anyway. However, just to ensure I'm not at a disadvantage,

'OK, Peter, let's do that but first, as you'll know where I live, can I please have your address too? I know that might seem a bit odd but ...'

'No, not at all, Amelia; I understand and think you're being quite sensible.'

He walks across to reception and borrows pen and paper.

'Here.' He hands me a note, 'my address in Coventry but I must warn you that I'm seldom there so if you're hoping for a tour of Coventry some time I'm afraid you'll have a long wait.'

He notices my disappointed expression and quickly continues. 'But that's not to say it won't happen, just that we'll have to plan it, that's all; no spur of the moment thing.'

'OK.' I smile my thanks as I place his note in my handbag and briefly wonder if he has another woman tucked away in Coventry; not that I care. Peter collects my coat and helps me into it.

'Right, are you ready to brave the elements?'

I take a deep breath, nod and together we fight our way out the hotel entrance doors against the full force of the wind and into swirling whiteness.

The relatively short distance home seems to take for ever but eventually we almost fall into my hallway, giggling from release of tension after the drive. Leaving Peter in the bathroom I walk from room to room closing the blinds and curtains. I'm in the bedroom as he enters with his case. Of course, I hadn't thought, he would have a case from his week's stay in London.

Leaving him to unpack a few things I turn at the door, 'Put your case in the wardrobe; there's not a lot of room in here and we're likely to trip over it if you leave it on the floor.'

'Sure, no problem.'

'Good, I'll make us some more coffee.'

Cuddling up together on the sofa, Peter nuzzles my neck.

'I'm hoping you won't make me sleep on the sofa.'

'Oh, I think such a lovely evening deserves a better ending than that, don't you?' and together we make our way to the bedroom.

◆

Waking up the following morning with Peter beside me, I lie there, looking at him whilst he sleeps. How strange that the man making his hasty exit from the Renaissance Hotel should be so very similar, whatever must be the odds of that? I recall Peter's reaction when I related my tale, it was only fleeting but I'm convinced he was momentarily concerned.

I study his features some more. In repose he seems so very familiar; maybe it is simply that he reminds me of Mick, my policeman boyfriend. I drowsily ponder my impression; no, no good, it won't come to me; perhaps he reminds me of a film star, he definitely has the looks.

The day is cold but bright, ideal for the walk we've planned. After that it will be a pub lunch before Peter has to return to Coventry and I have to knuckle down to planning courses for the New Year but he's still asleep, a slight smile of contentment on his lips. I decide to leave him and quietly slip from the bed, intending to make us both a coffee and take them back to bed but, when I open the milk, 'Oh no, it's gone off.' I sneak back into the bedroom. Peter is gently snoring so I quietly don some jogging pants and a hooded top and leave, closing the door softly behind me. Mr Shah's corner shop is the nearest and he's bound to be open today, he only ever closes for Christmas. It isn't far; hopefully I'll be back before Peter wakes.

Outside there's a raw wind blowing swirls of snowflakes around my feet and up into my face as I pull my hood closer as my eyes begin to water from the cold. I reach the shop only to find it closed, a notice pinned to the door – "Closed due to illness". Damn, I'll now have to go a couple of streets further on to the petrol station.

As I stand in line, clutching my bottle of milk, my fingers aching from the cold, I can't believe the queue; has everyone run out of milk this morning? The chap at the counter seems to be having difficulty paying with his credit card; I hop from one foot to the other, impatience building and realise that the cold has given me the urge to pee. 'Come on, hurry up.' At last, milk paid for, I'm out of the shop at speed, jogging down the road and reaching my front door just in time as I make a dash for the bathroom.

Slowly thawing out, I make the coffees. Still no sound from Peter, 'Well lazy bones, you're going to wake up now whether you want to or not.' Carefully balancing both mugs I push the bedroom door open with my bottom and turn toward the bed. 'Time to wake up, Sleeping Beauty.'

The mugs almost tip from my hands; the bed is empty, just the impression on the pillow of Peter's head. 'Peter?' I put the mugs down on the dresser and go from room to room. 'Peter? Stop messing about. Where are you?' Nothing, no-one.

I don't understand; it's as if his absence won't compute. On impulse I return to the bedroom and sling open the wardrobe door; his case has gone, there's no trace of him. I start going round the apartment, scanning all the surfaces for a note, some explanation, but there's nothing. In desperation, I go outside to the back where he'd parked his car – gone.

Returning indoors, I slump down on a kitchen stool, stunned. There must be some rational explanation although I can't yet think of one. I grab my mobile and ring his number; dead, switched off. Not again! I realise that I didn't quiz him, as I should have done, as to why it had taken me so long to reach him before. That was a mistake.

I spend the morning going over the past couple of days; everything we'd talked about, our love-making, but there's nothing, no hint of this.

A crisis, that's what it must be, something to do with work and he was in such a state of surprise he just didn't take the time to leave me a note. He'll ring when he's sorted himself out. I've just got to be patient.

◆

A week has gone by and there's been total silence. I've dialled Peter's number several times but his mobile's dead. I'm really anxious now and I know my anxiety isn't so much *what* has happened to him but *why*. He obviously left of his own freewill, case packed, driving away. Something is seriously amiss and I can't help thinking it can only be to do with me but *what*?

I can't remain in this passive mode, I must act and the only avenue I can think open to me is to go to Coventry, to the address he gave me and see if that throws up any explanation.

I make good time on the journey, the satnav route to Peter's apartment taking me past the bombed out skeleton of the old cathedral with the new rising majestically beside it, but I hardly notice.

The apartment is one of approximately 40 units in a modern, glass and steel structure. I find a short term parking space a little way down the road and walk back, all the time looking for Peter amongst the pedestrians hurrying along the pavement.

As I suspected, the development has security entrance doors; keeping my fingers crossed I press the tradesman's button. The automated voice responds 'Tradesman, unlocked.' With relief I push open the door and make my way to the lift.

Stepping out on the third floor I cast about for number 36 and find it's a corner unit looking out over the park at the rear. Heart thumping, I press the buzzer.

'He's not there.' I start as a door behind me slams shut and turn to face a young woman in her early twenties, busily locking her door. 'Left a couple of days ago.'

'Do you know where he's gone?'

'No, sorry but I think it's for a while; he had a couple of suitcases with him. Are you a friend?'

'Yes, I am.'

'He didn't tell you he was going away?'

'No, he didn't.'

'Well, if it's any consolation I think it was quite sudden. I bumped into Graham in the corridor the day he came back after New Year. He was as white as a sheet, looked as though he'd seen a ghost, hardly acknowledged me and he's usually so friendly.' She shrugged, 'Sorry I can't be more helpful.'

'Excuse me, did you just say "Graham"?'

'Yes, Graham Baxter.'

An uncomfortable pricking sensation traces its way up my spine at the familiarity of that name.

'What does he look like?'

'That's a strange question if he's a friend of yours.'

'I know, just humour me, please.'

She considers for a moment.

'Well, he's quite tall and slim, close cut beard; why do you ask?'

I ignore her question and reply with another.

'How long have you known him?'

'I don't really *know* him; he's just a neighbour; moved in about six months ago. Is there a problem?'

'No, no, not at all; thanks for your help.'

She gives me a knowing look.

'That's OK. Hope you sort out whatever it is. Bye.'

'Bye and thanks.'

For several minutes I just stand in the corridor outside Peter's apartment at a loss as to what to do, trying to make sense of what I've just been told but it doesn't make any sense. I really don't need this now; I've got enough to do juggling Barry, Lily and Munroe. Peter was meant to be no more than a brief diversion. Damn him! I could spit.

I wander out of the building; I might as well make my way home.

Traffic is bad, the return journey seems to take forever and I feel so tired from all the tension, I decide I'm being silly to keep driving; I need to stop off for a while, have some coffee and something to eat to wake myself up before I continue.

Turning off the main road I travel a couple of miles before finding a quiet pub, mock Tudor exterior with a welcoming scent of wood smoke from the large, open fire in the lounge bar. Gratefully I settle into a low, dilapidated armchair and order a coffee and homemade beef and ale pie.

Casting my mind back over the past couple of weeks I replay the conversations with Peter. When we were in Sheffield didn't he tell me his family had moved from Dorset to London when he was sixteen because of his father's work? Yet, over Christmas, I'm sure he'd said that his family had emigrated to Australia when he was fifteen and now it appears he's using another name, one that has significant and sickening connotations for me. What the fuck is going on with him? I don't like this; I don't like this at all.

Lost in thought I start as the landlord bends down to retrieve my empty plate and cup.

'Could I have another coffee please?'

'Of course you can; you travelling far?'

'Not too far to home now. I think I'll just give it a bit longer to let the rush hour traffic ease a little.'

'Very sensible; no pleasure driving in all that; I'll get that coffee.' So saying, the landlord ambles back behind the bar and I return to my anxieties. Graham Baxter was the name of Addie's brother!

CHAPTER 6

First day back at college and the staff are girding their loins for the battles they know are about to commence. I notice Ben, Barry's head tutor, waiting patiently for the kettle to boil for coffee.

'Hi, Ben, did you have a good Christmas?'

'Oh, hi, Amelia, yes, fine thanks. The usual pairs of socks, cufflinks and men's hankies with my initials in the corner,' Ben grimaces, 'would you like a coffee?'

'No, I'm fine thanks and by the way, I *loved* the Belgian chocs.'

'You're very welcome.'

'Are you OK, Ben, you look a bit down? The thought of another term isn't that bad, is it?'

Ben takes a sip of coffee. 'No, it isn't that. To be honest, I'm a bit concerned about Barry Mason.'

'Why, what's the matter?'

'Well, he contacted me over the break. You know he's one of the most promising students I've ever had on my course.' I nod in acknowledgement.

'I've spent a lot of time with him over the past year, encouraging, mentoring, so we've built up quite a close relationship. Anyway, I got this phone call out of the blue. He'd been taken in by the police for questioning about that tramp, you know, the one they found in the park. It seems the tramp was Barry's father.'

'Really? But I thought the tramp's name was Howden. I heard it on the TV.'

'Yeah, it is but it turns out Barry was fostered, long-term fostering, and when he reached adulthood he chose to take his foster parents' name.'

'Oh, I see. I suppose the police just wanted him to make a formal identification.'

'I expect so, I don't really know about these things. The point is, Barry rang me from the police station in a bit of a state. It seems that he's had no contact with his dad in years.'

I shrug. 'Well, that's not surprising, is it? According to what I heard on the news report his father was responsible for his mother's death.'

'Yeah, precisely, but unfortunately the police seem to think that makes Barry a viable suspect for his dad's murder.'

'No, they can't think that, surely? Barry? He's always struck me as such a gentle soul.' My mind is running riot. I can't have this, I really can't. Barry's crucial to my plans. Hopefully there isn't any forensic evidence. I distinctly recall that Barry was wearing gloves and as far as I know, I was the only other person in the park. Oh no, wait a minute, there was that woman dog walker who recognised me. I try to think back, the police didn't mention anything about her seeing the tramp, only that she saw me by the main gates. Hopefully, I'm all she saw.

'Amelia, are you alright?'

I shake my head to clear my thoughts, 'Yeah, sorry Ben. I was just thinking about what you've said. What's happening with poor Barry now? It must be a dreadful shock for him.'

'Well, the police let him go; no real evidence from what I can gather. Trouble is, I don't think Barry's got much of an alibi and in the absence of anyone else – you know what the police are like – need their clear up rates.'

I know only too well. I expected the police to discover Barry's true identity eventually. I'd managed it easily enough, and although they probably traced him through Social Service records, I'm actually surprised it's taken them as long as it has. I suppose, given the history, I'm not altogether surprised that they'd consider him as a suspect but I don't want it to go any further, not yet anyway. I need to divert the police attention onto someone else and I believe I have the ideal candidate.

In the evening I telephone the police station. 'Hello, could I speak with Detective Constable Wilson please? It's to do with the death of the tramp in Melsham Park.'

I've only been waiting two minutes, but it feels like hours. I'm praying DC Wilson is there; I certainly don't want to be put through to Chief Inspector Munroe.

'Hello, DC Wilson here. How can I help?'

'Constable, it's Amelia Thompson, you may recall that you interviewed me about the tramp in the park.'

'Of course, Miss Thompson, the lady with the gold pencil, how could I forget? What can I do for you?'

'I think I may have some information that could help your enquiries but I'd rather speak face to face, if that's possible. It feels less uncomfortable than over the phone.'

'That's no problem; I could call round this evening if that's convenient.'

'Yes, that would be ideal.'

'OK, I'll be there about seven.'

'Thank you, Constable.'

Perfect. That gives me a couple of hours. I have a quick shower and dress in figure hugging jeans and sheer white blouse revealing just enough of my lacy bra through the material to catch the eye. Along with a little make-up and some musk-based perfume, I'm ready.

I make sure my lounge is side-lit, enough to dispel the harshness that the centre light gives but not so low it appears deliberately seductive. I pour a glass of Pinotage and wait.

At exactly 7pm DC Wilson arrives looking as freshly scrubbed as the last time I saw him; I feel that if I ran my fingers down his arm he would squeak.

'Detective Constable Wilson, please come in.' I smile warmly, 'Please, go straight through into the lounge.' I notice him casting his eyes about the room, hopefully he's appreciating the subtle ambience created by the muted side lights; it gives a quite different impression to the starkness of the bright sunlight that flooded the area on his previous visit.

I indicate my partly drunk glass of wine, 'Can I get you a drink or are you not allowed, being on duty?'

He hesitates. 'As it happens I'm not actually on duty; I thought I'd call in on my way home but even so, I'd better not. Thank you, anyway.'

'Oh, a pity, I much prefer to drink with company.' I stroll over to the cabinet, 'Are you sure I can't tempt you?'

'Positive; thank you.' I top up my own glass adopting a look of hurt disappointment. I can sense I've made Wilson feel uncomfortably awkward, as he endeavours to adopt a business-like stance. 'Now, I believe you have something you wish to tell me.'

I indicate the sofa, 'Please, do sit.' I take the chair opposite, leaning forward a little to look directly into his eyes.

'I feel very awkward about this, in view of what I told you and Chief Inspector Munroe when you questioned me before. That's why I'm *so* glad *you* are here, I fear Chief Inspector Munroe wouldn't be quite as understanding, he alarms me a little.' I give a rueful smile and cast my eyes down in a display of awkwardness.

Wilson can't hide a slight smile of agreement. 'He can be a little abrupt but he usually gets results.'

'You mean, he "always gets his man"'.

'You could say that but please don't be concerned; it's much more important that we have all the information you can give.'

I emit a gentle sigh, 'That day in the park, when that man was killed, I *did* see someone else.'

Wilson gives me a querying look.

'I didn't say at the time because I wasn't absolutely sure but I've thought about it since and, coupled with some things I've recently heard, I think I might have been correct.'

'Go on.'

'There's a student at college, Gary Stevenson. He's not someone I teach so I don't know him that well, just in passing really. His mother is the Principal's secretary, Janet Stevenson.'

Wilson gives a slight nod of recognition.

'Anyway, in a college environment one often over-hears bits of gossip, students don't seem bothered about being overheard sometimes; it's mostly nothing but occasionally… Are you quite sure I can't get you a drink, as you're off duty?'

Wilson hesitates again, obviously torn between offending me and abiding by the rules. 'Well, just a tiny amount then.'

'Thank you, it's *so* much nicer than drinking alone.'

Handing him the glass I casually sit beside him on the sofa.

'You were saying?' Wilson, suddenly conscious that his eyes are focused on my chest, immediately directs his gaze up towards my face, colouring with embarrassment. I pretend not to notice.

'It was what I overheard that really made me realise what I'd seen. It seems, if gossip can be believed, that Gary deals in drugs, only in a small way I'm sure but, nonetheless. When you and Chief Inspector Munroe asked me if I'd seen the tramp loitering around the college grounds I was telling the truth when I said I'd seen a man in the distance but wouldn't be able to recognise him again but what I hadn't said at the time because, quite honestly, it hadn't really registered, was that I once saw Gary Stevenson talking with him and then, I remembered, as I left the park that day I'd seen

Gary again, just leaving by the side gate that leads directly back to college.'

Wilson puts on a slightly stern face, 'It's a pity you didn't mention this when we first spoke with you.'

'I know.' I lay my hand briefly on Wilson's arm in apology but he recoils as if stung and then looks embarrassed, realising he's offended me. I mirror his embarrassment and continue, 'I'm so sorry but at the time I didn't think it important. After all, I didn't see Gary talking with anyone in the park. It's only what I've overheard since that's made me wonder. Do you think it might be important?'

'It's certainly a line of enquiry we need to investigate.'

'Will people have to know that it came from me, it could make it very difficult for me in college and …' I pause and allow a slight note of desperation into my voice, 'I'd really prefer that Chief Inspector Munroe wasn't aware that I'd, what's the term, "withheld information?". I find him rather intimidating; I wouldn't want to give him cause to think badly of me.'

Wilson considers for a moment, 'I'll see what I can do but I can't promise.'

I bite my bottom lip in feigned anxiety.

Wilson smiles, 'It's difficult to immediately have total recall; people often remember things later, usually when they're not really thinking about the incident.' I get the impression he's going out of his way to reassure me, as if my peace of mind matters to him. 'Most people find being questioned by the police puts them under pressure and blanks things out they later remember. Well, I'd better make a move. Try not to worry; you've done the right thing.'

'Thank you, Constable. Oh, I hope you don't mind my asking but do you know when I might have my gold pencil returned, it has great sentimental value to me.'

'I don't see any reason why we need to hold onto it now but I'll have to check if it can be released.'

'That would be wonderful; perhaps you could return it personally?' I give what I hope is a coy smile.

Wilson looks torn between his pleasure at my inference yet slightly uncomfortable and unsure. 'I'll see what I can do.' Heaving himself up off the sofa he walks towards the door, 'I'll be in touch.'

'Yes, please do.'

Closing the door behind him I believe I've made a little chink in his formal police armour. It's a pity he's such a stickler for the rules and seems to have a moral rod up his back but I'll keep chipping away; I enjoy a challenge.

Returning to the lounge I notice Wilson's wine glass and feel a surge of annoyance. 'The crafty beggar, he hasn't touched it!' Well, DC Wilson, I obviously do need to give you some serious attention.

I pour myself another glass but as I sink down onto the sofa, tucking my legs up under me, I find my mood plummets as my mind returns to Peter.

It's now been almost three weeks and I've still heard nothing. Every time I allow my mind to wander in that direction I feel sick as my stomach knots with anxiety. What I can't dispel is the notion that his sudden disappearance is to do with *me* and the only way that makes sense is if he truly is Addie's brother.

I've been turning our various conversations over and over in my mind. He said he's a partner in an architectural practice based in London yet he lives in Coventry. OK. It's do-able but it's a pretty long commute. Still, then again, he said they had projects all over the country so perhaps he doesn't have to spend much time in their main office but is out on site more.

I've been looking at the RIBA website and ringing round architectural firms and asking if he works for them under both the names he seems to be using, Peter Everard and the name his neighbour gave, Graham Baxter, but nothing has turned up. None of this is helping to quell my concern especially as I'm now almost certain it *was* him doing a runner out of the Renaissance Hotel.

My initial intention of nothing more than a one night stand seems to have turned into a fucking nightmare.

◆

Next morning, driving in through the narrow gates of the college I almost hit the wall as a cyclist hurtles past and weaves in front of me, narrowly missing the front of my bonnet. I slam on the brakes. 'You stupid idiot!' but he's already gone, skidding around the corner of the building towards the bicycle sheds.

I head for the staff room desperate for a strong coffee to settle my nerves.

'Are you alright Amelia? You look stressed.' Ben smiles as he bends down to get the bottle of milk out of the fridge for my coffee.

'So would you if you'd just had an idiot student on a bike play chicken as you drove in.'

'Oh dear, I think I can guess who that was; Barry Mason?'

'Couldn't say, he was too fast, I didn't get a proper look and anyway, I was too busy trying to avoid a collision.'

Busying himself with the kettle and coffee mugs, Ben continues.

'You know Barry has this business of his dad and the police to deal with? Well, I think it's pushing him off the rails a little bit. He seems to have adopted a "What's the point of anything?" attitude and I'm not sure how best to help him.'

'Oh, I see. Well, in the circumstances I'll forgive him for almost causing me to dent my car. Maybe he needs some sort of distraction, something where he can get rid of his frustrations and anger without risking himself or anyone else.'

'Yeah, I agree but what? I don't think he's got much spare cash so it'll have to be something relatively cheap. I did consider suggesting he volunteer at the local animal sanctuary but I think he's pretty busy helping out at that smallholding where he lives.'

'I didn't know his foster parents ran a smallholding. I guess that's why he's got such an interest in wildlife and conservation.'

'No, nothing to do with them, I'm not sure why he moved there; from what I've heard he was really happy at his foster parents; seemed his decision to move out was made quite recently. Barry's a bit of a dark horse at times; doesn't disclose much.'

Ben runs his hand over his hair in exasperation.

'I need to do something; he needs some help even if he won't admit it.'

I nod my agreement and take a few seconds thinking time.

'Is it a mountain bike he rides? I didn't get much of a look.'

'Yeah.'

'Well, this is just a suggestion but I think I read in one of the local newsletters that gets pushed through my door at regular intervals that there's a mountain bike club fairly local. I think they meet down near the lakes. Shouldn't cost much; he's already got the bike.'

'Amelia, that's brilliant. It might be just the thing; I'll have a word with him, thanks.'

Ben brightens up considerably.

'Oh, look at the time; we'll both be late for class. See you later, Amelia.'

Hurrying down the corridor, a pile of marked papers clasped to my chest, I recall that before Christmas I saw Lily and Munroe at the bike shop in town. Of course, that's no guarantee that Lily is interested in cycling, they could have just been idly browsing but there's a chance I can use this to my advantage. I have to get Lily and Barry together somehow and the article in the newsletter indicated that they need helpers in the clubhouse and at off-road meetings so even if Lily doesn't cycle I can try that angle.

In any case, I don't want Barry getting too stressed out by the police investigation; he'll be of no use to me if he totally loses it and it's more likely that he'll slip up under the pressure of Munroe's questioning.

My class are pretty boisterous, still finding it hard to settle after the long Christmas break, so that by the time the bell goes I'm decidedly frazzled and bad tempered. I can't go through the rest of the day like this; I'll have to devise something a bit more entertaining for the afternoon in the hope of keeping the students' attention.

Rummaging through the college library's DVD collection I discover a DVD on the work of Vermeer. That will do perfectly.

Returning to the classroom I go to see Janet; as Principal's secretary she's in charge of all audio-visual equipment and I need her authority to have the caretaker set things up in the classroom but her office is empty. I hesitate, a bit flummoxed – Janet's always here – she never has time off. I'm standing wondering what to do next when the adjoining door into the Principal's office opens.

'Miss Thompson, Amelia, you look lost.'

'Hello Principal.'

'Paul, please.'

'Paul, I was looking for Janet. I need her to authorise my use of the DVD equipment. I want my class to watch a film this afternoon.'

'I can authorise that for you. I'm afraid Janet won't be in for a while.'

'Is she unwell?'

'No, just erm … Just a family matter I believe.'

'Nothing serious I hope.'

'I expect not. Now let me get you that authorisation slip.'

As I stroll back down the corridor in search of the caretaker I want to skip with delight. Janet's 'family matter' can only mean one thing. Thank you, Detective Constable Wilson, thank you so much.

◆

That evening I'm feeling a little more confident as I make my way to my therapy session but I still need to sort out my reaction to Peter's strange disappearance.

I find Barnaby makes a very useful sounding board. It's a strange phenomenon but as I speak my thoughts out loud to him they seem to bounce back from another dimension, as if I'm hearing them for the first time and I can then view them objectively; impossible when they're rattling around in my head.

I snuggle back into Barnaby's winged leather arm chair; it feels like an old friend.

I'm grateful that the initial silence of my sessions continues unchallenged; it gives me time in which to settle and compose my thoughts. I know Barnaby thinks I'm a troubled individual, a bit too close to the edge for him to feel entirely comfortable with me but today I don't want to play games. If Peter's real name is Graham Baxter and he is Addie's brother, then my anxiety is justified yet that only makes sense if he knew who I was but how could he and if he didn't know who I was, what possible reason could he have for disappearing so suddenly? I need to sort out in my mind just what it is about his disappearance that unnerves me so.

'This year, I didn't spend Christmas and New Year on my own; I had company.'

Barnaby raises an eyebrow, smiles and indicates he wants me to continue.

'It was a man I'd met quite recently.'

'Ah, a beau.' Barnaby smiles at his deliberate use of the word.

'Oh, Barnaby, what a lovely, old-fashioned word! Yes, that's exactly what he was, my beau.'

'You said "was"'.

'Because he is no more, gone, disappeared, like smoke on a breeze.' I waft my hand upwards.

Barnaby waits.

'Strange, isn't it, the way people just disappear from my life? Puff and they've gone.'

'What people?'

'Matt, his girlfriend, Addie, my parents, now Peter; take your pick.'

Barnaby rests his elbows on the arms of his chair and puts his hands as in the act of prayer, tapping the tips of his fingers together, a thoughtful expression on his face. 'Everyone loses people Amelia, some die, some move on, things constantly change; the whole world is in a state of flux, nothing is constant.'

Sometimes, Barnaby's patronising claptrap makes me want to throw up.

'The thing is, Barnaby, I can't find a reason for his leaving. Matt and Addie died and I miss them both terribly. As for my parents they never really wanted me, they only wanted Matt so, with him gone, they withdrew from me even further but Peter…'

I gaze into the middle distance, Peter's head on the pillow as distinct in my mind's eye as when he physically lay beside me and once again that uneasiness in my gut, that feeling of familiarity right from the start and yes, that inexplicable sense of danger.

'Barnaby, do you believe that for everybody in the world there's a double, someone who looks exactly like them, a doppelganger?'

Barnaby's face is a picture of surprise; I can see him wondering where on earth my question has come from. 'Well, I've heard the theory; I suppose it's possible that there isn't an infinite number of variations. Why do you ask?'

'Oh nothing; it's not important.'

There's a pause, that's somehow heavy with meaning. Eventually Barnaby's voice seems to come to me from afar.

'It seems Peter's disappearance bothers you.'

'Well, yes, of course it does. Wouldn't it bother you if someone you'd just slept with left without a word?'

'Were you close?'

I manage to stifle a snort of derision.

'No, not particularly; I hadn't known him long enough to claim we were close but I did think he really liked me.'

Barnaby still doesn't comment but continues with his questions, 'Would you have liked the relationship to have continued?'

I think back to my concern when I realised Peter would have to spend the night at my apartment. 'No, I didn't want it to last.'

'So, why are you so upset?'

'I'm not upset, I'm angry.'

The realisation surprises me.

Barnaby scribbles, probably writing "Anger Issues" on his notepad.

'It was a pretty shitty thing to do or do you think that sort of behaviour's OK?'

Barnaby doesn't answer, simply looks across at me with an expression of sympathy, the patronising creep. I know what he's thinking; that the only thing that's been damaged is my pride.

My hands grip the arms of the chair, nails clawing at the leather surface as I acknowledge that I am angry, so *very angry*. Peter was never truly important to me; I'd initially only considered him as a one night stand. It's just that I'd been thrown off course by my desire for company at this difficult time of the year. Christmas always fucks me up. How could I have been so stupid, so weak, I've wasted time, valuable time and I'm furious, both with myself and with him.

I give a slight involuntary shudder.

'Amelia, what is it? Are you alright?'

Barnaby looks at his watch, unable to disguise his relief that our session is over. I think I frighten him sometimes. I smile, stand and shake his hand,

'Thank you, Barnaby, you've been a great help.'

I walk out to the car, a cold calmness descending. I was right, talking with Barnaby has helped; it's changed my anxiety into anger and that's much easier for me to deal with. Now I must get back on track. The evening classes for the watercolour painting begin next week. I must be there. It's time to renew my acquaintance with Lily Munroe.

CHAPTER 7

I spend part of the weekend traipsing round the shops getting set up for the next week's painting class; palette of watercolour paints, brushes of various thickness, a piece of cloth for a cleaning rag. I wonder if I ought to buy some kind of smock to protect my clothes but decide rather than risk looking a complete idiot I'll wear things I no longer care much about.

Entering the classroom Tuesday evening I pause by the door as I scan the room and am pleased to see Lily already there. To her left an elderly man is busily setting out his painting equipment but the easel on her right is free. I'm just about to take a step forward when I'm shouldered aside by a young woman with strikingly pink hair and a tattoo on her neck. I sense that she's heading for the vacant easel next to Lily. Hurrying after her, I tap her on the shoulder.

'Excuse me, I think you just dropped something.'

She stops and turns to look as, indicating the paint brush I've just dropped on the floor, I hurry past her and swiftly place my things on the easel's shelf.

'No, it's not mine.'

'Oh, it must be mine; sorry.'

She shrugs, glances at my items on the easel and, giving me a hard stare, wanders across to another position.

I look across at Lily and smile as I remove my coat and scarf.

'Hello again, I'm Amelia, we spoke at the enrolment evening.'

'Oh, yes, I remember, I'm Lily. How are you?'

'I'm fine thanks. Did you have a good Christmas?'

'Just a quiet family affair as usual but it was pleasant enough, how about you?'

'Like you, fairly quiet.'

Lily's innocent 'family affair' sends a surge of resentment through me. I expect DCI Munroe enjoys playing happy families. I'm just about to quiz her about presents when the classroom door's flung open and a large woman in her forties bounces in.

'Good evening everybody. I'm Madeleine McLevitt and by the end of the course I shall have turned you all into competent watercolour artists.'

I make a face at Lily, 'She's optimistic.'

Lily nods in agreement, 'I wish her luck!'

Madeleine McLevitt is a throwback from the sixties era; clothed in a multi-coloured flowing kaftan, headscarf and beads, adorned with large rings and bracelets, she flounces to the front of the class and seems to fill the room with her presence. What she lacks in refinement she more than makes up for in enthusiasm.

I take an instant liking to her and am even more enamoured when she makes it plain we won't be painting the usual 'still life' bowl of fruit. No, under her tutelage we'll be expressing our inner selves through the medium of paint on paper. I'm not so sure I want to display my inner self but I expect I can fake it convincingly enough.

As class ends I glance across at Lily's effort and feel a pang of jealousy as I have to acknowledge that it's far superior to my own offering. Despite my interest in art and art history I've never been an artist myself, something that has always irked me.

Lily smiles as we walk out together.

'Did you enjoy this evening?'

'Yeah, I did. Your friend was right; she's a great teacher.'

'Yeah, that's what I thought. Do you think we ought to tell her that the sixties are over?'

'No, leave her be; she's more fun as she is. I wonder where she gets her kaftans.'

'Probably makes them herself!' Lily giggles as she heads for her car. 'See you next week.' She pulls up her collar against the cold January night and hurries across the car park.

Lily really does seem to have a sweet nature, so like Matt's girlfriend, Addie; that's promising; she's likely to be just as malleable.

My drive home takes a little longer than usual due to a couple of sets of roadwork traffic lights going against me so it's nearly ten o'clock by the time I pull into the car park at the rear of the house. Walking around to the front garden as the back door is merely a fire escape route; I have an uncanny sense of being watched. The hedge bordering the pavement is high, I'd have to stand on tip toe to see over it, but in places it's become quite thin allowing the light from the street lamp to illuminate the garden path. As I approach the front door a shadow flits over the path in front of me. I gasp barely suppressing a scream, as next door's cat brushes against my legs, mewling to be let in out of the cold.

'Oh you scared me, you naughty thing,' I give Angus a gentle prod with my foot, 'Go on, home with you; you're not coming in here.' Turning my key in the lock, I let myself in and as I turn to close the door I'm sure I glimpse someone standing on the opposite side of the road. I hold the door slightly ajar and peer through the crack. The person turns and walks on; I'm being silly, it's probably just someone on their way home from the Cat n' Fiddle pub.

◆

I'm annoyed that I didn't manage to keep Lily talking for longer; I was hoping to find out more about her interests. I know where she goes to hang out with her friends; that she prefers pubs to wine bars and hates rap music; all little snippets I've gathered over the years of observation but finding common ground to get her and Barry together is difficult.

Still, no point agonising over it; I decide to concentrate meanwhile on Barry. I need to distance him from the police enquiries; DC Wilson appears to have done his bit but it'll help if suspicions about Gary Stevenson are reinforced.

About halfway between college and the park there's a cosy little café run by a jolly man who bumbles between the tables carrying plates laden with deliciously unhealthy food. The place is always a welcome fug of warmth and aromas and the coffee is an excellent, high quality brand that's a surprise to find in such an establishment. I know Barry often eats there because I've seen him on my way to the park at lunch time.

As morning lessons end I indicate to Barry to remain behind. He slouches on one of the tables, his dark eyes observing me under long, silky lashes; a slight smile on his lips.

'Barry, I need to have a talk with you but not in college.'

Barry looks surprised.

'That's not allowed, is it? Being alone with a student off campus; people might get the wrong impression.'

'Not alone, Barry, just away from the college; the café near the park will do. I'll buy you lunch.'

Swinging his long legs, Barry levers himself up off the table.

'Trying to bribe me for sexual favours are you?'

I give him a cold stare.

'I've never had to bribe anyone in my life. Just go, Barry.'

'OK, if you're buying.'

He stands waiting.

'You go ahead; I'll be there in a few minutes.'

I watch from the window as Barry saunters across the college car park and out toward the café; hands dug deep into his jeans pockets. It's easy to see why he generates such interest from the opposite sex. If only I can get him and Lily together…

By the time I arrive at the café Barry has seated himself at a table by the window.

'Have you ordered?'

'Yeah, it's on its way; didn't know what you wanted though.'

'OK, I'll go and get something.'

As I wait at the counter I look back at Barry just as he turns his head to stare out of the window but not before I notice his expression; a look of self-satisfied smugness.

Sitting down opposite, I warm my hands on my coffee mug.

'I heard about your father and the police investigation; I'm so sorry Barry, it's a rotten business.'

'Thanks.' His mumbled response is grudging in the extreme but I plough on.

'They don't still think you had anything to do with it, do they? I heard they were questioning someone else now.'

'Yeah, they are.'

'I heard the name Gary Stevenson; isn't that the college secretary's son?'

'Yeah.'

'I wonder why they suspect him. Do you have any ideas?'

Barry shrugs his indifference. I *know* he knows Gary trades in drugs and does a lot of that business in the park, practically every student in college knows.

'You know, Barry, sometimes it can be very hard to prove one's innocence, especially if you don't have a strong alibi. Most of us don't go through life ensuring we've got alibis in case something bad happens and we're all aware of how persistent the police can be in their pursuit of an individual, especially if suspects are few and far between. There've been enough miscarriages of justice to prove that. Sometimes you have to take steps to safeguard yourself.'

Barry fixes me with his gaze; at last I feel I have his full attention.

'All I'm saying is that if you have any information about Gary Stevenson that supports the police suspicions you'd be doing yourself a favour to tell them. This is a very serious matter; you can't allow some sense of misplaced loyalty to jeopardise you.'

Barry leans forward placing his arms on the table and quietly asks, 'Why are you so concerned about me?'

'Because I know how these things can go so badly wrong. It doesn't matter how I know, that's personal, but trust me, Barry, I do know and I wouldn't like that to happen to you. You owe it to yourself to ensure the police are on the correct track, don't you agree?'

Barry nods, 'I guess so. Is that it?'

'What else could there be, Barry?'

He smirks as he levels his eyes at my breasts but before he can answer, a tap on the window causes us both to start and look up. Jess Saunders is waving at Barry but noticing his aggravated expression glances across in my direction and pulls a face. Ignoring her I stare pointedly at Barry.

'If you feel the need to discuss anything, at any time, you know my door is always open. Now I must get back.

Think on what I've said, Barry, it could really matter to your future.' I gather up my coat and scarf and hurry outside. The wind has turned and is sending icy blasts down from Siberia, or so it seems after the warmth of the café.

Jess smirks as I pass and so, putting on my teacher's voice, I command, 'Just make sure you're not late back.'

As I hurry along, my mind whirring, I wonder just what kind of relationship there is between Jess and Barry. Still, I feel the conversation has been fruitful. The deeper I can sink Gary Stevenson the safer Barry and my plans for him will be and the more traumatic it will all be for Gary's mother. I smile; a little collateral damage in her direction will taste particularly sweet.

◆

A couple of days later I'm sipping coffee in the staffroom during the break period when Ben strolls over. 'Mind if I join you?'

'Of course not, how are things?'

'Fine, fine.'

'How's Barry? No more near misses on his bike I hope.'

'No,' Ben grins, 'I told him about the cycle club you mentioned. He seemed interested so hopefully he'll do something about it. Actually, he's been a bit more upbeat recently, like he's come to terms with his father's death and got the police questioning into perspective. He doesn't divulge much but I think he can sort of see the police suspicions from their point of view and understands why they had, at least, some valid reasons to question him. I expect the questioning of Gary Stevenson's helped as well; shows that Barry isn't the only one in their minds.'

'Are they still questioning Gary then? I'd noticed Janet isn't back; it must be very hard for her.'

'According to the bush telegraph, yes they are. From what I've heard, the police got a tip off that Gary deals drugs and someone I don't know who saw him talking with the tramp. Since then they've had at least one other report confirming Gary's extra-curricular activities so I think they'll be investigating him for a while yet.'

'Good gracious, Ben, how do you find all these things out?' I reach for the biscuit tin on the table between us, I think this calls for a treat.

'Been here a long time now,' Ben rummages in the tin for his favourite biscuits, 'learnt who to listen to and who not. You'd be surprised how accurate some of the "rumours" turn out to be.'

'You sound like you're working for MI5!'

Ben grins, 'It feels a bit like that sometimes, trying to filter out the wheat from the chaff. Move over George Smiley!'

'I should think our illustrious Principal is finding things difficult without Janet running everything for him.'

'Oh, I don't know. I should imagine he's enjoying the freedom.' Ben's look is one of mild disgust.

I lean forward across the coffee table and lower my voice to a conspiratorial whisper. 'Whatever do you mean?'

I know Ben is far from enamoured of our Principal for, as Head of one of the larger departments, he was in serious contention for the position but in the event, lost out to Paul Whitlow who was brought in from outside. The general consensus of opinion was that some palms within the Board had been crossed with silver; Paul Whitlow's father-in-law being one of the Trustees and a very influential and wealthy businessman in the local community.

'*If* rumours are to be believed,' Ben continues, 'Paul Whitlow suffers from roving hands.'

'What! Not *Janet* surely?'

'Oh, God, no,' Ben looks aghast at my assumption, 'even *he* wouldn't go there. No, I mean students.'

'Really? Hasn't anyone reported him?'

'It seems he's quite adept at choosing his quarry, you know, girls with, shall we say, hand-knitted morals. After all, this is a Further Education college; all the students are technically adults above the age of consent.'

'Even so, it's still an abuse of his position.'

'Indeed it is but you wouldn't get anywhere reporting him; too well connected as they say.' Ben gives a dismissive, resigned shrug of his shoulders, 'The world today is all about *who* you know rather than *what* you know.'

I nod my agreement, giving Ben the sympathetic vote, but am quietly thinking that, actually, I get by quite well on *what* I know and this latest snippet of information might prove extremely useful.

On the way home I call in at the supermarket, I'm running a bit low on wine and they're doing a special promotion of a good vintage greatly reduced, which is not to be missed.

Getting back to the car with my trolley, I'm loading the wine and my evening meal into the boot when I experience a mild, pricking sensation at my back, like all my nerve ends have suddenly become hyper-sensitive. It's almost as if someone is breathing down my neck. I turn and look around but can't see anything unusual, just people sorting out their shopping or fiddling in purses for the £1 coins for the trolleys. I sniff, maybe I'm getting a cold; I do feel a bit chilled. Better get home into the warm.

I push the trolley back to its enclosure and retrieve my £1. Returning to the car I glance around me as I open the driver's door. I can't dispel this feeling of being watched. I turn the ignition, switching on the headlights and the heater fan, I so dislike driving on these dark, winter nights; I need to get home. I'm probably just over tired.

Driving home I put a CD on to distract my thoughts and sing along to the familiar words. I've gone a couple of miles when I glance again in the rear view mirror, I'm sure that car was behind me at the traffic lights. It seems to be driving much too close to my rear bumper. I speed up a little to put some distance between us and when that doesn't work I touch the brakes gently to put on the rear brake lights, a warning to drop back a little. I can't make out the car properly, only its headlights.

Using my brakes seems to have worked, the driver pulls back and as I turn into my road I'm pleased to find that he doesn't follow. Curious though. I think a glass of wine is needed.

◆

Tuesday rolls round quickly and I find I'm looking forward to the art class and meeting up with Lily again. She has such a sweet, endearing nature; the way she is always so ready to help, so immediately open when forming a new friendship. I find it hard to contemplate how a man like Munroe could have fathered her; her nature must all come from her mother's side.

Madeleine McLevitt flounces into class, all psychedelic colours and theatrical gestures – god, I love her! She's such a breath of fresh air. I wish I had the confidence to act in such an extravagant manner.

I do better tonight and actually receive some praise from Madeleine. Lily is also very complimentary. 'That's really good Amelia, I love the effect of the purple.' The non-competitive sort, Lily has no problem encouraging others, even if it means they might one day outshine her. I suppose it's a nice character trait but hardly one that will propel her forward in this world. I've always found a little ruthlessness goes a long way.

'Thanks, Lily, do you fancy stopping off for a coffee before going home?'

'Yeah, why not? I feel quite hungry, could do with something to eat.'

'Yeah, me too; why don't we pop into Pizza Express?'

'Yeah, good idea.'

Pizza Express is only a few yards down the road so we leave our cars in the car park and walk. It's a cold night but at least it's dry.

'I could do with a glass of wine,' I say, settling down at a table, 'do you want one?'

'Oh, I don't know,' Lily hesitates 'Dad's *really* against drinking and driving.'

'C'mon, it's only one small glass.'

'Well, maybe just a *very* small one.'

I can tell Lily is torn between pleasing me and defying her dad. I give another little push.

'He'll never know. Just suck a peppermint on the way home.'

Lily gives a small, conspiratorial smile, 'OK, why not?'

Tucking into pizza and wine Lily visibly relaxes. 'God I'm enjoying this; I didn't realise I was quite so hungry.'

'Mmm, me too,' I put on an interested expression, 'Have you made any holiday plans yet this year?'

'No, not yet; my friends all like to go somewhere hot and just lay on the beach and go clubbing at night but I get so bored with all that. I keep looking at activity holidays but it's a bit scary doing something like that on your own for the first time.'

'Yeah, I suppose so. What sort of thing do you want to do?'

'Haven't a clue.' Lily gives a chuckle and raises her eyes heavenward.

'You must have some idea; kayaking in Canada; white water rafting; a walking holiday in the Andes?'

'No, none of them; God, Dad would have a fit; he'd never let me go.'

'Why not? You'd be in a group, wouldn't you?'

'I don't know why; he's just so ridiculously protective, it's suffocating sometimes.' Lily looks downcast.

'But you're eighteen, aren't you?'

Lily nods.

'Then you can do what you want.'

'It doesn't seem to work like that in our household.'

Lily gives a deep sigh and sips her wine.

'Well, what about if it's not so extreme?'

'If you're going to suggest a painting holiday I'll hit you!'

'No! I was more thinking of something that you could do closer to home and maybe slowly build into something a bit more adventurous.'

'Such as?'

'Cycling.'

'Oh no, I don't fancy riding for miles on our roads.'

'No, I didn't mean that kind of cycling; I meant mountain biking; off road riding. Can you ride a bike?'

'Of course I can; haven't got one though.'

Lily looks dejected.

'Oh, that is a problem.'

I stare into my wine making a show of considering for a few minutes.

'I could lend you mine.'

'Really?'

'Yeah, why not? I hardly use it; it still looks brand new.'

Lily looks keen for a few seconds but then doubtful.

'No, perhaps not, I don't really fancy going off on my own through woods and that; might not be very safe.'

God, this is hard work! Has she really got to eighteen and still be so timid? Obviously been wrapped in cotton wool all her life; perhaps I should thank my parents for their lack of protectiveness and care; it certainly toughened me up.

'Mmm, true; how about a club?'

'Don't know of any.'

'I'm sure there's one locally; I read about it somewhere. What was it called? Endover something; I know, "Freewheelers", that was it, "Endover Freewheelers". They have a clubhouse down near the lakes. I'm sure I read somewhere that they were needing volunteers to work their coffee bar and help out at events. You could do that for a bit; see if you like the people and get a feel for what they do. Then, if you want to give it a proper go, you can borrow my bike. It could eventually lead to cycling holidays.'

Lily sits chewing her bottom lip, turning the conversation over in her mind.

'I bet Dad'll say no.'

'Don't tell him.'

'Yeah, but he always seems to have a way of finding things out.'

Lily looks really pissed off.

'Oh Lily, it's stupid; you're eighteen. You've got to cut the cord sometime.'

'Yeah, I know you're right.'

'C'mon, let's have another glass of wine; you need cheering up.'

For the briefest second Lily hesitates, then

'Yeah, sod him; I will.'

An hour later, arms linked, we hurry back to the car park. 'I've really enjoyed this evening, let's do it again sometime.' Lily suggests.

'I'd love to. Are you doing anything Saturday week, perhaps we could meet up then? There's a café near Melsham Park, we could meet there about twelve noon.'

'I think I know it; isn't that the one that does those enormous all day breakfasts and that delicious coffee?'

'Yep.'

'In that case, you're definitely on, I'll see you there Saturday. Bye.'

Dear Lily, so easily swayed from the straight and narrow path her father wants her to walk. It's like taking candy from a baby.

CHAPTER 8

Oh hell, I've over slept; I must have forgotten to switch the alarm on last night. I just have time to make and grab a piece of toast, stuffing it in my mouth as I head for the car. No time for my usual coffee in the staff room, instead I hasten straight for my class, rounding the corridor at break neck speed when I skid to a halt, swiftly backtrack a few steps and hide behind the corner.

Ben is in the corridor with Barry.

'That's fantastic! Thanks.'

'It's OK, Barry; just make sure you make the most of the opportunity.'

They turn and continue down the corridor toward the Small Animal Unit. What on earth can all that be about? I must make sure I speak with Ben during the break but for now I need to get to my class.

As it happens I don't manage to see Ben until lunchtime. 'Where were you at coffee break?' I ask as I pass him his mug.

'Just trying to get some things organised in the animal unit; I'm going to be a bit short-handed for a while.'

'Why? What's happened?'

Ben leads the way to a couple of armchairs in the corner.

'It's great news for the students; just means extra work for me.'

'I'm intrigued.'

I settle back in the chair and wait.

'The college has been given a rare opportunity to send some students on a week-long residential course at a wetland nature reserve on the Fens. It's a brilliant chance to see and work with the Rangers at close hand and get to grips with all the issues involved in wetland conservation. The Trust is also considering offering a place on their workforce to the most promising student on completion of qualifications and those jobs don't come up that often.'

'So, who have you picked to go?'

'Ted Cummins, Barbara Watson, Eddy James and Barry Mason. It wasn't that difficult; all four stand out above the rest and are the sort who'll make best use of it. I just got the names confirmed this morning by Paul Whitlow.'

I try to sound pleased.

'That's great, Ben and good that Barry's included, what with everything else going on for him at present. When do they go?'

'In a couple of weeks, so I'll be cramming them with as much relevant information as I can before then.'

'Sounds like you're going to be busy. By the way, did Barry join that cycling club I mentioned?'

'Yes he did and likes it by all accounts so thanks for that, Amelia.'

'You're welcome.'

'Oh well, time to go; can't keep sitting here chatting with you all day, however enjoyable it is.'

Ben picks up his coffee mug and rinses it at the sink. Watching him leave for his next class I feel my frustration will boil over. Damn! The last thing I need is for Barry to disappear for a week just as I'm hoping to manoeuvre him and Lily into meeting. How the hell can I put a stop to it? As much as I've been trying to divert the police attention away from Barry I've a sinking feeling that the only way I'm going to prevent him clearing off to the Fens is to involve the police. Bloody ironic but I just can't think what else I can do.

I wait until the end of day and ring DC Wilson.

'Constable Wilson, its Amelia Thompson. I'm sorry to trouble you again but I wonder if there's any chance of the police returning my gold pencil soon.'

'As it happens I was intending to call you today. Your pencil is no longer required as evidence so I'll be able to return it to you this evening, if that's convenient.'

'That's wonderful, thank you.'

'I'll be there about six-thirty.'

'That's fine. Thank you again, Constable Wilson.'

Despite Ben's conviction at the Christmas party Jess and Barry are still together several weeks later. It's a damn nuisance, I could do without the bother but if I'm to get Barry and Lily together Jess *must* be history.

As I leave for home I notice Jess and a couple of other girls in a conspiratorial huddle at the far side of the college car park. They're all so engrossed that no-one notices my approach as I walk slowly toward my car and am just in time to see a small packet being passed from Jess to one of the other girls and money handed back. Drugs; that could prove very useful.

When I arrive home, I'm pounced on by Mrs Lewis,

'Amelia my dear, how are you?'

'I'm fine thank you, Mrs Lewis, I hope you are too.'

'Oh yes my dear, I'm well, quite well.' Mrs Lewis hesitates as if deciding whether to continue.

'Is there something you wish to tell me, Mrs Lewis?' I'm willing her to hurry up; I want to get into my apartment and get changed before DC Wilson arrives.

'Oh dear, I do hope I haven't done anything wrong; I didn't mean to and he was such a nice man.' Mrs Lewis' hands flutter up to her head as she starts nervously pulling at a strand of grey hair that's come loose from the ruched band at her neck. I've always thought the style looks incongruous on such an elderly person; she'd do far better to have it cut short, her hair's too thin now to be worn long.

'What "nice man" is this, Mrs Lewis?'

'I was in the front garden, doing a bit of pruning to the roses near my window; if I wait for the landlord to do anything they'll be all straggly come summer.'

I drop my heavy bag onto the floor at my feet and shift my weight onto the other leg; it looks like I'm in for the long haul. Mrs Lewis notices and gives a nervous cough, 'He surprised me a bit…'

'Who, the landlord?'

'No, no, the man, I didn't hear him approach you see. I think the postman must have left the gate unlocked so I didn't hear the usual warning squeak as it opened. Anyway, I turned round and there he was, right up close behind me. Gave me a real start I can tell you but he was very nice, so polite, apologised straight away he did.'

I barely suppress an exasperated sigh, 'Mrs Lewis, forgive me but, what is the point of all this?'

Mrs Lewis gives a guilty, apologetic smile, 'He was asking about you, my dear.'

I feel the blood drain from my face as I stare open-mouthed at Mrs Lewis,

'Wanted to know when you'd moved in, if you ever had any family visit.'

'Did you tell him anything?'

'No, well, only a little; I said you'd moved in about a year ago and I didn't know anything about your family.'

'Did he want to know anything else?'

'He did ask if I knew where you'd lived before.'

'What did you say?'

Mrs Lewis refuses to meet my eye, 'I said I believed you'd lived in the Dorset area; you'd told me if you remember, that evening shortly after you first arrived when I gave you a cup of tea, you were telling me about your childhood there.'

I vaguely remember and curse myself for revealing even *that* much about my past. 'What did this man look like?'

'Oh, I don't know; I'm not very good at noticing things.' Mrs Lewis looks panicked, 'He was tall, I remember that I had to look up to him and I think he had dark hair, or maybe, no, I think it might have been a woolly hat, it was very cold this morning.' My lips in a tight line of fury I simply stare mute at Mrs Lewis as she makes an effort to recall more detail. 'I think he wore glasses but …' Mrs Lewis puts a hand to her lips in thought, 'no, maybe he didn't; it's no good, I can't remember.'

Being tall was no help, everyone was tall compared to Mrs Lewis' tiny stature; the rest was less than useless. 'Did he say *why* he wanted to know these things about me?'

'Well, no, I don't think he did.'

'Didn't you ask?' Anxiety causes my voice to increase a few decibels at which Mrs Lewis flinches and takes a couple of frightened steps back.

'I'm so sorry my dear. I guess I'm just a silly old woman.'

I don't bother to disillusion her instead, picking up my bag, I give what I hope is a withering look and turn away,

'Good night, Mrs Lewis.'

Entering my apartment I slam the door behind me, stomp into the lounge and throw my bag onto the sofa. Stupid old bat!

Who could this man have been? Can't be Detective Constable Wilson, Mrs Lewis would have recognised him from her earlier encounter. It wouldn't be Ben; he'd have no reason to call round and certainly wouldn't be asking questions about me, he'd ask me himself. I suppose it could be Barnaby but to be asking questions about my past behind my back would be seriously unprofessional and I can't believe he'd do that. Surely, it can only be Peter. Mrs Lewis wouldn't know him, she never saw him but she said the man had dark hair, but then it might have been a hat and that would have hidden Peter's blonde hair. But, if it was Peter, why hasn't he made contact and why on earth would he be asking such questions about me unless he knows who I am? The thought shudders through me.

I keep turning everything over in my mind. Knowing that someone has been asking questions about me coupled with the sense I've had recently of being watched is unnerving. I feel as though I'm being stalked and I don't know how to handle it. I don't want to report it to the police as the last thing I need is their focus upon me and anyway, I don't suppose for a moment they'll do much about it. Maybe I'll speak with Barnaby. It's about time for my next session and it may help me to rationalise my thoughts but for now I need to get ready for DC Wilson's visit.

Rushing through my shower, I've just finished drying my hair when my doorbell chimes.

'DC Wilson, please come in.'

I stand back holding the door open as DC Wilson sidles past, barely able to avoid brushing against me in my narrow hallway.

Following him into the lounge I relieve the DC of his raincoat,

'Will you join me in a drink? I noticed you left the last one I gave you.'

Wilson squirms under my gentle reproach, as embarrassment heightens the colour in his cheeks emphasising his chubby, smooth, baby-like features. He coughs lightly and sheepishly apologises, 'Sorry about that. I appreciate the offer but I'd better not.'

I cross to the drinks cabinet and pour myself a glass of Pinotage.

DC Wilson rummages in his jacket pocket and pulls out a small plastic bag, 'Here, as I said on the telephone, I managed to get this released.'

'Oh, how wonderful, thank you so much,' I cradle the gold pencil to my chest, 'I know Chief Inspector Munroe considered that I'd just been careless; I've no idea when it could have fallen out of my bag; I don't use it that often and I simply hadn't realised it had gone.'

I allow a tremble of sadness into my voice,

'I didn't feel your Inspector was very sympathetic to my loss.'

'The Boss isn't one given to displays of emotion or sentimentality.'

God, this man is loyal to the point of nausea!

'Well, I'm glad you're not *all* like that in the police force, sometimes a little empathy can go a long way.' I smile warmly, 'May I ask what's happening with the investigation into the tramp's murder? Have you arrested anyone yet? Or perhaps you're not allowed to speak about that.' I've positioned myself on the sofa beside

Wilson, my legs tucked up underneath me as I lean in toward him.

'Well, I can tell you that you were right about Gary Stevenson dealing drugs in the park but we've no evidence to link him to the murder.'

'Oh dear, I'm sorry I got it so wrong but the more I've thought about it, you know, tried to visualise, the more sure I am that I did see him talking with the tramp in the college grounds and leaving the park by the side entrance. I think the general feeling amongst the students at college is that he's probably guilty. He's not well liked. Still, are you looking at anyone else?'

'I can't possibly discuss that.' Wilson's tone admonishes me in no uncertain terms.

'Of course not, I apologise. It's just that Barry is such a lovely lad and I hate to see him suffer so. It's all over the college that the tramp was his father. Once he'd been brought in by the police to identify the body and was questioned he seems to have been quite open about everything. Barry's the opposite of Gary, very well liked; taking the Small Animal and Wildlife course.'

Wilson looks mildly apprehensive. 'Appearances can be deceptive you know. In an investigation of this nature, we can't afford to take anything at face value.'

'No, I suppose not but I'm glad you don't regard Barry as a suspect anymore.'

'What makes you say that? We're still following several lines of enquiry.'

'Well, yes but it's just that as Barry's going away for a while I assumed he was no longer under investigation.'

'Going away? Where?'

'To the Fens; it's a week-long residential conservation course. I assumed the college would have notified you to check that it was OK.'

Wilson looks decidedly annoyed.

'No, they haven't.'

'Oh dear, I hope I haven't got anyone into trouble. It's probably just an oversight on the part of the Principal. Have you ever been to the Fens, DC Wilson? I have once; it's a huge area; one could easily get lost in it.'

Wilson, looking concerned stands, obviously anxious to get back and report my news to DCI Munroe. I hurry through into the hall,

'I'll get your coat.'

As I hand it to him I reiterate,

'I do hope I haven't spoken out of turn, Constable.'

'No, we need to know these things; thank you for your time, Miss Thompson.'

As I walk him out into the entrance lobby I place a brief kiss on his cheek, 'That's for returning my pencil.'

His surprise is evident and he tries to hide his embarrassment by joking, 'That's the first time I've been kissed by a person involved in an investigation! Goodnight, Miss Thompson.'

I've just reached my apartment when I hear Mrs Lewis' door across the hall open.

'Amelia, my dear, may I have a word?'

Closing my eyes I take a calming breath and turn to face her, my features a mask of indifference.

Mrs Lewis twitters nervously, 'I don't want to keep you, it's just I think I've remembered something.'

'About what, Mrs Lewis?'

'About the man who was asking me questions about you.'

I fold my arms across my chest and wait; I'm *not* going to make this easy for her.

'It was his jacket, a sort of puffed up thing.'

'Lots of people wear those, Mrs Lewis.' I let out a sigh of exasperation.

'Oh yes, I know but it was what was on it that caught my eye. A sort of emblemy thing, embroidered I think it was, in some sort of gold coloured thread.'

I realise I'm going to have to ask or she'll never get round to the point. 'So, what was this "emblemy thing"?'

'Oh, it was lovely, really life-like I thought. I remember I remarked on it.' Mrs Lewis notices my angry stare and hurries on triumphantly, 'It was a kangaroo! Does that help?'

I steel myself to not display any sign of recognition, 'Not in the slightest, Mrs Lewis. Goodnight,' and so saying I turn my back on her and walk into my apartment.

Leaning my back against the inside of my front door, I think back to my conversations with Peter. At one point he'd said his family had emigrated to Australia although that didn't seem to tie up with his comment that they'd moved near London for his father's work. I'm beginning to feel that everything he said was ambiguous.

I try to visualise the run to Peter's car on New Year's Eve through the snowstorm. He'd pulled on a thick padded jacket over his suit. I close my eyes and try to recall sitting beside him in the car. I'm almost certain I can see gold stitching on his right lapel although I can't be sure what it is. I let out a weary sigh; perhaps I'm just reacting to the power of suggestion.

CHAPTER 9

Next morning Ben's in the staff room banging mugs and the milk bottle onto the kitchen area surface with a complete lack of regard either for the noise he's causing or the risk he's running of smashing things.

'What on earth's got into you this morning, Ben?'

'I've been trying to placate Barry; not an easy job.'

'Why? What's got his back up?'

Ben leans heavily on the work surface, his frustration obvious.

'It seems the police have been in touch with Principal Whitlow and insisted that Barry doesn't go on the residential course I told you about. They're saying he's still very much part of their investigation and they're not prepared to take the risk of him absconding.'

'But surely he could abscond from here if he wanted to. It's ridiculous.'

'I know but they're adamant, apparently. What's made the whole thing worse is that when Whitlow told him, Barry thinks it's all Whitlow's doing.'

'Why should he think that?'

'It's all to do with Whitlow's roving hands and Jess Saunders.'

'Ah, I'd forgotten that.'

'Ah indeed. Having the reputation she does I don't suppose Jess is that averse to Whitlow's attentions but Barry went ballistic when the rumours reached him. You heard he strode into Whitlow's office and landed him one, almost broke his nose by all accounts.'

'Yes, I did; I'm surprised Barry wasn't thrown out of college.'

'I think Whitlow was too scared of his behaviour becoming public, he's been involved with more than just Jess remember.'

I nod my acknowledgement, 'So ever since I suppose Whitlow's been on Barry's case.'

'That's it, I'm afraid Barry's his own worst enemy sometimes.'

Ben emits a defeated sigh.

'Better get back to the animal unit. The mood Barry's in I don't suppose he's doing much work. See you later, Amelia.'

'Yeah bye, Ben; see you.'

Settling down at the table, I spread some marking out before me and reflect. My little chat with DC Wilson obviously worked and Barry's going to remain around. Good. Also, the antagonism between Barry and Principal Whitlow over Jess is potentially useful. If I'm careful I can use it to cause trouble between Jess and Barry which, coupled with her drug dealing, may be enough to break up any relationship.

As arranged I'll be seeing Lily on Saturday at the café, hopefully she'll have done something about the cycle club. Of course, if she does take it up it's going to cost me as I'll have to buy a sodding mountain bike but it'll be worth it if it gets her and Barry into contact.

The rest of the day passes uneventfully and I'm easily in time for my meeting in the evening with Barnaby.

As usual the room is warm and enveloping. I settle in the leather chair opposite Barnaby, coyly adjusting the hem of my skirt as I sit and notice Barnaby's eyes slowly travel up from my fashion boots to my face. Very unprofessional but I've been aware for some time that he finds me attractive and have enjoyed playing the tease.

I smile as I ponder how to begin. Barnaby still plays this game of sitting in silence until I feel obliged to commence. Goodness knows where he learned that technique, probably some correspondence course!

I close my eyes for a brief moment and barely suppress a giggle as the words "Are you sitting comfortably, then I'll begin" go through my mind.

Forcing myself to adopt a concerned expression I cast my eyes down into my lap.

'I know this sounds silly,' I twist the ends of my scarf between my fingers, 'but just recently I've had the feeling that I'm being watched.' Glancing up, I'm surprised to see a slightly startled look flit across Barnaby's face. Keeping my eyes fixed on him I continue. 'The first time was when I was driving home from my evening class'

Barnaby visibly relaxes, as if what I've just said is a relief, but he says nothing.

'Then, another time, I was loading my car at the supermarket.' I'm watching Barnaby intently. He shuffles the papers he's holding and makes as if to write but leaves his pen merely hovering above the page. Softly, he clears his throat.

'Have there been any other times?'

'Yes, a couple. Do you think I should inform the police?'

'Erm, have you actually seen anyone? Anyone you could identify?'

'Well no, it's just been a feeling really, a sort of sensation. I'm probably just being paranoid. What do you suggest I do?'

Barnaby considers.

'If you haven't actually seen anyone, I can't think there's anything the police can or will do. Perhaps you are just imagining it; you have seemed to be a little on edge at our last couple of sessions.'

'Yes, I suppose so. I did think someone was outside my apartment one evening though, on the other side of the road.' I'm looking at Barnaby intently. He keeps crossing and uncrossing his legs and changing position in his chair as though he can't get comfortable.

'I wouldn't worry too much, Amelia, but let me know if this feeling occurs again. It might help to talk about it in more detail.'

I can tell Barnaby is decidedly uncomfortable with the subject and his jittery reaction suggests that he knows more than he's letting on. Although I still doubt it's him I think I'll play with him for a little longer.

'You know, Barnaby, despite what you say, I think I will go to the police over this stalking business. After all, if anything dreadful does happen to me at least they'll have been made aware and I won't feel quite so impotent; I'll feel I've done something, however slight, to protect myself. Don't you think that's what I should do … be more proactive?'

Barnaby looks a little hot and is absently scoring his pen so deeply into his notepad he's almost gone through the paper.

'Of course, I expect if I do report it they'll likely want to talk with the men I know. It'll be the', I put on an authoritative voice, "Where were you Wednesday evening, Mr Branding?"'

Barnaby squirms under my gaze as my eyes demand a response.

'I, erm, I should have to consult my diary.'

'Oh dear, Barnaby, that sounds suspicious; it isn't that long ago, can you really not remember?'

Just then the doorbell chimes. 'My word, I didn't realise the time, that's my next appointment.' He keeps his head turned away from me as I gather up my belongings so I stand resolutely in front of him, forcing him to turn to face me.

'Thank you for your help. I'll be sure to keep very alert next time I have the sensation of being watched. I'm sure eventually I'll know whether it's all in my mind or not, don't you agree?'

Barnaby swallows hard, 'Absolutely but it probably won't happen again.'

'No, probably not.'

'Goodbye, Amelia.'

'Goodbye, Barnaby.'

What a strange man Barnaby is; can he really be so besotted with me that he's following me about? Does spying on me give him some kind of warped thrill? I'm not sure if I'm concerned or merely amused.

Perhaps we ought to reverse roles and I should counsel him.

◆

It's Saturday and I'm due to meet Lily in the café by the park.

Sitting in the warm fug, relishing the aroma of excellent coffee and the good old English fry-up that the café is renowned for, I'm keeping my fingers crossed that today works out as I'm hoping.

Lily should be here shortly so I order myself a coffee and start browsing the local newspaper someone has discarded at the table. Flicking through my eye is caught by a tiny piece on page 8. Referring to the murder of the tramp and the police questioning of Gary Stevenson it states "*When asked if she was aware that her son had, for some months, been dealing drugs in Melsham Park, Mrs Janet Stevenson swore vehemently and struck out with her handbag, hitting our reporter in the face and causing a gash below his right eye. Mrs Stevenson has subsequently been charged with assault and is due to appear before magistrates next week.*" I splutter into my coffee, unable to suppress the snort of laughter that explodes from me, just as Lily enters.

'Crikey! Are you alright? You're choking.'

I hold up my hand; 'I'm fine,' as I fumble for a tissue to wipe my streaming eyes, 'went the wrong way.'

'Can I get you another? It looks as if you've spilt most of that one?'

'Yes please. Do you want anything to eat?'

Lily casts her eye over the loaded plates on other tables. 'God, it is tempting; oh, why not, shall we have two full breakfasts?'

'Definitely.' I may be fussy about my food but there are times when a jolly good blow out of unhealthy eating is just what the doctor should order.

I tuck the paper into my shopping bag as Lily joins me at the table. I feel I want to frame that article. 'How are things with you? Did you find out about the mountain bike club?'

'Yeah, I managed to find a contact number and gave it a ring. The guy was really helpful. I told him I hadn't done anything like it before and was a bit nervous so he's suggested I go along on Monday night; they're having a meeting to discuss future events. He says I can then meet some of the members and maybe help with the teas and coffees but I don't have to if I don't want. He says to use it to chat to some members and get an idea of what it's all about, then I can decide, no pressure, so that's what I'm going to do.'

'That's brill. Don't forget, if you do go for it, you can borrow my bike.'

'Are you sure?'

'Yeah, I told you, I don't use it; it's just gathering dust.'

Just then, two laden plates are plonked onto the table in front of us.

'Wow, look at that!' Lily grabs for the tomato sauce with delight.

We linger over our meals, neither wanting to leave the cosy warmth of the café but eventually we decide we have to make a move. Wrapping coats and scarves close against the cold wind we step outside.

'I'm off this way to town.' Lily indicates to her left.

'OK, I'm off home out of this weather. See you at art class Tuesday evening and good luck Monday.'

'Cheers; see you Tuesday with all the news.'

Lily turns and strides off in the direction of town. I watch her for a few seconds; so far, so good. Let's hope Barry's at the club Monday evening and that his recent upset over the Fens trip doesn't make him give it a miss. That really would be Sod's Law.

◆

At home that evening I'm feeling quite pleased; it seems that the police investigation into the tramp's death, if the newspaper report is accurate, is still focused on Gary Stevenson. I pull the newspaper from my bag; must cut out the article and put it in Matt's album. I want to keep a full record of events; I shall enjoy reading them in years to come.

I reach into the wardrobe and carefully pull the album toward me. Holding it close to my body I move to sit on the bed, intending to insert the newspaper cutting, when I notice the corner of a photograph sticking up over the edge of a page. Odd, it must have come unstuck although I don't see how; I've always been very particular when creating my tribute to Matt.

I lay the album on the bed and carefully turn the pages, in case anything else has come loose.

The errant photograph is the one of Matt and Addie; the only one I have of them both. I look at the page where the photo should have been; it hasn't just come unglued, it looks as though it's been pulled out, part of the page is still attached to the back of the photo. I don't understand, how could this happen? I gaze at the photo, trying to resolve the conundrum. Matt and Addie are grinning like a pair of Cheshire cats, Addie's hazel eyes glistening, the camera flash highlighting the flecks of gold; just like …

No, I won't believe it. I feel the blood drain from my face. I try to control my breathing; I must think, I must remember, I must go back to my childhood, back to the day of Addie's funeral. Surely it can't be. No, think. I close my eyes and try to force the memories to come.

I'm nine, I'm standing close to Matt, right up against him; he's holding my hand as though if he lets go he will crumple. I've never been to a funeral before; I keep staring at the coffin as we follow it into the chapel, picturing Addie lying inside. I wonder what she's wearing, what style her hair is in. I want to open the lid and peek.

Matt is gulping back sobs. There's a keening sound somewhere in the chapel; I search for its source; it's Addie's mother, grief wrenching that awful noise out of her and beside her a boy, maybe eleven or twelve years old, her arm around him, drawing him close.

Addie's family go to sit in the front pew with my family directly behind. The priest drones on but I'm not listening. I keep fidgeting, raising myself up on tiptoes, desperately trying to see between the people in front. I want to see the coffin slide through the curtains; I want to be sure she's gone.

Slumped on my bed, the image in my head plays out like a video before my eyes. The boy in the front pew turns and looks directly at me, his expression one of knowledge and accusation, his hazel eyes glistening, the sunlight through the oriole window exaggerating their flecks of gold as I recall my mother's comment.

'How unusually striking Addie and Graham's eyes are; you can tell instantly that they're brother and sister.'

A coldness creeps over my skin as I lie on the bed and close my eyes, willing the darkness to smother the images from so many years ago.

I don't know when I manage to drift into blissful unconsciousness, all concept of time is lost but eventually I wake when it's dark outside. My mouth tastes foul and I ache as though I've had the flu.

Slowly I make my way through to the kitchen, my hand trailing the walls for support. Coffee, I need a strong coffee. I perch on the stool, my elbows on the work surface, a hand supporting my head as I sip the hot soothing liquid and try to think.

OK, Peter is Addie's brother, Graham, that explains the Dorset connection but why would he be in Sheffield? He said it was to do with work but I've not been able to find any architects' firms, in London or Coventry, who know of him. Didn't Addie's family have relatives in Sheffield? I vaguely recall something like that. That could be an explanation.

Did he know who I was when we met in the hotel? No, I can't believe that he did, his manner toward me was genuine, I'm sure of that. For me not to have sensed an undertone he would have had to be a consummate dissembler. I'm convinced he didn't know my true identity at that point.

Our time together over Christmas and New Year gave no hint of any ulterior motive; his behaviour was always that of an attentive, decent man. So why was he rummaging in my wardrobe? He must have done so when I was out that morning getting fresh milk; no, wait a minute, he wasn't snooping. I remember now; when he'd first arrived I'd got him to store his case in the wardrobe; my bedroom is fairly small and to have a case left on the floor is a definite trip hazard. So, he'd probably woken up whilst I was out, decided to start packing for leaving later that day and accidentally found the album. His case may well have caught on it, the wardrobe isn't that deep. The whole thing could have been a genuine accident.

Pragmatically I spend the weekend turning everything over in my mind. What am I to do? More to the point, what is Peter, or it now seems certain, Graham, likely to do? Maybe he has just disappeared, sickened by the realisation of who he's been having an intimate relationship with; wanting to put as much distance between himself and me as possible. Yet again, he could decide to take matters into his own hands; like me, he could decide on his own form of retribution.

I reach for Matt's album and hug it to my breast once more. I will *not* let this man or anyone else prevent my pursuit of Munroe. I will take whatever steps are necessary. This game is not yet over.

◆

Why is *everything* so complicated? I thought my plan was pretty straightforward but now I have Jess *and* Peter to contend with. It wasn't like this when I dealt with Addie. Admittedly, I hadn't foreseen the consequences, I don't think you do as a young child, you just see everything in clear cut, straight line terms of what you want to achieve but the actual act itself, well that went smoothly enough.

I feel like death Monday morning but know that I can't let the shock of the weekend delay me, I must force myself into college however difficult it is.

My class this morning is the small group of ten that includes Barry Mason. A bit of a mixed group with some taking art history as their main subject whilst others, like Barry, are using it as a filler subject. Despite the diversity of interests they all get on quite well and are definitely the fount of all knowledge when it comes to college gossip and rumours, so I tend to allow them some leeway when settling down to work. They never seem to mind talking in front of me or indeed, sometimes including me in their discussions, all of which can prove extremely useful.

As I enter the classroom I can tell they've got something interesting on their minds. All attention seems to be focussed on Barry with Terri Westacott looking particularly concerned, sympathy evident in her manner as she murmurs something in his ear.

I pretend not to notice and instead walk over to my desk and begin hauling exercise books out of my bag. After a few moments I look across at the huddle of downcast heads, 'Good morning everyone, is there a problem?'

'It's Barry.' Terri thumps Stephen Blake on the arm and glares.

'Is it anything I can help with?' I direct my query, 'Barry?'

Barry merely shakes his head but Terri whispers something and Barry then nods in agreement.

'It's the police.' Terri has obviously elected herself spokes-person. 'First they stop Barry going on that field trip and now they've told him they've let Gary Stevenson go, not enough evidence. They're doing him for the drug dealing but not the...' Terri is trying desperately hard to protect Barry's feelings, groping around for the best words, '...not for Barry's dad.'

I feel my heart sink; I was hoping the Gary diversion would keep the police occupied for longer. Now they'll probably turn their attention back onto Barry, a fact of which, by the look on his face, he's all too aware.

'That's disappointing but I'm sure none of us would want Gary blamed if he's innocent.' The looks on the faces opposite me make it plain they'd be only too pleased if that were the case. 'We may have to accept that it's one of those times when the culprit simply can't be found. I know it's hard but I'm sure the police won't give up easily. As long as their investigation is still open...'

'Oh, it's that alright, they've started questioning poor Barry again.' Terri is fuming with righteous indignation, 'As if he'd have anything to do with it, it's a disgusting idea.'

Barry shifts slightly in his chair, raising his head just enough to catch my eye and I feel his unspoken suspicion that somehow I know the truth.

'Yes, it does seem harsh. Barry, if there's anything I can do you only have to ask. Now, I'm sorry people but we really must get down to some work, exams are looming.'

I hope that Barry will linger and speak with me as class ends but he simply walks out of the room with barely a backward glance.

I hate Mondays and am always glad when they're over as my timetable for the day seems to be crammed with my most difficult classes and this Monday is particularly depressing, what with the news of the police investigation and the persistent rain and greyness necessitating artificial light all day.

Driving home through the drizzle and glare of oncoming headlights I find I'm frequently checking my rear-view mirrors. Despite my suspicion that my stalker was Barnaby the threat of Peter/Graham is now constantly in my mind and is making me doubt. I can see why he would be asking questions, just to dispel any doubts he might have but what does he intend to do, when and if he does dispel his doubts?

CHAPTER 10

I can't get Peter/Graham out of my mind; the whole situation is bizarre. Despite my earlier conviction part of me won't accept that he's Addie's brother; it would be a fantastic coincidence if he is; after all, it's a fairly common name but then, the photo …

I turn it over in my mind for the umpteenth time. The appearance of Addie's eyes in the photo could simply be a trick of the camera flash. I wish now I had kept some more snaps of her so I could compare. I try to picture her as she was, in real life, but it's all so long ago; I can't be sure. I know Mother made the comment about the siblings striking eyes but she was always given to exaggerated theatricals; making more out of something than was actually there. I'm even beginning to doubt my memory of the exact colour of Peter's, or should I be saying, Graham's, eyes now. God, this is driving me insane.

As for the photo being pulled out of the album, I initially just leapt to the conclusion that it was a deliberate act but maybe it was a genuine accident. It could easily have caught as he pulled out his case; he may not even have noticed it.

But, if he isn't Addie's brother then who the hell is he, why did he disappear so suddenly without explanation and why is he asking questions about me?

He claimed he worked for an architectural firm, but I can't find any firm who knows of him in either London or Coventry, he's using the name Graham Baxter at his apartment and has moved out. Is that move temporary or permanent? I need to resolve this; it's becoming too much of a distraction. I'll go back to his apartment in Coventry, talk with the neighbours. I can't think of a reason why he would have lied to me unless he already knew who I was when we first met; that he knows my connection with Addie. Perhaps seeing the photograph simply confirmed his beliefs. Oh God, I don't need this uncertainty.

I ring into work sick next morning and am on the road to Coventry just after the rush-hour. The journey doesn't take quite so long this time, probably because I'm more familiar with the route and I find my way to the apartment block easily. Once again I'm in the timespan that allows me in via the Tradesman's button and make my way up to the third floor.

Without expecting any result I nonetheless press the buzzer of number 36. I listen carefully but there's no sound of movement inside. I walk across to the apartment that the young woman I spoke to last time emerged from but there's no response there either.

Feeling defeated I go to number 38 and ring, this time with success. A few seconds pass before I hear footsteps approaching and the door is opened to reveal a middle-aged woman, busily brushing baking flour from her hands.

'I'm sorry to trouble you; I wondered if you know if number 36 is available. A friend told me it's empty.'

'Yes, that's right; it is. Last chap left without paying his rent, by all accounts. Landlord's none too pleased.'

She chuckles on this last comment as if the landlord's upset is a delight to her.

'No, I bet he isn't.' I smile in response, 'Have you got the landlord's contact details? I'd like to make enquiries.'

'Oh, you need to do that through the estate agents, Browns on Wigmore Street; they handle most of these units.'

'Thank you, that's really helpful; I will. Do you know when the previous person left? I just wondered how long it's been empty.'

She bites her lip, considering.

'Must be about a month or more by now; I didn't have much to do with him but I wasn't surprised when I heard he owed; never seemed to be doing any work; was here at all times of the day and night.'

'Really, some people.'

She smiles in agreement.

'Thanks again. I'll contact the agents.'

'You're welcome.'

Back at the car, I check the map. Wigmore Street is only a couple of roads away so I shove more coins into the parking meter and walk.

Browns Estate Agents is easy to find but it's now the lunch-hour and there's only a young woman holding the fort.

'Hello, I wanted to make enquiries about renting an apartment in Cadogan House. I understand number 36 is available.'

The young woman smiles nervously.

'I'm not sure I can help; I only started working here this week. Can you come back about two fifteen?'

I give an exaggerated sigh.

'No, not really; I'm here in my lunch-hour; are you sure you can't find the Particulars for me?'

'I'll try.'

She turns to the filing cabinet and starts flicking through its contents but then stops.

'Did you say number *36* Cadogan House?'

'Yes.'

'I've just remembered, I think Norman has that file out; some problem with the previous tenant.'

She moves across the room and begins sorting through the papers at a desk in the far corner.

'Here it is.' Relieved, she holds up a file just as a phone at the front of the office starts to ring.

'Oh, I'd better get that. I won't be a moment.'

So saying she drops the file back on the desk and moves to pick up the phone, standing gazing out the window with her back to me.

Quickly I open the file, pulling out a front sheet which sets out client details and contact numbers. Stuffing it into my bag, I lightly tap the young woman on the shoulder.

'I'll come back tomorrow.'

She nods and continues her phone call as I hasten down the road. Back at the car I take the paper out of my bag and read.

The tenant is given as "Graham Baxter of 421, Chelsea Avenue, Bristol" but the contact number I recognise; it's Peter's mobile. So, there appears to be no doubt that the man I know as Peter Everard is leading a double life and whether he is Addie's brother or not, he's asking questions about me for a reason.

I simply can't afford the time to travel to Bristol and with the sparse information I have, I doubt if it will yield anything more helpful. I decide, on balance, to give things more time. I have enough reason now to be very much on my guard and it could be that Peter/Graham will make some move that will give me more insight into his motives and intentions. In any case, I need, firstly, to be certain that my stalker really *is* him. I can't afford to make a mistake as, if I concentrate on him I'll lose the momentum with Lily and Barry and that's much more important.

I turn the ignition and pull out into the traffic.

Back in college next morning I look out for Barry. He doesn't have any classes with me today but, since learning of the renewed police interest in him, I'm concerned as to how he may be reacting.

By the end of the day, having seen nothing of him, I make my way down the corridor toward the Small Animal Unit in the hope that he's still there, Mr Simpson's book nestled in my bag as the excuse to speak with him, but the unit is empty, everything shut down for the night. Damn! I head back to the staff-room in the hope of catching Ben to find out when Barry's likely to be around but Ben's not there either.

'Has anyone seen Ben?' I ask the room in general.

Muriel Perkins, English Lit., raises her head from the essays she's marking, 'I heard he's down at the police station with Barry Mason; shouldn't think he'll be back in college tonight.'

'Oh, OK, thanks.' Christ! Bloody Munroe, why can't he just back off for a while? Fuming I stride out to my car and hurl my bag onto the passenger seat. As I walk round to the driver's door a slight movement in a first floor window catches my eye. I pause, trying to work out which room it would be and then realise, it's the Principal's office. He's obviously forgotten that, on a dark evening like this with his office light on, the room is illuminated like a stage show and I can clearly see Jess Saunders as she reaches up to wrap her arms around his neck. So, that little liaison is still ongoing; that could prove useful.

Next day Barry still doesn't seem to be in college although Ben is, looking decidedly haggard.

'Ben, you look completely wasted; must have been a good night!'

'I wish it had been. I spent most of last night at the police station whilst they questioned Barry again. My back's killing me; their chairs must be the most uncomfortable they could find!'

'Where is Barry? They haven't kept him in, surely?'

'No, eventually let him go about three o'clock this morning. I told him to stay at home today; he's that knackered he'd be a liability around the animals anyway.' Ben runs his hand through his hair, 'Don't think I'll be much better either.'

'It is good of you to support Barry but a bit above and beyond the call, don't you think?'

'I suppose so,' Ben lets out an exhausted sigh, 'but who else has the poor sod got? The chap he lives with, well lodges with really, doesn't seem to want to be involved, just wants a regular income from a trouble-free lodger and help on his smallholding.'

'What about Barry's foster parents? They must have been pretty close if Barry wanted to take their name; maybe, they could give him some support.'

'Possibly, but I believe they're quite elderly and Barry's pretty protective of them by all accounts.'

Ben takes a deep breath.

'No good, can't put it off any longer.' Stifling a yawn, he shuffles off in the direction of the Small Animals Unit.

Does everything have to conspire against me? If Barry doesn't come into college tomorrow but stays holed up at that dreadful smallholding, it's going to make it very difficult for me to see him.

◆

I can't believe that Tuesday's art class has rolled round again so quickly. Despite my best intentions I even have to admit to a stern looking Madeleine McLevitt that I haven't managed last week's homework. It's so embarrassing, I don't appreciate being made an example and feel like pointing out that I'm an adult, here voluntarily. However, I manage to curb my tongue when I notice the conspiratorial looks of sympathy from the other class members.

As Madeleine returns to the front of class Lily puts a comforting hand on my arm and whispers, 'Never mind her, I've got something to tell you. Can you stay for coffee after class?'

'I think I need something stronger after that reprimand.'

'Pub it is then.' Lily's giggle is infectious and I have to cover my mouth with a hanky as I acknowledge the absurdity of my annoyance. It's only a stupid art lesson, after all.

The art classes are held in a building close to the town centre so Lily and I have a choice of three pubs within walking distance. Opting for the Tudor Tavern we make a beeline for the dilapidated sofa that flanks one side of the log-effect gas fire. I much prefer the real thing, the scent of wood smoke I find particularly comforting, but this imitation throws out a good heat that's extremely welcome after battling our way here through the wind and rain.

'Stay there and I'll get the drinks this time.' Lily strolls up to the bar and orders a couple of house reds. Obviously, her recent rebellion at the Pizza Express has had a lasting effect. I notice her smile, directed at the barman, is so obviously lacking in guile the young man is instantly enamoured and ready to fall at her feet. I wonder when I lost that ready openness and willingness to take others at face value; nowadays, each of my smiles is calculated and handed out sparingly.

Lily places the wine glasses on the low table before us and drops onto the sofa beside me. 'Did you want some crisps?' she asks.

'No, I'm fine thanks. C'mon, don't keep me in suspense, what have you got to tell me? I'm assuming it's to do with the cycle club on Monday night.'

Lily takes a sip of wine and turns to face me, her eyes dancing with excitement.

'Too right! It was good; they're a great crowd; it felt like I'd been there for ages. I definitely want to join, so can I borrow your bike? They're going out on a ride next Saturday.'

'Yeah, 'course you can; I said, didn't I? I've got to return some books to the library Friday evening so if you can meet me in the car park, say about 6pm, you can have it then. Our cars are about the same size and it fits in mine fine, with the back seats down, so it should be OK in yours.'

'Brilliant, no sweat. I can keep it at my friend, Shirley's, so I don't have to worry about dad seeing it and asking awkward questions.'

Lily takes another sip of wine, a slightly smug look on her face, but remains silent.

'So, what are they like at the club; I bet they're a load of geeks and nerds in Lycra!'

'No, cheeky bitch! They're not like that at all. There's several nice guys, really fit; I'm gonna have to start regular exercise if I'm gonna keep up.'

Lily's grin widens as she looks at me.

'C'mon, spill; there's something more, isn't there?'

Wrapping her arms around her body, Lily leans forward.

'Yeah there is. The leader chap has suggested that I ride along with another new member and he's just *so tasty*; I mean seriously so.'

'Trust you! I suppose you can't wait for Saturday now?'

'Too right, I can't. You should have seen the looks I got from some of the other girls; jealous as hell.'

'So what's his name?'

I secretly cross my fingers.

'Barry something; didn't really catch the rest.'

At last, something seems to be working in my favour. It's about time!

A little later, when Lily has popped into the Ladies prior to driving home, I ponder how things are progressing.

Lily is attractive, fun to be with and the cycling is a shared interest. She may not be as free with her sexual favours as Jess but a lot of boys find that a challenge such that it keeps their interest. Barry may well be getting a bit bored with Jess, she's not the brightest spark in the fire and I can't imagine her being prepared to cycle or take any interest in animals. It'll probably only take a bit of a nudge from me to cause a permanent split and I already have the ammunition.

Walking back to the car park, arms linked, Lily gives me a friendly squeeze. 'Y'know, Amelia I'm so *very* glad we've met.'

'Yeah, me too.'

Pulling out of the car park I wonder just how much a mountain bike is going to cost me but it'll be money well spent if it gets Lily and Barry together. One thing's for sure, I'll never want to ride the bloody thing!

◆

I find I'm becoming quite edgy; I want to know if the police feel they have anything more definite against Barry other than a bad parent/child relationship.

In the meantime, I have my small art history class; perhaps I can glean some information from them. As I enter the room, I'm met with the most subdued, forlorn faces.

'Whatever's the matter with all of you? My lessons don't make you that miserable, do they?'

I'm rewarded by a few weak smiles as Terri Westacott speaks up, 'We're just all really concerned about Barry.

He's been really down since the police started questioning him again. Stephen met with him yesterday and he's talking about giving everything up and just disappearing.'

Oh no, I can't have this. If Barry does a runner my whole scheme is lost. Fingers crossed, I quiz further.

'Did you manage to persuade him to stay, Stephen?'

'I think so, for now anyway. I told him the police won't get anywhere if he's innocent and they obviously haven't got much on him or he'd be arrested by now, not just helping with enquiries.'

The innocence of the young; they still have that unassailable belief in fair play and justice with all that nonsense about innocent until proven guilty. So naïve, its heart breaking.

'It sounds like you gave some good advice, let's hope Barry heeds it.' They all nod their heads in agreement.

'He did say he might come with me to play football, there's a match on Sunday,' Stephen volunteers, 'so that's something.'

'That's good. OK class, down to more mundane matters I'm afraid. Turn to page three please. I think we need to go over this section again.'

There's a collective groan. 'Yes, I know. I'd rather not be doing it too, so let's all knuckle down and get through it as quickly as possible.'

The rest of the day feels as though it will never end so when the final bell sounds it almost takes me by surprise.

I need to slow the police investigation and the best way to do that is to give them another lead to follow and DC Wilson is my best bet. Reaching for my mobile, I dial the Endover police station.

CHAPTER 11

I've been giving DC Wilson some thought. I'm sure he's attracted to me; the sideways looks that he thinks I don't see, his attempts at reassurance; his willingness to call at my apartment. He's obviously very much on the career ladder and isn't going to jeopardise that without a very compelling reason. I'd been hoping to seduce him but my powers have so far failed.

Punctually at seven o'clock DC Wilson arrives, clean shaven to the point of baby's bum smoothness and smelling sweetly of talc!

All this newly scrubbed cleanliness, coupled with his slightly chubby features, has the unfortunate result of making him look considerably younger than he actually is. I find his whole appearance so disconcerting I feel I should be offering him a Farley's rusk rather than a glass of wine.

'DC Wilson, come in. It's really good of you to come over again at such short notice. I do hope I'm not wasting your time. Please, go through.'

I follow him down my narrow hall and indicate for him to sit on the lounge sofa. 'Would you like some wine?'

'Not for me, thank you. Perhaps we could just get on?'

Wilson's tone is abrupt, formal; not what I expected at all.

'Oh, very well, if you're sure; perhaps a cup of tea? I think I could do with one.'

Looking as though he's deciding between being polite or not he opts for politeness, 'Yes, thank you.'

In the kitchen I hurry with the tea. Maybe he prefers the mothering sort, that baby face certainly suggests so. Calling through into the lounge, 'Do you take sugar?'

'Yes please.'

Carrying the tray through into the lounge I find him, notebook in hand and pen poised; obviously he wants to get through this meeting as swiftly as possible, which I find mildly insulting.

I settle on the sofa beside him, tucking my legs under me, which causes the side split of my skirt to reveal an expanse of thigh which I pretend not to notice. 'You look tired; are you very busy at work?'

Wilson presses his lips firmly together, giving nothing more than the merest nod, forcing me to continue.

'I heard at college that you've been questioning Barry Mason again. I probably shouldn't say this but continuing to pursue that line of enquiry isn't doing the police reputation much good with our students. They think he's being unfairly treated and you've got no grounds.'

Wilson's tone is defensive, 'There are grounds; whatever your students like to think.'

'Oh, I'm sure there must be, I wasn't implying otherwise. It's just that Barry's never pretended to anyone that he'd got any time for his dad but it's a big jump from that to killing someone, don't you think?'

'Possibly.'

Playing for time, I pour the tea and watch, mesmerised as Wilson piles three heaped spoonful's of sugar into his cup.

'My word, you do have a sweet tooth.'

Wilson doesn't comment, simply fixes me with an impatient stare so I've no choice but to continue again.

'Surely the most likely thing is a failed drug deal.'

'We tried that angle, if you remember, with Gary Stevenson,' Wilson takes a gulp of tea and carries on impatiently, 'but it didn't amount to anything. Although he eventually admitted dealing drugs he swore he'd never even spoken with the tramp let alone assaulted him and we had no real evidence to the contrary.'

'Yes, I know, I feel very badly about that, but Gary isn't the only one locally who deals drugs, not even the only one in the college, I'm sorry to say.'

'Can you be more specific?'

I keep my eyes cast down, fidgeting with the hem of my skirt in awkward silence.

He checks his watch, 'Please, Miss Thompson, I really haven't got the time for this.'

This is not going as I'd imagined. I feel like I'm losing the initiative.

'This is so uncomfortable for me,' I make a show of wrestling with my conscience, 'I feel like I'm the college sneak.'

Wilson looks at me sternly.

'Well, I do know of someone else who deals, I've seen them myself in the college grounds and I also know that person is often in the park but obviously, I can't claim to know if they've ever had anything to do with the tramp.'

'If it helps, I can tell you that the post mortem showed drugs in the tramp's system.'

'Oh, I see, well in that case.' I hesitate some more, managing a slight anxious break in my voice, 'This is very difficult for me, especially after I seem to have got it wrong about Gary Stevenson being involved. Your DCI will be charging me with wasting police time if I'm not careful.'

'He'll be even more annoyed if he finds you've been withholding important information.'

I swallow hard; Wilson's tone is almost offensive. 'I will tell you, but you've got to promise to keep me out of it.' I pause, waiting for Wilson's assurance but it doesn't come. I'm not happy with the way this is panning out but now I've got this far I can hardly back-track. 'It's Jess Saunders. She's a second year secretarial student but I know she hangs about with a lot of local lads; I really don't think she'd be capable of attacking anyone herself though.'

'You'd be surprised what some females are capable of,' Wilson's voice carries a bitter edge that suggests his comment is decidedly personal.

'Yes, I suppose so, in the right circumstances. I don't think I could though. I don't think I have a malicious bone in my body.'

Wilson stands, obviously intending to leave.

'I'm sorry, prattling on like this, of course, you want to leave. You must have someone waiting at home for you. I'm sorry to have taken up so much of your time. I'll be getting you into trouble with your other half.'

'No, I just need to get back to the station.'

'Forgive me for saying so, but I wouldn't have thought you were the type to be married to the job.' I shift a little on the sofa, ensuring the side split of my skirt has fallen open again.

He looks slightly miffed, 'I'm not, it's simply the nature of the job; it requires long hours.'

'Oh yes, I understand completely, teaching is the same, people simply don't realise the pressures that can put on a relationship.'

Wilson remains non-committal, 'No, I guess not.'

I get up from the sofa and move across, to stand close to him, sensing a degree of sadness in his voice.

'It's difficult, isn't it, balancing a career and a relationship.'

Wilson merely nods slightly as I lay my hand gently on his arm. Taking a step closer I look up into his pale eyes, concern evident on my face. For a brief second he inclines his head toward me and I feel the cool sweetness of his breath on my cheek. Then, as if startled awake, he takes a step backward away from me.

'Thank you for your help with our investigation, Miss Thompson; we'll keep in touch.'

Damn! I must be losing my touch. Annoyed, I re-emphasise.

'You will follow up what I've told you about Jess Saunders, won't you, constable?'

'Yes, we'll definitely look into it.'

'And you won't mention that the information came from me?'

Now it's Wilson's turn to look annoyed.

'As I said before when we discussed Gary Stevenson, I can't promise that.'

I stare hard into his face.

'I'm sorry you feel like that. If it becomes common knowledge that your information has come from me it may jeopardise the position of trust I currently have with my students.'

Wilson doesn't respond so I continue.

'I'm not surprised people are unwilling to assist the police in their enquiries when the police have so little concern for their informants' welfare.'

Wilson bridles.

'That isn't the case, Miss Thompson. We do appreciate your help and I will do my best to keep your involvement quiet but I can only reiterate, I cannot promise. I'll see myself out.'

I remain where I am until I hear the front door close behind him. What a supercilious shit he is. I glance across the room at the tray of tea cups, resisting the urge to pick the lot up and throw it against the wall. Instead, I go to my drinks cabinet and pour myself a large glass of Pinot Noir.

Slumping on the sofa I review the evening. I think Wilson will follow up the Jess lead I've given him but I'd also hoped that, with a little seduction, I could have persuaded him that they were completely wrong to suspect Barry at all but that ploy seems to have failed miserably. I close my eyes and take another sip of wine.

The unexpected ringing of my door bell startles me. I can't imagine who … If it's Mrs Lewis with one of her made up emergencies I swear I'll strangle her. It goes again; it's no good, I'll *have* to answer.

Hurrying down the hall I don't think to peek through the spyhole, convinced as I am that it's Mrs Lewis. I fling the door open in barely concealed temper.

DCI Munroe seems to fill the entire opening, blocking out light and casting a shadow down the length of my hall, staining my carpet like a malevolent slick of oil that's soaking into the fabric of my life.

'Miss Thompson, I wonder if I might have a word?'

I stare at Munroe, dumbfounded, shock momentarily preventing coherent thought.

'Are you alright?' he puts a foot into my hall, his action snapping me out of my stupor as I instinctively block his way.

'Yes, yes I'm fine. What do you want?'

'I've a few more questions I need to ask in connection with our current investigation. May I come in?' He makes a slight move forward, putting his hand out to prevent my closing the door.

'No, it isn't convenient.' I'm holding the door with both hands, my foot also acting as a stop. I can feel his determination from the pressure he's exerting on the door against me.

'Your convenience is not my concern; this is a murder enquiry. Now, we can either do this here or you'll have to accompany me to the station.'

'Am I under arrest?'

'No, we'd simply appreciate your help with our enquiries. However, if you refuse, I may have to draw unfavourable conclusions.'

'Can't it wait until tomorrow?'

'Miss Thompson, if I felt it could wait I wouldn't be here now, would I?'

Fuck it! 'Very well, Inspector, it seems I have little choice.' I reach behind me, taking my coat and keys off the hooks. I absolutely do not want him in my apartment leaving behind that disgusting taint of pipe tobacco lingering like some malignant ethereal wraith.

'You can come in my car. I'll have an officer drive you home.'

As I follow him down the path, I see Mrs Lewis' curtains twitch. The old girl must be beside herself with curiosity.

Munroe opens the front passenger door, 'No, I'll sit in the back,' and without giving him time to object I open the rear door and drop angrily onto the seat.

The drive to the station passes in an agony of excruciating silence, forming a barrier more solid than the Berlin

Wall. My nose twitches as I recoil at the scent that lingers on his clothes and hair. I study the back of his head which seems to be insecurely fixed on top of an overlong neck.

I wish I was a panther; I'd pounce and claw and bite into that scrawny neck until the head hung loose, a single strand of spinal cord all that's left to connect it to the body.

He swings the car into the police car park, braking unnecessarily sharply but at least it jolts me out of my imaginings. 'Follow me.' He punches in a code at the inner door leaving me to catch it as it swings back, making no attempt to hold it open for me. I have little choice but to obediently follow.

'Should I remain four paces back and to the left?' My sarcasm is wasted; he simply bulldozes his way into an interview room and points at a chair on the opposite side of the table.

'Take a seat; I'll get a WPC in here with you. I'll be back in a moment.'

I sit, fiddling with my keys, deciding to leave my coat on; the room is chilly and I realise I haven't eaten yet this evening. The WPC enters.

'Do you think I could have a cup of coffee please?'

She takes up position in a corner of the room as if she's on sentry duty but says nothing. I thought they only behaved like that in TV dramas. Moments later Munroe returns, tossing a file onto the table between us.

'Before you start, could I please have a cup of coffee and some biscuits; I haven't eaten yet this evening.'

Munroe nods at the WPC who obediently leaves the room. He obviously doesn't demean himself by talking to underlings more than necessary.

I lean back on my chair, pulling my coat closer around me and stare blank-faced at Munroe as he makes a show of shuffling through the file of papers. His fingers are long, the joints slightly swollen preventing them straightening out properly; they put me in mind of a hawk's talons. His head bowed over the papers, I notice he's going thin on top, quite a large area too. If it continues he'll end up with a monk's tonsure. An image of him forms in my mind, dressed in a brown cassock, his claw-like hands tucked into the sleeves as he shuffles along intoning some religious dirge. All false piety and reverence; what a hypocrite!

The door opens and the WPC enters bearing sustenance. I give her a grateful smile as I wrap my hands around the mug of steaming coffee. She's obviously been kind enough to go down to the staff canteen as its proper coffee, not that dreadful vending machine slop. There's also a small packet of biscuits. Taking them out of the wrapper I crunch my way through the first one before Munroe begins his questioning.

'Miss Thompson, you are in the park near the college most lunch-times, even in cold weather.'

I remain silent.

'Please, Miss Thompson, just answer the question.'

'I wasn't aware it was a question, I thought you were making a statement.'

'Being obstructive will simply keep us here longer.'

'I'm not,' indignation makes me bristle, 'ask me a question and I'll do my best to answer it.'

'Barry Mason is in the park a lot too.'

I'm beginning to get really exasperated; is he doing this on purpose? 'Are you asking me or telling me?'

Munroe ignores the question. 'Have you ever met him there?'

'No.'

'You seem to have a lot of interest in him, for a student who is only taking your subject as a "filler".'

'Why do you say that?'

Munroe straightens up in his chair, raises his eyes from the papers on the table and looks directly at me. 'Have you ever been round to Barry's house?'

The question hits me like a fist; how did he …? 'No.'

'The college secretary, Mrs Janet Stevenson, claims that you looked at Barry's personnel file when she was out of her office.'

How could she have? My mind is in overdrive; Munroe can't know anything for certain, this is a fishing trip; I'll just keep denying everything.

'No.'

'Why did you want to see Barry's file?'

'I didn't, I haven't; she's mistaken.'

'I don't think so,' Munroe makes a show of examining the papers again, 'she's apparently very fussy about her filing and noticed, when she returned to her office, that Barry's file was slightly out of line in the drawer, as if it had been put back in haste.'

'Then perhaps someone else had been in her office after I left but before she returned.'

Munroe looks fractionally put out, 'I suppose that's one theory.'

'A perfectly valid one I would have thought,' I mentally clock up one to me.

'So, you've never been to Barry Mason's home?'

'No! How many more times?'

'His landlord tells us that a young woman was there asking questions about Barry.'

'Well, it wasn't me.'

Munroe pauses for effect, 'Barry's a handsome young lad.'

'Are you asking me or telling me?'

Once again, Munroe ignores my question. 'I imagine he's got quite a few admirers amongst the female students.'

'I expect so. Look, what is this about, Inspector?'

'Not that much difference between Barry's age and yours, is there? He's almost twenty and you're not much more yourself, are you?'

'What? What exactly are you trying to imply?'

Munroe places his arms on the table and leans towards me, thrusting his head forward, the tendons in his long neck standing out like twisted hemp. 'I'm not implying anything, Miss Thompson. I'm simply trying to ascertain why you are so interested in our murder suspect.' Munroe rifles through his papers again, pulling one sheet free. 'Mrs Stevenson is quite clear in her statement; that you got her to leave her office under a false pretext; that whilst she was out you looked at Barry's file; that you're often in the park at lunch-time where Barry also spends a lot of time and that she's noticed that you're often enquiring after him, particularly to his tutor, Ben Anderson.'

I'm seething; that malicious old cow! Keeping my voice calm and matter-of-fact I look unwaveringly into Munroe's eyes. 'Inspector, Janet Stevenson does not like me, she never has and has been unpleasant toward me since my first day at college. This is all nothing more than puerile nonsense fuelled by that dislike. I'm surprised you should be so taken in by it. Now, if you don't mind, I'd like to go home.' I stand, defiantly pushing my chair back and making for the door.

'Not just yet, Miss Thompson, I haven't finished.'

'Well I certainly have. If you have anything else you need to ask me you can do it at a more reasonable time when I will be happy to assist.' I put my hand onto the handle of the door.

'Very well, Miss Thompson; we'll speak again later.'

I glare at him as I pass. 'The WPC will arrange transport for you.'

Once home I hurry up the path only to notice Mrs Lewis' curtains twitch again; doesn't the old girl ever sleep? I'm beginning to feel as though the whole world is spying on me.

❖

God, I'm tired; last night's events and lack of sleep have left me decidedly woolly-headed. I'll be very surprised if Wilson doesn't come through and follow-up with the Jess Saunders lead I've given him. Apart from keeping the police investigation away from Barry it's very satisfying to think that I'm wasting DCI Munroe's time.

Thursday morning is cold and grey, in keeping with how miserable I'm feeling. Barry is obviously keeping a very low profile and that worries me. Nibbling at my breakfast toast I'm aware that I can't just sit around and wait for him to put in an appearance; I'm concerned he might do a runner, as implied by his classmates, and I also want to know just what the police have on him, if anything. Somehow I have to instigate a meeting and can see no option but ringing into college sick, yet again. Firstly, I have to locate Barry so it looks like a visit to his home is needed.

I realise there's no way I can simply knock on the door of the cottage even if I can put on a convincing show of concern for him. The mud and dogs are more than enough discouragement without the risk of coming face to face with that smirking, obnoxious brute of a landlord who may well recognise me. No, I shall have to stake the place out. Let's hope I don't have to wait too long.

The drive doesn't seem so bad this time, now that I'm more familiar with the twists and turns of the country lane. I manage to find an entrance to a field a short distance past the smallholding where I can hide the car behind a hedge and if I get out and stand I can see the front door of the cottage. I'm hoping that before too long Barry will come out and I can follow him and engineer a meeting.

A cold wind whips across the open fields and despite my warm clothes and boots I find it's not long before my feet and fingers start to go numb. A couple of times the door opens and my hopes lift only to plummet when it turns out to be Barry's landlord. Thank God I brought a flask of coffee but, trust me, I didn't think about its diuretic qualities which, coupled with the cold wind, is creating an increasing urge to pee. I keep jiggling about from one foot to the other until I have absolutely no choice but to squat down behind the hedge to relieve myself.

I stand, awkwardly pulling up and re-arranging my clothes when I'm dismayed to catch a glimpse of Barry's receding figure hurtling down the lane on his bike. Damn! I race round to the driver's side, slam the car into reverse then slam it back into forward gear and speed out onto the lane.

There's a screech of brakes and blare of horn, 'What the fuck d'ya think you're doing, you stupid cow?'

Shit! I catch the briefest flash of a blue transit van in the corner of my eye and slam on the brakes, nose-diving the car. The seatbelt cuts into my chest as I pitch forward; it's a miracle the airbag hasn't inflated. I'm terrified the van driver's going to get out and come across to me but he restrains himself to a few more choice words and an obscene gesture before pulling away.

Feeling sick I try to steady myself as I follow the van which completely blocks my view of the lane ahead. Eventually, at a T-junction the van turns away from the town and I just catch sight of Barry on the main road as he turns right towards the park.

I'm stuck at the T-junction. Oh, come on, let me out *please*! There's a constant stream of traffic both ways. I should have known; this road is always busy. Impatiently, I thump the steering wheel; doesn't anyone have any manners these days? I start to nose the car forward but the bastards simply loop round my bonnet. There's a slight gap in the stream so I recklessly pull out; that did the trick! At last, I'm heading on the main road toward town but I still can't make much headway as it's so busy and slow.

It seems to take forever but eventually I'm able to make the turn Barry took towards the park but by now he's nowhere to be seen. He could have gone in any of three directions from here. I slump in my seat; what now? I might as well find somewhere to park and go for a walk, I'm too strung up to simply go home; the sun is out and the wind has dropped, a walk will ease some of my tension and frustration.

I stroll through the main area of the park, past the children's playground and without really thinking about it, find my feet taking me in the direction of my encounter with the tramp. All evidence of a police presence, let alone a murder, has been removed. It all looks completely innocent and innocuous; it's hard to believe that 'murder most foul' took place here just a few weeks ago.

Sauntering toward the bench I sit, pondering the transient nature of things. Here, in this very spot, a life was violently snuffed out and yet nothing has changed. The rains have washed away any trace of blood, the grass has regrown and erased the indentations caused by the tramp's body, the birds are still singing and, oh look, there's even a snail sliming its way along, just as before. I idly wonder if it's the same snail but no, I carried out a much too efficient demolition job on its home. To have merely cracked or holed the shell would never have been enough; it would take time but the snail would put its little life and home back together and I couldn't allow that, now could I?

After this afternoon's fiasco I'm trying to work out how best to bring about my talk with Barry when my subconscious makes me stiffen slightly, all my senses on full alert. I glance about me but nothing seems to have changed and then … 'Jesus, Barry you frightened me! What are you trying to do? Give me a heart attack.'

Barry Mason is standing just behind to my left, a slightly arrogant look on his face. 'Sorry, I thought you'd have heard me.'

'No Barry, I didn't.' I take a deep breath to calm my nerves and turn to look into the overgrown area behind the bench. 'Where did you come from anyway?'

Barry indicates over my head, 'Over there, there's a small gate in the wall, leads into the back lane that runs down to the river.'

'Oh, I've never noticed it.'

'It's not really for general use. I only know about it 'cos I used to be friends with one of the park keepers a few years back. He used it as a short cut home.'

I look up into Barry's face, trying to gauge his mood.

'How are you, Barry? I hear the police have been questioning you again about your dad.'

Barry shoves his hands in his pockets and sullenly kicks the gravel at his feet, 'Yeah, well. They let Gary Stevenson go.'

'Yes, I heard. Barry, I want to talk with you. Would you sit down a minute?' I indicate the place on the bench beside me. Barry slumps down and lolls against the back of the bench, his long legs stretched out before him.

'It must be quite difficult for you to come back here, where it happened.'

'S'pose.'

'The thing is, Barry I have something of a problem.'

Barry inclines his head slightly and looks at me from the corner of his eye but says nothing.

I pause and look away, emphasising my discomfort at what I'm about to say. It's important that Barry believes that my desire to help him is genuine.

'Barry, I saw what happened.'

For a few seconds Barry doesn't move from his slouched position on the bench beside me. Then, slowly, deliberately, he pushes himself into an upright position and turns towards me. His height and steady gaze are quite intimidating.

'Really, and what was that?'

Keeping my voice low and matter-of-fact, 'I saw you hit your father and walk away.' I pause, waiting for a response but there is none. 'I really am very grateful for what you did for me that day, I won't ever forget it.'

Barry's eyes narrow as he stares at me.

'What did I do for you?'

'You don't have to pretend with me, Barry, I was here, remember. To come forward and protect me like that, it was so … good of you. I was so scared after the tramp … I'm sorry, I mean, after your father assaulted me, I know if you hadn't done what you did, I'm sure he would have come after me and if he'd caught up with me … well, I dread to think what might have happened.'

Barry's gaze is unwavering as he tries to piece together the implications of what I'm saying.

'That's why I've never said anything to the police. I know it was an accident. I'm sure you never meant to kill him, you were simply protecting me and it was just unfortunate. You don't have to say anything Barry. I understand.'

'That's very kind of you. So, what do you want?'

Edged with sarcasm, his tone is mildly offensive.

'Nothing, I just wanted you to know that if it comes to it, I'll tell the police that you were helping me; that it was an accident.'

Barry's expression gives nothing away; he looks at his watch and stands, towering over me, his face impossible to read.

'That's very good of you. I've got to go now.'

'Before you do go, Barry, there is something I'd like you to do for me.'

He eyes me warily.

'I thought there might be.'

'It's nothing to do with this, I promise, so there's no need to be so cynical. It's very simple; I understand from Ben that you've recently joined a local mountain biking club.'

Barry gives an almost imperceptible nod.

'The daughter of a friend of mine joined recently too but she's a bit nervous. I'd appreciate it if you'd keep an eye out for her, help her settle in. Her name's Lily, she's about your age, copper-blonde hair, quite pretty actually so you shouldn't find the task too onerous.'

A slight flicker of recognition passes over Barry's face; he's obviously already noticed her at the Monday meeting. Good.

'Will you do that for me?'

'OK.'

I watch as he collects his bike and wheels it through the herbaceous border and out the small, concealed gateway. I find I'm trembling slightly, my jaw shuddering on each intake of breath.

Slightly shakily, I walk back to the car. I need a drink, God, do I need a drink but before then I've got to become the proud owner of a sodding mountain bike!

I drive into town and head straight for the bike shop. I know little about mountain bike attributes and care even less but I manage to make up a plausible story about needing one that will alter enough so I can share it with my sister who's a few inches taller than me, The salesman is particularly helpful and by the end of the day I'm scores of pounds lighter in the pocket but it'll be worth it if it gets Lily and Barry together.

I drop the back seats and, with the salesman's help, get the bike into the car covered with a large blanket. It'll have to stay there until I can deliver it to Lily tomorrow evening.

◆

Waking Friday morning I have to admit that yesterday's contrived meeting with Barry was not as illuminating as I'd hoped. The conversation hadn't gone the way I'd intended. The only thing I do know is that he hasn't yet done a runner. I'm slightly nervous that, despite my assurances, he'll decide I'm a threat to him which could put me at risk but then, if the police do charge him, I can also provide his mitigation. On balance, I think I'm safe.

However, I still need to get him alone and persuade him to talk to me as I'm anxious to know how far the police investigation has gone. In the meantime, I've continued my sick leave and plan to visit Barry's foster parents whose address I'd noted from his personnel file. Maybe they can shed some light; Ben did say that Barry was protective of his foster parents but nonetheless there's a chance he's confided in them. It seems reasonable to assume he would seek some support from somewhere and according to Ben Barry hasn't been very open with him.

I dress warmly and hurry out to the car.

'Hello, my dear, off out again?'

That damn woman, she must spend all day with her nose pressed against her windows; it's surprising she doesn't look more like a pug dog.

'Mrs Lewis, yes I am and I'm also in a hurry.'

'Oh, I don't want to keep you, my dear. I just wondered if everything is alright. I saw you go off with that policeman Wednesday night. Are you sure there's nothing I can do to help? If you need to talk about anything …'

'I'm sure you mean well, Mrs Lewis but really, I'm fine; I don't need any help so please don't concern yourself further. Now, I really am in a hurry.'

I keep walking toward my car in the hope of shutting her up but she's relentless.

'It's just that I saw that man again, the one who came round asking questions about you.'

The unexpectedness of Mrs Lewis's statement causes me to pause, my key in the door lock.

'Really? When was this?'

'Erm, it would have been last Tuesday evening, about eight o'clock. I always spend Tuesday evenings at the art college; they hold a bridge club in one of their back rooms; it's been going for years.'

'Oh, I wasn't aware the college did that.'

That Mrs Lewis may have seen me at the art college before is slightly unnerving but I shrug the feeling aside; what does it matter? Mrs Lewis continues.

'It's my little treat.'

Noting my impatience she hurries on.

'Anyway, I was waiting for the bus to come home, the stop is just opposite the college and I saw you leave with another young woman; very pretty girl, lovely copper coloured hair. You were walking down the High Street and that man, the one who asked questions, he was a little way behind you both.'

'Are you sure it was the same man? It could have been anyone who just happened to be walking in the same direction.'

Mrs Lewis looks slightly put out, 'I know my eyesight isn't all it might be but I'm not going senile. I'd noticed him particularly because he'd been waiting by the bus stop, the one that heads north of town but when the bus came along he didn't get on and I know it was the last one. When you all came out of the college, he turned and walked along behind you until you both went into that pub, the Tudor Tavern, then he turned round and walked back and got into a car. He turned on the car's interior light and seemed to be writing something. I didn't see what he did after that because my bus came.'

I'm rooted to the spot as sinister fingers of dread tighten my throat, threatening to choke me with the possible implications of what Mrs Lewis has said.

'I just thought you ought to know, that's all,' Mrs Lewis is apologetic, 'I don't mean to interfere; I'm just anxious for you.'

'No, no, it's alright, Mrs Lewis. I'm sorry if I snapped. Did you notice what sort of car it was, the colour maybe?'

'Oh no, dear, it was dark and I don't know anything about cars. I think it was quite big.'

'Never mind, I do appreciate you telling me but I really must be on my way now.'

'Alright, dear, take care.'

I open the car door and drop into the seat, starting the engine and slowly moving forward. Mrs Lewis gives me a friendly wave as I round the corner of our building. I find it amazing the way Mrs Lewis can sometimes be so lucid and at others vague. I wonder if she's in the early stages of dementia, yet her news has rattled me. Obviously, my stalker is still on the prowl and I'm more convinced than ever that he is Addie's brother, Graham, which is how I must refer to him from now on.

CHAPTER 12

Driving into town I use the facilities at Marks & Spencer's to change. This time I indulge in a shoulder-length blonde wig, T-shirt and casual but smart trousers topped with a three-quarter leather jacket. Blue coloured contact lenses complete the picture. It doesn't take long; once again the transformation even surprises me.

It's not very far to Mr and Mrs Mason's. From the outside, everything about the house and garden exudes loving care; raised flower beds and brick weave paving making maintenance easy, the beds showing the first sign of spring bulbs pushing through the weed free soil. Someone here has green fingers and a sense of respectability even on a low income.

I press the bell, listening to the tinkling tune within. A few moments later the door opens to reveal an exceptionally tall elderly woman, her height accentuated by how very thin she is, almost stick-like. Her nose is narrow, hooked at the bridge from wearing specs, probably since childhood. She totters a little, holding onto the door frame for support.

'Yes?'

'Good morning, Mrs Mason, my name's Linda, from Social Services. I wonder if I might have a word with you about Barry.'

I briefly flash a card as identification and make a display of shuffling my briefcase from one hand to the other, giving the impression of authority.

'Barry doesn't live here anymore; Social Services know that.'

'Yes, of course we do but we assume he still keeps in touch with you and Mr Mason?'

Mrs Mason gives a slight nod in affirmation so I continue.

'Good, then I'd just like a very quick word if I may; just to be sure that everything is OK, that Barry is still doing well; just to keep our records up to date.'

Mrs Mason looks slightly dubious but decides not to make an issue of it on the front doorstep and grudgingly steps back a little to let me in.

I follow her as she weaves slightly down the hall and into the lounge, her hand tracing the wall for support.

There's a two-seater sofa and two easy chairs; one a riser on which rests some knitting.

'What are you making?' I ask conversationally pointing to the knitting and settling down on the sofa opposite.

Picking up the needles, being careful not to drop any stitches, she says, 'It's a waistcoat for my Bert; he's always burning holes in them.'

She sees my querying look.

'From cigarette ash.'

I smile my understanding.

'Can I get you a cup of tea or coffee?'

'No, I'm fine thank you, Mrs Mason.'

I pull a folder out of my briefcase and start rifling through some papers.

'So, does Barry visit you very often?'

'I wouldn't say often, wouldn't want him to; he's got his own life to lead now but he keeps in touch.'

A glittering band from the light of the standard lamp by Mrs Mason's chair catches my eye.

'That's very pretty. Was it a gift?'

I indicate the bracelet on Mrs Mason's bony wrist.

'It was.'

Mrs Mason fingers it lovingly.

'From your husband?'

'No,' Mrs Mason sounds slightly amused, 'it was from Barry; he always remembers my birthday. Came in a very pretty box too; that jewellers in the Mall do things up so nicely.'

So, not a gift for Jess after all; that's promising.

'Well, Barry obviously has good taste, Mrs Mason. How lovely that you're so close after all he went through with his natural parents. I take it you've not noticed anything different in Barry's behaviour since the unfortunate death of his father?'

''Unfortunate' isn't a word I'd use. He was a worthless individual. Why do you want to know anyway? Barry's an adult now; don't see why Social Services should concern themselves anymore.'

'We don't like to desert families completely once the foster child reaches adulthood, Mrs Mason. Whatever you may think, we do genuinely care and will help in any way we can, especially when the family are coping with such distressing circumstances. We know that the police have been questioning Barry. That can have an effect on the whole family.'

Mrs Mason clasps her hands in her lap in an endeavour to control her emotions.

'What I can't understand is why the police should suspect our Barry had anything to do with it. He don't have anything to do with drugs, hasn't for years.'

'Barry took drugs in the past?'

Mrs Mason looks alarmed.

'No, I never said that. He got in with a bad lot for a while, that's all. It weren't that surprising considering what he'd been through and what he'd seen.' A look of anger on her face, 'They used him, sneaked some drugs into his jacket pocket when the police was questioning a crowd of them. He were only sixteen. Them little beggars only got what they deserved.'

'And what was that, Mrs Mason?'

Mrs Mason looks slightly alarmed and tries to backtrack.

'He were only young, got a bit of a temper, inherited from his father no doubt.'

'Are you saying Barry could be violent?'

'Only with just cause; we told him it was wrong, of course, but he was like a lot of young boys, a bit hot-headed. He's not like that now, mind.'

'Was he formally charged with anything?'

Mrs Mason eyes me suspiciously.

'Isn't it in your files?'

'Oh, I expect so. I'm quite new to this case. I'm afraid I haven't had the time to read everything yet.'

Mrs Mason looks a little doubtful but lets it go.

'Are you sure I can't get you a cup of tea; Bert'll be back soon and he'll be wanting one.'

'That's very kind but no, thank you. Tell me, Mrs Mason, why did Barry move out, if you all get on so well?'

'It were when he discovered his dad was in the area. He was protecting me and Bert; my health's not been so good; things upset me easily. Eddie's a friend of ours; when he knew what was going on he offered Barry a room for some help with the animals. We knew Barry would be safe there; Eddie's not the kind of man you mess with.'

The image of Barry's landlord as he leant over my car crosses my mind. I can well believe that it would be unwise to provoke him.

'So, was Barry's dad threatening him?'

We both start a little at the sound of a key in the front door lock. With some relief Mrs Mason pulls the lever of her chair, raising it into the eject position.

'That'll be Bert back from the allotment; better put the kettle on.'

Mr Mason enters, as tall as his wife but with a more solid frame, an imposing figure as he stands in the doorway of the lounge.

'Bert, this lady's from Social Services. She's been asking questions about Barry.'

Mr Mason gives me a hard stare.

'What would Social Services be wanting to do that for?'

Mrs Mason looks guiltily at her husband, suddenly afraid that she's done the wrong thing. I hasten to explain.

'It's nothing to be concerned about, Mr Mason. It's just that I'm new to Barry's case and it helps to speak directly, rather than just read the file.'

Not convinced he counters.

'Seems a strange way of going about things to me; what did you say your name was?'

'Linda.'

I turn to address Mrs Mason.

'Well, I won't take up any more of your time. Please contact us if you think we may be of help in any way.'

I hastily gather my things and head for the door but Mr Mason remains where he is, blocking my exit. He smells earthy and I notice mud on the bottoms of his trousers, his large hands ingrained with dirt. Leaning down to my eye level he spits.

'Are you a bloody reporter?'

I take a couple of involuntary steps back, trying to distance myself from his vehemence.

'No! No I'm not. Would you let me pass, please?'

'Cos if you are, you'd better not be writing any lies about our Barry; he don't need you lot raking up the past again. He's a changed lad, grown up, responsible and I won't have nowt else said about him.'

'Please, let me pass.' I motion with my hands as if I could brush him aside, 'I have another appointment to get to.'

Still glaring, Mr Mason steps aside.

'I'll see myself out.'

'You do that!'

I almost run down the hallway, fumbling with the Yale mechanism of the front door in my confusion. I plunge outside, hurrying down the path as the door slams behind me. Reaching the car I sling my briefcase onto the back seat, breathing heavily as I turn the ignition.

Was it worth it? Yes, I think so. Barry's got some history with drugs and another episode of revenge-driven violence as well as his attack on his father when a child; all of which will help me paint him in an unfavourable light when the time comes.

Returning to Marks & Spencer's I change clothes again. Time is speeding by and I need to be in the library car park by six o'clock for my meeting with Lily.

On the stroke of six Lily arrives, obviously still keen on the cycling. I wave my hand to indicate where I'm parked as she pulls up alongside.

'This is really good of you, Amelia.'

'No worries; I said, I've hardly used it.'

Together we manoeuvre the bike out of my car.

'Gosh, it looks brand new. Are you sure you don't mind me using it?'

'How many more times? It's fine. I'm not even sure I want it back. I can't think now why I bought it.'

Lily lowers the back seat of her car and we lift the bike in.

'If I get on OK, maybe I could buy it off you?'

'Don't see why not; it's not much use to me.'

That could be useful; at least I'd get some of my money back!

'What time's the ride tomorrow?'

'Not 'til the afternoon. Shirley's going to keep the bike for me so I can pick it up from there.'

Lily slams down the hatchback.

'Will you be at art class on Tuesday?'

I nod.

'Good, I can tell you about it then. Bye and thanks again. I owe you.'

As I watch her drive away I cross my fingers and trust to providence that she and Barry connect and to help with that I need to put a sour taste in Barry's mouth where Jess is concerned.

All day Saturday I'm on edge, wondering how the cycle ride is going. Lily said that Barry had more or less been assigned to her; I can only hope that's the case and that there's at least the start of a mutual attraction.

By Sunday morning I'm prancing around like I'm treading on hot coals. Not knowing what's happened on Saturday is driving me insane and, in any case, I need to see Barry so that I can poison his relationship with Jess.

The football match; Stephen Blake said they'd be playing football today. The local ground's not far away, I'll see if I can catch Barry there.

I pull into the car park just as the match appears to be starting. I can't see clearly enough from here but I don't want to get too close as I don't want Barry to see me or he's likely to try to avoid me. No, I need to catch him by surprise but I do need to be sure he's actually playing. I don't want to sit here for ages only to discover he didn't turn up.

Pulling my hat down to protect my ears from the cold wind, I get out of the car and walk to the end of the car park but several spectators standing around the edge of the pitch are blocking my view. Reluctantly I follow the line of the hedge and manage to position myself behind a large oak tree. Peering round its enormous trunk I get a better view and am relieved to pick out Barry as he races down the pitch toward me.

I leave the car park and drive a couple of hundred yards down the road, pulling into a layby from where I can see the main exit of the football ground. I believe that it's the only exit so I should be able to see Barry when he leaves and be able to follow him.

I resign myself to a wait, turning on the local radio to pass the time. At half past the local news comes on; no mention of the tramp's murder, obviously the story has died a death as far as the media are concerned. One thing of interest though is an item about drug dealing amongst the local youngsters. There are indications that it's becoming something of an epidemic in the area. Let's hope it'll help lend weight to my character assassination of Jess Saunders.

If I have to wait much longer I'll die of boredom! Rummaging in my handbag for a mint I glance up in time to see Barry cycling out, heading in the direction of Melsham Park. Keeping back I follow him; it's much easier today, being Sunday the traffic's lighter.

Eventually he cycles into the park. I wait until he's out of sight then follow on foot. I've a shrewd idea where he'll be heading.

As I stroll through the gardens I notice that tiny shoots of spring bulbs are peeking through the cold earth. All this new life thrusting forth makes an incongruous contrast to my planned intentions but then, I suppose it's just all part of the natural cycle; as one life ends another begins etc. etc. I can't deny it gives me a little bit of a thrill to be an active part of the Architect's Great Plan.

As I suspected, Barry is sitting on the bench that has, by chance, become such a focus of our lives. He looks up as I approach, wariness lending a coolness to his dark eyes masking any hint of his true feelings. I smile a greeting but he merely looks down at the ground, grinding his heel into the gravel. His attitude creates what I fear will be an impenetrable wall but I must try; without him my scheme will fail and that I simply can't accept.

'Hello, Barry.' I take the place beside him.

'Why are you following me?'

He doesn't even do me the courtesy of looking in my direction.

'I'm not following you; you know I come here a lot; it's my thinking space. Why do you keep coming back here?'

Ignoring my question and without asking if I mind, he takes out a cigarette and lights it.

Conversationally, I continue.

'I hear the police investigation has moved on again; they seem to be focussing on a drugs angle for your father's killing. They're questioning people whom they know have a connection with drugs, even if only in a small way.'

'Yeah, we both know I know about Gary Stevenson but they've dropped that now so what's your point?'

Feigning annoyance I reply.

'There's no need to be rude, Barry, of course I know that. I wasn't thinking of Gary.'

'Who then?'

I look mildly surprised.

'Well, Jess Saunders, I would have thought you'd know.'

It's Barry's turn to look surprised but his expression changes quickly to one of anger.

'Why do they suspect Jess?'

'I don't know; I'm not privy to the police investigations. I can only assume someone's snitched on her. Jess isn't the most popular student in college, you must know that, and her relationship with the Principal hasn't made her any friends either.'

Barry kicks at the gravel, grinding his toe into the stones until he's cleared a patch down to the soil.

'That was over ages ago.'

'Was it? It's not what I've heard.'

Barry's look is thunderous.

'What have you heard?'

'Only that it's her relationship with the Principal that allows her to get away with so much; you know, the missed classes, smoking in the grounds, alcohol on the premises, that sort of thing.'

'Who's been telling you all this?'

'Oh, Barry, no-one's been *telling* me anything! It seems it's simply common knowledge; it's even discussed in the staff room … things that have been overheard, I mean.'

Silence hangs heavy between us as Barry considers.

'Of course, if you really care about Jess you could always stop the police investigation; you could tell the police what actually happened.'

Barry looks up from the mess he's been making of the gravel path and stares fixedly at me.

'So could you.'

I keep my expression neutral as I respond.

'Yes, I could but I don't want to do that because I lied when they first interviewed me in order to protect you. I claimed I'd seen nothing. If I go to them now, with a completely different story, they'll probably charge me as an … what's it called? … "Accessory after the fact" and I'll definitely lose my job and probably never be able to teach again.'

There's a long pause while Barry seems to weigh up my argument.

'What if they charge me with murder anyway, what'll you do then?'

'Then I'd come forward, of course I would but while there's a chance that they can't prove anything and you're not arrested, I don't want to jeopardise my future simply because I was trying to help you. Surely you can understand that?'

Barry gives a brief nod, a thoughtful expression on his face, then he simply turns, collects his bike and walks away, back through the small gate behind the herbaceous border.

I remain on the bench, replaying our conversation. It seems the mention of Jess' continuing liaison with the Principal came as a genuine surprise, more so than the drugs and I don't think Barry's inclined to put his neck on the line for her, which is all to the good.

Fingers crossed the cycle club ride with Lily went well; his bike was filthy so it seems likely he went.

◆

Monday morning I'm in college with time to spare before my first lesson so I decide to take a stroll along to Janet's office and rub in a little salt in revenge for her maligning me to DCI Munroe. When I enter, Janet is ensconced behind her desk just stuffing the remains of a large jam doughnut into her mouth.

'Hello Janet, it's good to have you back,' plastering a sweet smile on my lips, 'the past few weeks must have been a dreadful strain.'

Janet struggles up out of her chair and waddles the few steps across the room to extract a tissue from the box on top of the filing cabinet. Dabbing at her lips, she looks cautiously at me, obviously wondering if she really can take my concern and sympathy at face value.

'And how is Gary now? I do hope he's over his ordeal.'

'Yes, he is thank you.' Janet peers at me, her eyes narrowing with suspicion until they're almost lost in her fleshy face, 'If you don't mind my saying, you seem to have a lot of interest in this investigation.'

'I'm sorry you think that, Janet. I was only trying to lend you some support, as one colleague to another. I apologise if you feel my concern is misplaced.'

Janet hesitates and then decides to accept the truth of my statement and continues in a more conversational tone. 'I've heard a rumour that the police are focussing on Jess Saunders now.'

'Yes, I've heard that too.'

'Makes it plain it wasn't my Gary; he was treated very badly.'

'Indeed and so were you. It seems so unfair after all your years of loyal service; I really would have thought that the Principal would have been far more supportive.'

'I told my Gary, he should tell the police that she'd tried to get him involved in her drug dealing but he won't.'

'It does seem unfair, I agree, but I imagine the police will be a lot gentler with Jess, what with her being so friendly with the Principal and him with all his important connections.'

Janet's eyes are glistening with the injustice of it all, 'What do you mean?'

'Well, don't quote me but the grapevine whispers are that she and the Principal are rather, shall we say, close. If it's true, he's bound to try to help her, don't you think?'

Janet slumps down in her chair, chewing at her bottom lip. I quietly leave the office. Job done I think.

As for DC Wilson, what a sweet little puppet he is. I do so enjoy pulling his strings. Talking of pretty puppets, it's Tuesday's art class tomorrow. Hopefully, Lily will have encouraging news for me of her Saturday cycling with Barry. It all seems to be falling into place quite nicely.

◆

As I drive toward the studio Tuesday evening I can feel excited tension increase in me. I have a real sense of everything coming together such that my skin tingles with delicious anticipation. I'm so keen to hear Lily's report that I arrive at class far too early and have to kick my heels for half an hour, drinking vile coffee from their vending machine.

Slowly, the other hopeful artists arrive but I'm dismayed that Lily isn't amongst them. Every time the door opens my head swivels round expectantly only to be disappointed. By the time class commences and Lily has still not put in an appearance I can't concentrate on anything Madeleine McLevitt's saying.

'I'm so sorry, Madeleine I'm not feeling very well. I think I need to go home.'

Madeleine hurries over to where I'm standing, all concern and kindness. 'Will you be alright to drive or shall I call you a taxi. I'm sure I can square it with the night porter so you can leave your car overnight.'

Shaking my head I give a brief smile, 'Thank you, but I think I'll be OK, I just need some air.'

'Well, if you're sure,' Madeleine helps me pack up my things and comes with me to the door. I step outside leaving Madeleine directing her best wishes for my speedy recovery to my retreating back.

Getting into the car I thump the steering wheel in frustration and anger. Where is she? It's obviously no good my just sitting here fuming, there's nothing I can do tonight, I might as well get home and have something to eat. Maybe I can catch Lily tomorrow as she leaves work for her lunch break, it's worth a try. As a precaution, I've never phoned or messaged her just in case Munroe ever gets hold of her phone; I don't want the risk of leaving any obvious connection.

As I pull into the drive at the side of my apartment block my headlights arc across a shadowy figure a few yards away. Hurriedly I park, grab my art paraphernalia off the back seat and walk briskly round the house to the front door, the threat of Graham still present as I fumble my key into the lock.

'Excuse me.'

'What?'

'I'm sorry, I didn't mean to startle you; I'm looking for number 83.'

I turn in the direction of his voice and with relief realise that the man doesn't look anything like my fears; he's clean shaven and much too stocky, older too.

'"83"? That'll be on the other side, in the direction of town. The numbering down this road is rather odd.'

'Yes, it certainly is. Doesn't help being in the dark either, can't see a lot of the numbers. Anyway, thanks for your help. Goodnight.'

'No problem, goodnight.'

I push the door and step inside, taking a deep breath as I do so. The stranger seemed genuine but I don't feel I can trust my own instincts anymore. Pulling back the door curtain to one side, I press my nose to the glass and peer down the street. He's disappeared quickly, he can't be at number 83 yet, it's quite a way down the road. I raise myself onto tiptoes to try to get a better angle.

'Are you expecting someone, dear?'

I drop back heavily onto my heels in surprise, letting go of the curtain at the same time.

'Oh, Mrs Lewis you made me jump, I didn't hear you come out.'

She repeats, 'Are you expecting someone?'

'No, no. I simply thought I heard a strange noise as I came in but it was probably just next door's cat, Angus, messing about in the dustbins.'

'Yes, he's a little mischief, isn't he? I do fuss him but I don't feed him, you know. It isn't me that encourages him over here.'

'I'm sure you don't, Mrs Lewis.'

Mrs Lewis starts to wring her hands lightly, 'I don't want you to think me a nuisance.'

'I don't.'

'It's just I do get anxious these days; what with the murder of that poor man in the park and the local news; the drug dealing and everything and, it's probably my imagination, but there often seems to be a man just loitering around here, strolling up and down the street or just standing at the corner, like he's waiting for someone.'

Graham, it has to be.

'Try not to worry, Mrs Lewis there's been a lot of new developments in Endover recently. It's probably just many more people about than you're used to.'

'Yes, I expect that's it. Thank you, Amelia my dear. Goodnight.'

'Goodnight, Mrs Lewis.'

I push my door and step inside, taking a deep breath as I do so. If only I'd actually seen Graham, or indeed, anyone else following me I could confront them but all I've ever had are vague sensations and Mrs Lewis' reported sightings.

◆

Wednesday lunchtime, sheltering in the opening of the Marks & Spencer store, I have a clear view of the front door of the solicitors where Lily works. Despite being shielded from the worst of the wind I find it isn't long before I'm feeling really chilled. I dig my hands deeper into my coat pockets and stamp my feet in an effort to keep warm. I do hope she hurries up, I'm due back in college by two fifteen but I don't want to let this opportunity slip or I'll have to wait until next Tuesday's art class.

Oh, damn it! A delivery van pulls up right outside, completely blocking my view. I've no choice but to hasten across the road. Rounding the back of the van I glimpse Lily's red coat disappearing round the corner.

Hurrying after her, I'm just in time to see her enter Dougie's café. Good, she appears to be on her own so I casually enter and stroll up to the counter, turning in fake surprise as Lily touches my arm. 'Amelia, hi.'

'Oh, Lily, didn't see you there. Are you OK? I missed you at art class last night.'

'Yeah, I'm sorry about that but I was out on a date and art class came a very poor second.'

Lily gives me a wide grin as she hugs her coffee cup.

'A date? Who with?'

'You remember I told you that the leader of the cycle club had suggested another relatively new member and I sort of pair up for the ride on Saturday.' 'Yeah.'

'Well, it's him!'

'Wow, that's quick work.'

Lily giggles.

'Yeah, I know, but we just sort of hit it off straight away. We exchanged phone numbers and Sunday evening he rang to ask me out.'

I allow myself a moment of smug congratulations; my character annihilation of Jess seems to have worked better than I'd hoped and Barry isn't about to let the grass grow under his feet.

'So, tell me, how did the ride on Saturday go? You obviously managed it OK.'

'It was great, I loved it. I'm so grateful to you for suggesting it and the loan of the bike. Just think, if you hadn't I'd never have met Barry.'

'So where'd you go on Tuesday night?'

'To that new club that's opened up in the Old Town; it was brilliant. He's a really nice guy and we've got so much in common.'

More than you know I think but simply nod encouragingly.

'Will you tell your mum and dad that you're going out with him?'

'No, not yet; I don't want Dad doing his usual snooping and coming up with reasons why I shouldn't see him.'

'Eh? I don't understand, why would your dad snoop and how, anyway?'

Lily makes a dejected sigh as she concentrates on stirring her coffee.

'I haven't told you this before but Dad's a police officer, a Detective Chief Inspector to be precise.' She glances momentarily up at me, trying to gauge my reaction. 'I tend not to tell people; it kind of puts them off.'

'Oh, I see, at least, I think I do. Are you saying your dad does a police check on all your boyfriends?'

'Just about, yeah.'

'God, Lily, that's awful! How can you stand it?'

'I'm getting pretty sick of it.'

'I'm not surprised; I'd keep it to myself for as long as possible if I were you. Are you going to see this Barry again?'

'Yeah, next weekend. Barry lodges with some chap who's got a smallholding just outside town. They've got a few animals there so Barry's invited me over to have a look round.'

An image of the dogs, mud and that obnoxious landlord flashes across my mind, 'Sounds fun but how are you going to keep it secret from your dad?'

'My friend Shirley, she'll cover for me, she's a good mate.'

'Good for you.'

I pick up my bag and coat, 'Whoops, look at the time, we'll both be getting the sack if we don't hurry. Good luck with everything. Will you be at art class next Tuesday?'

'Yeah, I plan to. See you there.'

'Bye and enjoy the weekend. I shall want to hear all about it on Tuesday.'

Strolling back to the car I have to restrain the urge to give a little skip of delight.

CHAPTER 13

Ensconced in the winged leather armchair I cast my eyes about Barnaby's consulting room. I sense a difference but I can't determine what it is. The room still bears the faint scent of previous clients mixed with the pot-pourri and oil burners, the curtains are still drawn, blocking out all presence of an outside world. The light is still of a slightly reddish hue, like watered-down blood, as if the room has absorbed the leeched-out agonies of Barnaby's clients and is now pulsing with its own life-force yet, there is something not quite the same.

I'm grateful that Barnaby still continues with his silent approach, waiting for me to utter the first words; it gives me time to ponder this conundrum.

I look around the room again, allowing my eyes to come full circle to rest on Barnaby. He seems a little ill at ease under my gaze and then I realise what has changed; he has positioned his chair further away, only a little, about six inches. I can make out the indentations in the carpet where its feet originally stood. How very strange. I wonder if this is a move purely for my benefit or if he has decided to withdraw from all his clients.

I smile sweetly, 'Good evening, Barnaby.'

'Good evening, Amelia. How have you been?'

'Very well thank you, very well.'

Another silence ensues whilst I pointedly stare at the indentations in the carpet, sensing Barnaby's awareness of my discovery as he shifts uncomfortably in his seat. Without looking up I ask, 'Do you think it's important to remember things from your childhood?'

'Is it important to you?'

Oh, Barnaby; always answering with another question. I imagine it was a guideline printed in big, black letters from his online correspondence course. He is definitely no psychiatrist or psychoanalyst, I knew that when I first came to him. He's a counsellor; an amateur whatever his framed certificate on the wall purports to indicate.

'I've been thinking recently about my brother's girlfriend, Addie.'

Barnaby waits quietly, trying to adopt a look of impartial interest yet I sense his disquiet underneath. He can't deal with things too deep.

'She was very lovely, you know; have I told you that before?'

Barnaby briefly shakes his head.

'Yes, very lovely, in a pale, translucent way. She was tall and slender and seemed to waft across the floor, as though her feet were suspended a few inches above its surface; such fluidity of movement, such grace and femininity. I *hated* her.'

Barnaby's startled expression makes me aware of the vehemence that I've inadvertently let slip so I immediately hasten to dispel his fears. 'Of course, I was only eight years old when Matt first brought her home so I suppose that was a natural reaction. You have to understand that up until that point I'd been the centre of Matt's attention. He'd been a wonderful brother, making up for the lack of attention I received from our parents and she was so *unlike* me; fair to my dark, tall to my short stature, I was a tomboy, she was elegance personified. I thought Matt's choice was a rejection of me.'

I let the words drift quietly away and sit in contemplative silence. Barnaby is observing me, a thoughtful expression on his face as he tries to think up a placating comment. 'But you were only a child, some jealousy was natural. How did things progress?'

'Addie tried really hard, really worked at being friendly. I think she saw herself as an older sister, even as a replacement mother figure. God knows, my own mother didn't demonstrate any maternal feelings towards me. I think Addie felt sorry for me.'

I fall silent again as I cast my mind back over the many ways Addie tried to include me, to make me feel welcome around her and Matt. If I'm honest, she couldn't have been nicer but despite it all I could feel Matt drawing away and I wasn't going to allow that.

I shift a little further back into the enclosing security of the winged chair, its leather back moulding to the contours of my spine, becoming part of me, like a second skin.

'Of course, it didn't help that Mother and Father liked her so much. They fawned over her and her family who were more up market than ours and I think our parents saw it as a step up the social ladder. They were so thrilled when we got an invitation to her parents' house, you'd think they'd just been invited to tea with the Queen.' I can hear the sneering disdain in my voice even after all these years and I sense that Barnaby has noted it too. He's scribbling something in his notebook, probably to the effect that I can't let go of childish resentments. So, I decide to give him something more to mull over.

'Addie collected porcelain dolls, had a whole cabinet of them. She took me into her bedroom to show me. It was the day she and Matt announced their engagement.' I close my eyes and allow the image of that cabinet and its contents to materialise in my imagination. 'She told me that they weren't playthings, their arms and legs didn't move like a toy doll but if I promised to be very careful I could take them out one at a time to look at them. It was then her mum called, so she left me to go downstairs, saying she knew she could trust me to do as she'd said. I remember I sat for some time in front of that cabinet, not touching anything. I was deciding on the doll that looked most like Addie and, when I'd decided, I took it out of the cabinet and deliberately wrenched its leg off. Then I carefully placed it back, tucking the leg under its long skirt. No-one would know until you lifted it up.'

As I re-imagine, the exquisite sensation of malicious triumph is as vivid and palpable all these years later and I can't prevent a smile of satisfaction spreading over my face.

I can tell Barnaby is discomfited and is desperate to somehow lighten the situation.

'But things improved, didn't they? You've told me in the past how much you miss both Matt *and* Addie so you must have grown to like her over time.'

I ignore him and fall into silence once more. I'm recalling turning back from the cabinet to go downstairs. I'm startled to see a boy, about three years older than me, standing in the doorway; his look a mixture of anger and disbelief as he stares fixedly first at me and then at the cabinet. Then, without a word, he turns and walks away. I still don't know how much he'd witnessed. I waited for days for the axe to fall; for me to be brought before my parents and Addie's family to account for my actions but there was nothing. With him being at boarding school most of the year, I didn't see him again until the day of Addie's funeral.

Barnaby gives a theatrical cough to marshal my attention. As I lift my head I stare unwaveringly into his eyes, 'You didn't answer my question.' My tone is accusatory and harsh; Barnaby seems to shrink before me.

'What question was that?'

'Whether you think it's important to remember things from your childhood?'

Barnaby really doesn't like being put on the spot; I wonder what it is about himself that he's afraid of disclosing. This counselling lark is just a means to enable him to hide; he can concentrate on others so he doesn't have to examine himself too deeply. I despise such weakness.

'Well?'

'I suppose it depends if you learn from them; every experience can be a learning tool, can help you understand yourself more clearly. Do you think your memories help you have a greater understanding of yourself, Amelia?'

'Oh indeed, I understand myself very well, Barnaby. Do you?'

He gets up from his chair and busies himself putting away his notebook and pen into the desk by his side.

'We have to finish now, Amelia; my next client will be due soon.'

'Of course,' I stretch languidly as I peel myself out of the leather chair, like a snake sloughing its skin. 'Thank you, I've enjoyed today's session. I hope you have too.'

'Enjoyment isn't really the object of the exercise, Amelia.'

'Mmm, I suppose not but it doesn't hurt. Good evening, Barnaby.'

Turning to close the door as I leave I see him moving his chair back, carefully placing its legs in the carpet indentations. So, it was purely for me, as if six inches would put him out of my range; doesn't he know a spider can cast her threads a lot further than that? Walking down the stairs I allow myself a smile of amusement.

I'd decided not to bring the car this evening. The weather was slowly warming up and I felt the walk to and from Barnaby's rooms would give me some uninterrupted thinking time.

Strolling along, I ponder Graham; the angry ten year old at the door, the accusatory twelve year old at Addie's funeral, the confused, bewildered twenty-something man. *Why* had he said nothing, done nothing? If he'd brought to light my true nature all those years ago perhaps everything that has ensued could have been avoided. You see, it isn't *all* down to me.

I do a bit of shopping on the way home; it's getting a bit late for cooking so I buy myself a microwave meal and side salad. I think I've got some Rioja left from the other night that will be a good accompaniment. I feel quite happy and despite Barnaby's disapproval, I did enjoy our session. It's been a long time since I've allowed my mind to go back over childhood events and it was gratifying to find that I didn't have the slightest twinge of conscience.

I'm just unlocking my apartment door when I hear Mrs Lewis' door behind me open and feel my shoulders involuntarily slump; it's all I can do to prevent myself laying my forehead against the door in despair.

'Hello my dear.' Since the business of her answering the stranger's questions about me Mrs Lewis is more jittery than ever, shuffling non-stop before me as though she's constantly treading on eggshells. I place my bags at my feet, forcing a weak smile as I try to be pleasant.

'Mrs Lewis, good evening.'

'Had a busy day, my dear?' Mrs Lewis notices my querying look, 'I simply meant that you're home rather late, later than usual I mean.'

'I wasn't aware you were keeping tabs on me, Mrs Lewis.' My annoyance is obvious.

'Oh no dear, I wasn't …I mean, I'm not. It's just that nice policeman was here earlier, looking for you and, when he didn't get a reply, he knocked on my door to ask if I knew when you were usually home.'

Apprehension seems to surge from my toes to my scalp. I haven't heard anything from DC Wilson for a while although I know from my conversation with Janet that he did follow up the Jess Saunders lead I gave him.

'Did he say what he wanted?'

'No, not really, just said he needed a word. I asked if it was anything I could help with; to be truthful I was a little lonely and was hoping for a bit of company, but he said no, he'd call back again over the weekend. I was glad in the end that he didn't come in because, as he turned to leave, I smelt the pipe tobacco on him, on his clothes, really strong it was.'

'Pipe tobacco? Are you sure?'

'Oh yes, reminded me of my father, he was a pipe man too; Old Holborn, I'd recognise it anywhere. Our house reeked of it when I was growing up, not something I want in my little flat now, dear me, no. Oh my dear, are you alright? You look quite pale.'

'Yes, yes, just over-tired I think. Good night, Mrs Lewis.' Without allowing her a chance to continue I hastily open my door and stumble inside, tripping over the bags at my feet in my haste to shut her out. Sinking onto the sofa I close my eyes and concentrate on regulating my breathing. In, 1,2,3; out, 1,2,3. Slowly, control returns. I walk through to the kitchen, unpack my shopping and pour a glass of Rioja, the first few sips calming my thoughts and allowing more rational thinking to come to the fore.

So, it wasn't baby-faced DC Wilson after all, it was Detective Chief Inspector Munroe. What the hell can he be sniffing around again for? It's possible Wilson has let something slip; he's such a ninny, I can imagine he'd fold if shouted at loudly enough.

I shove my meal into the microwave and decide what I'll do. I'm not going to stay at home over the weekend waiting for Munroe to turn up. No, I think I'll take myself down to the seaside, find a cosy little B & B and walk by the sea. That way, if I can't avoid seeing him, Munroe can at least wait on *my* convenience, not his.

I'm aware that as the past few months and my plans have progressed I've more control over my reactions; improving with age, it seems. As I speculate as to Munroe's reasons for wanting to speak with me again I find I'm rather looking forward to the encounter.

◆

I'm up early next morning, sling a few things into an overnight bag and am on the road down to Brighton by 8am. I haven't bothered to book anywhere; it's still very early in the year so accommodation shouldn't be a problem.

The thought of Munroe calling round to my apartment only to keep finding I'm not there is deliciously amusing; it's partly the reason I left so early, so Mrs Lewis wouldn't be aware. She'll probably think I've just gone shopping so is bound to encourage him to try again later. The more fruitless calls he makes the better.

Immediately I arrive in Brighton I head for the beach, stumbling and staggering down the steep mound of stones I plop down, huddling into my jacket, my knees drawn up to my chest. The wind is blowing off the sea, flinging spray into my face; I lick my lips to taste the saltiness. Pebbles, tossed up the beach by previous seas, are now clawed back by the waves, clattering and tumbling over one another in their haste to return, shiny and glistening, Neptune's very own Faberge eggs.

Pebbles all around me, I idly pick one up, marvelling at the exquisite smoothness of its surface as I gently put it to my cheek. I close my eyes and think of Matt and Munroe. Retribution has always been a convenient tag, giving me the illusion of a degree of normality but I've always known it was merely that; an illusion. The truth is I enjoy the game. Like chess, one has to develop a strategy, anticipate and manipulate the moves of one's opponent. Matt taught me to play, by the time I was nine I mostly won. You'd think he would have remembered that. It's playing the game that's been a constant force in my life, ebbing and flowing like the tides; a natural rhythm moulding me to its bidding. I can no more resist than the pebbles can resist the pull of the waves.

I sit for ages, not moving, until I feel my face going numb from the cold but eventually, reluctantly, I struggle to my feet and make my way back to the promenade where I find one of the little café huts open for business. Settling myself by the window, nursing a huge mug of steaming coffee in my hands, I gaze out at the sea. I've always found the rhythmic rise and fall of the waves mesmerising; it's the only time my mind is stilled and I'm completely in the moment.

'You here on an early holiday?' the chap has come out from behind the counter and is busily wiping the tables around me.

'No, just a quick weekend break; I don't suppose you know of a decent B & B that's open, do you? I know it's early in the season.'

'As a matter of fact I do. Mrs Foster keeps open all year round. Just down the road a little to your left – Sunnyside B & B, you can't miss it; bright red front door and chintzy curtains. If you're lucky, you might get one of her sea view rooms.'

He notices my slightly puzzled look.

'I was watching you, down on the beach and since you've been in here; can't take your eyes off it, can you?'

I smile my acknowledgement of the truth of his observation as he continues, 'I think for some of us it's simply in the blood; nation of island dwellers, sea all around us, part of our heritage.'

'Yes, I think you're right. It's always fascinated me, ever since I was a child,' I push back my chair, 'Thank you for the coffee, it was most welcome.'

'That's OK, Miss, here to please. You tell Mrs Foster that Stan from the Cockleshell Café sent you. She'll see you right enough.'

It doesn't take long to find Sunnyside B & B and Stan was right, Mrs Foster makes me feel very welcome *and* I get a sea view room. Fantastic. I get myself settled and then decide to go exploring The Lanes, Brighton's famous maze of tiny streets and curio shops. Even at this time of year there are quite a few people milling about, probably encouraged by the protection the area gives from the strong winds on the front.

It's as I turn the corner from one lane into another my attention is drawn to the cluttered window of a toy shop. Not something that would normally interest me but on this occasion … I'm not immediately aware of what has actually caught my eye, only that I feel compelled to press my nose against the glass, peering into the relative gloom and then I spot it – right at the back of the display sits a doll, its delicate features and wide, doe-like eyes making it difficult to accept that it's actually made of wood.

As I enter the shop for a better look the shopkeeper is immediately by my side. 'I see you've noticed our little marionette.'

'Oh, I thought it was just a doll.'

He moves over and lifts the toy out from the clutter around it, carefully disentangling its strings. Holding his arm aloft he makes the puppet take a few faltering steps toward me. 'Here, you try.' He places the string control contraption in my hand, 'This way; hook your little finger over here, that's it, now the index finger goes here and controls the legs.' He stands back to give me room as I hesitantly try to move the puppet forward. 'You're a natural!' he exclaims as within a few steps I have her striding confidently forward. I allow myself a smile of satisfaction, a natural indeed. It's no good, I can't resist. 'How much?'

'For you, my dear, £20.'

A few moments later and I'm leaving the shop, my purchase sitting carefully upright in a carrier bag. With its strings discreetly hidden, one would never know it was anything other than what it seems; a very pretty doll. I feel she's my kindred spirit.

The weekend passes all too quickly and I seem, too soon, to be on the road back home Sunday afternoon, my new friend strapped into the passenger seat beside me. The only thing casting a shadow is the impending visit from DCI Munroe but my break away has done me good, cleared my mind to a point where my confidence is paramount.

I haven't been home above a couple of hours when the intercom from the front door buzzes. 'Miss Thompson, it's Detective Chief Inspector Munroe, may I come in please?'

'What's this about, Inspector? I'm afraid it's not really very convenient at the moment.'

Munroe can't keep the annoyance out of his voice, 'I'm sorry about that, Miss Thompson, but this is important police business so I'm afraid your convenience is not my concern.'

Arrogant, patronising bastard! I grit my teeth and say nothing, simply press the door open button. I wait for his knock on my apartment door and then deliberately make him wait a few more minutes before letting him in.

Munroe strolls through into my lounge as though he owns the place and not waiting for me to make the offer, plants himself firmly in one of my armchairs. 'Please, make yourself comfortable.' He ignores my sarcasm.

'You're a hard woman to catch; this is the fourth time I've called round.'

I don't make any reply but stand poker-faced before him.

He waits; presumably hoping his silence will unnerve me and casts his eyes around my lounge, eventually focusing on my marionette, sitting tucked into the corner of my sofa. 'That's a very unusual doll.'

I've no intention of indulging in small talk with him so remain silent. He looks from the marionette back to me and then back again to the marionette. 'It's very pretty, beautiful copper blonde hair.' With effort, he turns his eyes and attention back to me. 'I wanted to ask you a few more questions about your visit to the park on the day Barry's father was killed.'

'Really? I'm sure I don't know what else I can tell you.'

'Well, let's just see, shall we?'

I take a deep breath and sit on the sofa beside my new friend.

'Do you have any idea why you didn't notice our victim that day or any other day, for that matter? We understand he was in the park quite often.' Munroe takes out his notepad and pen as I give a slightly bored sigh.

'None whatever, Inspector.'

'I do find it strange that a young woman, on her own, would choose to sit in such an isolated spot.'

I don't attempt to explain but simply let his comment hang in the air. Munroe decides not to pursue it.

'You teach Barry Mason don't you?'

'You know I do.'

Munroe wriggles himself further into my armchair as though he's settling in for the night.

'You seem to take a lot of interest in someone who, presumably, you don't tutor that often, who's basically only "filling in" with your subject.'

'You've accused me of that before. Why should you think that it's strange?'

Munroe doesn't answer, merely continues, 'According to his main course tutor, Ben Anderson, you've shown a great deal of concern for Barry's situation, often asking Mr Anderson how Barry is, what's happening.'

I can't believe that Ben has implied there's anything unusual in my interest. No, it's Munroe's twisted mind making connections where there are none.

'Inspector, Ben is a close friend and colleague and, as I'm sure you are aware, is also very supportive of Barry, doing his best to help what he considers a very promising student through extremely difficult times. When I chat with Ben about Barry it's simply my way of giving *him* support, as a friend and colleague. I'm quite sure Ben has never implied anything else.'

I'm furious, this is exactly the kind of bending of the facts he used on Matt.

'But you haven't just talked about it with Ben, have you?' Munroe flips open his notebook and makes a show of checking his notes, 'You've been seen in the local café having a cosy little tête à tête with Barry.'

I realise immediately where that little gem of information has come from, Jess Saunders. I let out an exasperated sigh. 'For goodness sake, Inspector; *once*, on impulse, I sat with Barry when I came across him, quite by chance, in the café one lunch time. He looked really down, miserable and so, yes, I took it upon myself to speak with him to see if there was anything I could do to help. Is that *so* unbelievable? Perhaps you didn't attend college, Inspector. If you had you'd realise that student/tutor relationships are nowadays conducted on an adult to adult basis. There has been nothing inappropriate or suspicious in my behaviour.'

'I didn't say there was,' Munroe counters.

'Well, you're certainly implying it.' I deliberately raise my voice, as though anger is getting the better of me as I stand defiantly in front of him, 'Is there anything else? I'd like to get something to eat.'

'Please sit down, Miss Thompson, I haven't finished yet.'

I sit back down, dropping heavily onto the sofa in a display of exasperation.

'I believe you aware that there is a drugs problem at the college.'

A statement, not a question; why that now?

'Of course I am, all staff is but it isn't something the Principal likes to advertise. We stamp on it when we can.'

'Very commendable, I'm sure.'

You patronising bastard.

'And you're aware that our victim was seen loitering about the college grounds for a couple of weeks before his death?'

'Yes, you told me but as I said at the time, I hadn't seen, or rather recognised him myself.'

'The post-mortem revealed traces of drugs in his body, so it seems likely that he was acquiring his supply from someone at the college.'

I shrug, 'I suppose so.'

'I believe you've been aware of certain individuals selling drugs on campus; is that correct?'

I can't for the life of me think where this is going.

'Yes, I have been aware and on occasion I've advised the Principal accordingly.'

'Really; is that so?'

'Why should you doubt me, Inspector?'

Ignoring my question, Munroe carries on.

'I believe there was an incident only recently involving a Jess Saunders and two other girls?'

'Well, I did see what I thought was an exchange of something but I was too far away to do anything about it other than report what I'd seen.'

'Miss Thompson, I've interviewed Jess Saunders. She admits to possessing a small quantity of an illegal substance for her own use and insists that you have, both on that occasion and in the past, relieved her of some of those items.'

Before I can answer he continues.

'I've spoken with the Principal. He's adamant that you have never spoken with him regarding this recent incident, or any other for that matter, or handed to him any confiscated drugs.'

'Well, I can assure you that I have, Inspector; whatever the Principal has said.'

Munroe carries on as if I haven't spoken.

'However, we know that our victim hung about the college grounds; we know, from speaking with other park users, that he was regularly seen in the park and low and behold, we also know that on the day of his death you were also in the same area of the park in which our victim's body was found. We also now have reason to believe that, at some point, you have had drugs in your possession. I'm sure you can see my difficulty, Miss Thompson.'

I swallow hard and force myself to answer.

'Inspector, Jess Saunders is a difficult young woman not averse to using her considerable charms to her advantage. She's managed to create a situation that could put our Principal in a very embarrassing, if not damaging, position.'

Munroe raises an eyebrow but says nothing.

'Surely I don't have to spell it out for you, Inspector. You've seen her; you must know what I'm referring to.'

Munroe remains non-committal. I emit a weary sigh and continue.

'Reporting Jess to the Principal would have little effect other than probably threaten my own career. I can only reiterate that I have reported any suspicious incidents to the Principal and handed over any substances I have confiscated. It's my word against his.'

Munroe looks a little sceptical so I continue the attack.

'Let me make it plain, Inspector. I have *never* taken drugs and *never* traded them and I am deeply offended that you could even begin to think that I would *ever* stoop that low. Worse still, you obviously consider me capable of murder and that, having committed such a heinous crime, I then go round ingratiating myself with the poor man's son! Just what kind of monster do you take me for?'

I've managed to work myself up into loud, high-pitched hysteria. Within a few seconds of my shrieking there's an urgent knocking at my door.

'Amelia? Amelia my dear, is everything alright?'

Mrs Lewis' frantic call is coupled with her even more frantic pounding. As I stumble toward the hall Munroe pushes in front of me, worry etching his face. Reaching the door first he tries to block Mrs Lewis' view into my hall as I sink down onto the floor, gulping air into my lungs, a feigned panic attack wracking my body.

'It's alright, Mrs Lewis, nothing to worry about.' Munroe is frantically trying to defuse the situation.

'It doesn't look alright to me.'

For once Mrs Lewis is all bristling determination as, catching Munroe by surprise, she ducks past him and hurries toward me. Wrapping a comforting arm around my shoulders she glares at Munroe.

'I think you'd better leave right now, Inspector.'

Munroe starts to try to explain then thinks better of it and simply turns to go as Mrs Lewis tosses at his retreating back, 'I shall be reporting you to your superiors.'

Oh, Mrs Lewis, bless you my dear, bless you.

CHAPTER 14

What a star Mrs Lewis is! She maintains she was in the hall sorting out the vase of cut flowers but I think it's far more likely she had her ear pressed up against my door as curiosity about Munroe's persistent visits got the better of her. No matter, for once I'm grateful, her intervention got Munroe completely wrong-footed and his discomfort was a joy to see.

It took me a while to convince Mrs Lewis I was fine and persuade her to leave but eventually I was on my own and able to reflect. It seems that Munroe is getting desperate, grasping at straws in his effort to solve the tramp's murder. I expect the pressure from his superiors is getting to him and if Mrs Lewis does as she threatened and reports him for his behaviour tonight he's likely to be even more stressed out. Good.

I glance across at my new little friend sitting on the sofa beside me, her wide eyes, copper blonde hair and delicate features, so like Lily and Addie. Turning her head toward me I smile. 'You can be my little helper but you need a name. I think I'll call you Liliad, for both of them.' I swear Liliad smiles back.

Still, bed I think. Monday tomorrow and I want to see how things stand with Barry. After this evening's debacle I'm sure Munroe will be directing his attention there again as he's running out of options which could mean that I'm running out of time.

The drive into college is pleasanter than usual, the early morning sunshine lifting my spirits after the greyness of the past few days. I think I'm also on a bit of a high what with my enjoyable weekend in Brighton, my new friend strapped into the seat beside me and the exhilaration I feel from my encounter with Munroe.

As I head down the corridor to the staff room I pass the canteen, already open for coffee and snacks for those students who skipped breakfast. At a table just inside the door I notice Jess Saunders, centre stage of a small group who are obviously hanging on her every word. I'm pretty certain no-one has noticed me as I passed so I stop just the far side of the open door and listen.

'So they put me into this interview room, there's just metal chairs, a metal table and painted this puke green colour, no window, stuffy as hell. It's so hot I take off my sweat shirt and am unbuttoning the top three buttons of my blouse when this young copper comes in. I see him trying not to look but he can't tear his eyes away from me tits!'

There's a collective giggle round the table.

'Then this older guy comes in, says he's,' she puts on a pompous voice, 'Detective Chief Inspector Munroe. Surly bastard he was. Anyway, they start going on about me dealing drugs, claiming I'd been supplying Barry's dad. They just wouldn't let up, wanted to know all the boyfriends I'd had. I said to 'em, "How long have you got?"'

Another explosion of giggles.

'In the end I thought, sod this, I don't owe Barry Mason nothin', 'specially after he dumped me, so I told 'em.'

'Told them what?'

There's a pause, presumably Jess playing it for all the effect she can get. 'I told them why I think it was Barry who killed his dad.'

I can hear the sudden intake of breath from the other girls.

'Why?'

''Cos of what Barry told me.'

There's a scrape of chairs; I subconsciously hold my breath, as if my breathing might prevent me hearing this valuable snippet, as the group obviously lean in over the table in a conspiratorial huddle.

'When Barry was a small kid living in Sheffield with his parents there was this old geezer lived next door, did a lot of wildlife watching, wrote books about it so Barry says. Apparently the old guy used to take Barry out with him when he went looking for animals and stuff. Barry reckons it was him started his interest in all this conservation crap.'

Jess allows another pregnant pause. Come on, get on with it, I can't stand here all morning. I hear some footsteps behind me and start rummaging in my bag as though I've simply paused to look for something.

'Apparently,' Jess continues, 'when his dad got out of prison he looked for Barry, found he was living around here and tried to blackmail him.'

'How?'

'Threatened to make out that the old geezer used to abuse him as a kid.'

'Did he?'

'Barry says definitely not.'

'So what's the problem?'

'Barry really cares for this old bloke, even all these years later. Didn't want him to be put through all the questions and suspicions; even if it isn't true, mud sticks and apparently the guy's quite well known in Sheffield. Barry's afraid the scandal would kill him.'

'Did Barry admit to killing his dad?'

Jess snorts, 'No, of course not, you idiot. He's not likely to do that, is he? He was just telling me why he didn't care about his dad being dead. Good riddance as far as he was concerned.'

'Yeah, but the police aren't gonna take your word for it, are they? It's hearsay, surely.'

Ah, at least one of them has some common sense.

'I know that,' Jess sneers, 'but the seeds planted, init? It's got to be in their minds; they can't un-hear it, can they? I don't care if all it does is get them questioning Barry more, serve the sod right.'

I hear the clatter of chairs being scraped back as the group begins to disperse, so quickly continue down the corridor to the staff room. So, that's the reason, is it Barry? At last, the final piece of the jigsaw. Makes sense, your vicious dad threatening someone you have such affection for; you must have felt justified in what you did but I can't let sentimentality push me off course. I need to keep moving forward; Tuesday tomorrow, art class and Lily Munroe. At least, she'd better be there, I don't want any more uncertainties.

◆

Lily is there when I arrive but not in the studio, instead she's waiting in the foyer. 'Amelia, I'm so glad you're here. I really need to talk with you.' Lily is all flushed agitation, 'I know it's a cheek, but do you mind missing the class?'

'No, of course not; let me just put this art stuff back in the car. Where do you want to go?'

'How about Dougie's; it's usually pretty quiet this time in the evening?'

Together we hurry down the road and manage to get the table at the back of the café, tucked into a small, discreet alcove. Lily orders a couple of coffees, making small talk until they arrive. Taking a sip she gives a drawn out sigh of despondency.

'So, what's all this about, Lily? I've been wondering how your weekend went. Your dad didn't find out, did he?'

'No, nothing like that, the weekend was brilliant. I got over to Barry's place about twelve on the Saturday. His landlord made me ever so welcome. It's a bit sparse there, but then blokes don't seem to care much about that, do they?'

'I suppose not. So what happened?'

'Nothing happened, not on Saturday anyway. Barry showed me around; let me help him with feeding the pigs and chickens and collecting eggs. Have you ever put your hand under a sitting hen?'

The very thought makes me shudder, 'No, can't say that I have.'

'It's wonderful. I was really scared I'd get pecked but Barry showed me how to do it; says you've got to be confident, not hesitate. Their feathers are so warm and soft, you can understand how a little chick would be so cosy and secure under there. They've definitely got their own personalities too.'

Personally, the only chickens I like are plucked, sealed in plastic and headless. Why do these nature lovers always have to anthropomorphise everything; personality – ridiculous!

'Oh, and the goats, especially the little kids, they're so adorable. I had loads of cuddles.'

I'm getting a bit bored with all this gooey stuff but it sounds as though Lily was in her element. Cupping her hands around her coffee she stares into the middle distance, apparently in a dreamy idyll of smallholding life. I haven't got time for this cloying sentimentality.

'So, Lily you obviously had a super time with all the animals but how are things with you and Barry?'

Lily leans forward over the table and drops her voice a little, anxiety and sadness evident. Taking a deep breath she continues.

'Barry told me he had the most awful childhood; his dad was a violent alcoholic. He was always knocking Barry's mum about and one night he hit her so hard she fell, hitting her head on the fireplace and died.' Lily's face is full of concern. 'Anyway, it all resulted in his dad going to prison and Barry being fostered out; that's how he came to be down in this area.'

Lily takes another sip of coffee, 'His dad eventually got out of prison and no-one heard from him for years until he turned up here a few months ago, looking for Barry.'

'That's really sad but what's it got to do with your seeing Barry now?'

'Do you remember about that tramp that was found dead in Melsham Park; it was in the local papers.'

I shrug, 'Not really. I don't read much local news.'

'Well, apparently the tramp was Barry's dad.'

'Oh my God, really?'

'Yeah and Barry says that the police seem to think, 'cos of the history, that Barry might have killed him.' Tears well up in Lily's eyes, as she fumbles in her handbag for a tissue.

'That's awful but I still don't understand …'

'Amelia, just think a minute. It's Dad, he's leading the investigation. If Barry ever finds out who my dad is he'll go mad, not to mention how Dad'll react.'

Lily's voice is close to a wail of despair.

'I don't know what to do. Barry's been in and out of the police station for questioning. He thought he was in the clear, the police have been questioning some people to do with drugs as they reckon his dad took drugs but Barry is *so* against them, he'd never … but then yesterday, he was actually pulled out of lessons, in front of all the other students. It was dreadful for him.'

'How do you know that, Lily?'

'He rang me, from the police station Monday night; they're allowed one call apparently.'

'Oh I see. I don't know what to say, Lily; no wonder you're upset. Have they charged him?'

'No, thank goodness. Barry said his tutor at college has been really supportive and has found Barry a solicitor to represent him. The solicitor told the police if they didn't have enough evidence to charge Barry they had to let him go which they've done but it doesn't look like they're going to give up any time soon as all their other leads have come to nothing.'

'I have to ask, do you think Barry could be guilty?'

'*No*, no way.'

'So what are you going to do? If your dad finds out you're seeing him …'

'Do you know, I don't care, I'm convinced Barry's innocent; I'd stake my life on it.'

I have to lower my head to cover up the slight smile I find curving my lips; Lily doesn't know how prophetic her words are.

'What happens next with the police?'

'I've no idea but I do know I'm going to stick by Barry come what may.' Lily wriggles a little in her chair, an excited tenseness in her manner.

'C'mon, give; you obviously have something up your sleeve.'

'OK, but you mustn't tell anyone, promise? Next weekend Barry's landlord is going away, leaving Barry to look after the place, so we've agreed, I'm going to be there too, staying over to help out. Shirley's agreed to cover for me again and Dad's working all weekend; extra-long shifts because they've got some staff off sick so Dad'll hardly be home, won't have time to miss me and as I've stayed overnight at Shirley's before, he won't think it's strange.'

'Wow, things are moving forward. Are you really that serious about him, Lily? You are sure about this?'

'Absolutely; he's a really nice guy; Dad's got it all wrong. Barry even moved into that place just to keep his dad away from his foster parents. No-one that's as caring as that would kill someone, however much he hated him. I think that's why his tutor is helping him so much; it isn't as if I'm the only person who thinks he's innocent.'

'Don't take this the wrong way, I can see that you're absolutely smitten with him but are you really sure?'

Lily's look is defiant.

'Look, Lily I'm only playing devil's advocate but you need to think very carefully. Your dad must have some serious doubt as to Barry's innocence if he keeps on questioning him, even if he hasn't got enough to charge him with.'

Lily's look is implacable.

'If you're going to be there alone with him …'

Lily stands up, reaching for her handbag.

'You're like Dad. What happened to "innocent until proven guilty"?'

'Oh, Lily please don't be angry. I'm just worried for you, that's all.'

I reach out and gently touch her arm.

'There's no need, Amelia. I'm a grown woman and I think I'm a good judge of character.'

'Yes, of course, I'm sure you are. Let's not let this spoil our friendship. Will you have another coffee with me?'

Lily drops her handbag back onto the table and gives me a tiny smile.

'Yeah, why not? I didn't mean to snap, I know you meant well; I'm just so on edge.'

'No worries. I'll get those coffees. I really hope it all works out.'

What I mean by 'it' is, of course, very different to what Lily thinks I mean.

'Thanks, Amelia.'

Later, as we leave I say, 'Please, keep me updated and I'll keep everything crossed for you.' I stand, pulling on my coat and rummaging in my bag for my car keys. 'Take care and I'll see you next week.'

'Bye, Amelia.'

Turning at the door I give Lily a warm, encouraging smile; after all, this could be the last time I speak with her.

As I walk back to the car park I reflect on what now needs to be done to ensure things go as I've planned.

Most importantly, nothing must interfere with Lily's planned weekend at Barry's so that means Barry must be kept out of police clutches until then. I can only hope the lawyer Lily mentioned is good at his job.

The drive home doesn't take long, for once all the traffic lights seem to be with me. Turning into our rear car park I'm perturbed to notice that the sensor lights aren't working so that once I've turned off the car headlights I'm plunged into darkness save for a little light coming from the rear flats' curtained windows.

Pulling my art things off the back seat, I slam the car door and turn hurriedly. Damn! My brush case has come unzipped and all the contents tumble to the tarmac, rolling this way and that as I try to stop them with my feet.

Squatting down to gather them up my blood chills as a shadow looms out of the semi-darkness, sliding over the brushes and my extended hand; viscous glue fixing me to the spot.

The shadow enlarges as it nears, creeping up my arm, slowly encompassing my upper body, to my neck, my head. I can't breathe; tension suffocates me as I keep my eyes fixed on the ground.

A large pair of Nike trainers fills the dark space before me, as a body squats down to my level.

'Want a hand?'

I almost stumble backwards as the spell is broken and I start breathing again but relief is only short-lived.

Barry! What the hell is he doing here? It's an effort but I manage to keep my voice steady.

'Barry, you gave me quite a fright. What are you doing here?'

He gathers up my brushes, slowly returning them to their case before carefully re-zipping it and handing it back.

'I need to speak with you. I've been questioned by the police again; they're not letting up. I think I need to tell them what you said, that you saw everything and that I was only defending you. It was an accident, not murder. I need to know you'll back me up.'

Christ! I can't allow this, if he owns up he'll be kept in custody and everything I've worked toward will be lost. Firmly, I respond.

'But they haven't charged you with anything yet, have they?'

Barry shakes his head.

'Then there's no need to pre-empt anything. I told you why I didn't want to say anything unless it was absolutely unavoidable. You can't expect me to put my future at risk unless completely necessary.'

Barry takes a couple of steps towards me, leaning forward slightly; his large frame physically threatening.

'So, you won't help me?'

'I didn't say that, Barry; just not right now, that's all; it isn't necessary.'

I hear Barry's sharp intake of breath and sense his body stiffen with barely controlled anger yet when he speaks his quiet controlled tone carries an ominous animosity.

'Did you pay a visit to my foster parents last week?'

Struggling to get incredulity into my voice I reply, 'Why would I do that?'

He doesn't answer my question but continues.

'Someone was there, a young woman, asking questions about me. You're always asking questions about me. You keep turning up where I am; at the café, the park, Ben says he saw you snooping around at the football match on Sunday.'

How the hell did Ben see me? The surprise almost trips me up.

'Whoever Ben saw it wasn't me; I hate football so why on earth would I be there? As for the rest, it's merely chance or are you saying I use the park or the café simply to bump into you?'

Barry shrugs defiantly.

'Well, all I can say is you must have a mighty high opinion of yourself.'

Barry stands silent for what seems like an age, just looking at me, stony-faced. Then, without a word, he simply turns and walks away.

I stand where I am for several minutes, staring dumbfounded at Barry's retreating figure. I don't know what to make of his silent departure but its undertone is decidedly threatening.

I realise I can't wait any longer; it must be this weekend.

As I let myself into the communal hall Mrs Lewis pounces.

'Oh my dear, I'm so glad you're back safe. I was worried about you.'

My resigned sigh must speak volumes as Mrs Lewis hurries to explain.

'It's just I was worried about that man, lurking around again. Has he spoken with you yet?'

'He's just one of my students from college, Mrs Lewis; nothing to worry about.'

I continue toward my door when the thought strikes me.

'Wait a moment, how did you see him? Your windows don't look out the back.'

'Out the back? Oh dear, no. I can't see anything out the back. He was at the front, opposite the gate, on the other side of the road.'

'Mrs Lewis, are you saying it's the same man who asked you questions about me?'

Mrs Lewis wrings her hands in confusion.

'Why, yes my dear, who else would it be? The man with the kangaroo emblem on his jacket.'

I can't believe it; as if I haven't got enough to deal with, it seems Graham is still hanging around, stalking me, yet I still haven't seen him myself, not for certain. If

I had I could confront him as I've had more than enough of this nonsense. If I can just get through the next few days and accomplish what I've set out to do then I can disappear; get free of the lot of them. I absent-mindedly put my hand up to my forehead as I try to think.

'Oh my dear, are you alright? Shall I call the doctor?' Mrs Lewis tries to take hold of my arm but I shake her off.

'No, I just need to get indoors, have something to eat. Goodnight, Mrs Lewis.'

Hurrying into my lounge I collapse on the sofa. I fear my world is threatening to disintegrate.

CHAPTER 15

This weekend, I *have* to make it happen this weekend. I daren't delay any longer for fear my control has already started to slip. Munroe's questioning is becoming more perceptive and from what Mrs Lewis told me, Graham is still around, watching me with God knows what sinister intentions.

With Lily and Barry going to be together at his cottage it's unlikely there'll be a more opportune time but the weekend is still three days away. Three days when I'll have to appear completely relaxed and at ease, giving no indication of the momentous importance to me of the coming two day break.

At college I keep a low profile, drawing as little attention to myself as I can. As for Barry, he's been in a couple of my classes since our evening encounter but remains non-communicative so I'm ignoring him as much as feasible, ensuring I address any comments to the class in general rather than any individual.

It seems to take forever but eventually Friday afternoon arrives and I feel my pulse quicken as I gather my teaching paraphernalia for the final time. I will not be back here after today.

Janet's office is situated at the 'T' of the corridor, looking up towards the main entrance/exit doors of the college. I'm just making the turn down the exit corridor when, 'Amelia, Miss Thompson, might I have a word before you go?'

I turn to see Janet sitting behind her desk, arms folded over her ample bosom, her moist lips curving into a satisfied smirk as she watches me retrace my steps towards her.

'Yes?'

'My word, you do have your arms full. I hope all those books have been properly signed out of our library.'

'These are my own books; I thought I'd do a bit of sorting out over the weekend.'

Janet merely nods.

'I've been doing some tidying myself, going over the staff files, making sure all details are up to date and so forth.'

'Really.'

Janet stares at me, her eyes mere slits above her pink, piggy cheeks.

'Did you have something you wanted to say to me? These books are heavy and I'd like to get them into the car.'

With deliberate slowness Janet opens a file on her desk and leans slightly forward, as if examining its contents for the first time.

'I was looking at the references you supplied at your interview. I see there's one here from a college in Dorset, Albany Teacher Training College.'

'And?'

Janet picks up the paper, holding it delicately between thumb and forefinger as if it's contaminated in some way.

'Signed by a Mrs Elizabeth Marshall.'

'And?'

'I've spoken with the college secretary on the telephone. She tells me that Mrs Marshall left the college over four years ago. She wasn't teaching when you were there.'

I take a deep breath as if in exasperation at her stupidity.

'Indeed. Well, Janet I suggest you check your sources more carefully in future. I think you'll find that the current secretary has only been at the college for the past year and so wouldn't be aware that Elizabeth Marshall returned to Albany as a supply tutor for a brief period which was when I came to know her. Now, if you don't mind, I really must be going.'

As I walk toward the exit I can feel Janet's eyes boring into my back like steel skewers. What I've just said is a complete lie as I'd forged Elizabeth Marshall's signature but it doesn't matter, Janet won't be able to do any further checking until Monday and by then I'll be gone.

❖

I spend the evening in reflective mood, wandering round the apartment, touching items with a strange feeling of fondness. I've liked living here, in this apartment and in Endover. It'll be a shame to leave it but my roots have always been shallow, just deep enough to anchor me for a few years. Now, I must move on.

My things are packed, I only have a couple of large, wheeled suitcases having deliberately kept my belongings to a minimum; the apartment being furnished I've only personal items to take with me.

Curled up before the gas fire, I know everything hinges on my planned performance before DCI Munroe tomorrow afternoon. My plans have cooled to a solid mass of icy determination. Control of the game and the ability to direct its players is everything.

Lying in bed Friday night I think everything through once more; it occurs to me that before I engineer my meeting with Munroe I need to be sure that Lily's at the cottage with Barry. I'll have to drive over and take a look tomorrow, there's no other way.

◆

Saturday dawns cloaked in a cat-like fog that curls around the corners of buildings; a sensuous, caressing movement that belies the bone-chilling damp of its substance.

As I drive further into the countryside that afternoon it swirls in the air like a muslin shroud. The overhanging branches of trees lining the narrow lanes are laden with moisture, heavy drops suspended along their lengths like bereavement tears. It all seems so very fitting.

The fog lights on the car only penetrate a short distance into the opaque greyness making the journey nerve-wracking but eventually I turn the final bend. Lights from the cottage windows are just visible through the murk, a cosy, mellow sight amidst this uncharitable dankness.

As well as confirming Lily and Barry's presence I want to see if I can locate a track that I'd noticed on the local map. If I'm correct, it will give me a good vantage point to observe things without my presence becoming obvious.

Skirting the front of the cottage I make my way into the next field. I'm relieved and a little surprised that the dogs haven't detected my presence but it's possible that they're out on a walk with Barry and Lily for as yet I've seen no sign of them either.

Keeping well away from the post and wire fence that marks the boundary of the smallholding I follow its line until I reach a temporary opening, just before a large barn at the back of the property.

I know from the map that the farm track running away to my right, climbs quite steeply uphill, skirting the edge of a couple of arable fields eventually emerging onto the tarmacked lane about a mile from Barry's cottage. Perfect. I can enter the track from the lane and drive to the summit of the rise where I'll have a reasonable view of the cottage.

Standing at the barn, I peer through a gap in the lapboard wall and discover Lily's car neatly tucked away. Good, she's definitely here and Munroe won't be made aware by the presence of her car on full view.

I recall my first visit to the cottage and what strikes me now is the total absence of birdsong. Despite my horror at the mud and dogs, the most lasting impression had been the abundance of melody as I'd opened the car door. Today, the fog seems to have taken the breath out of the world and everything is hushed with the oppressive silence of a funeral congregation.

Walking swiftly I retrace my steps, past the cottage. Safely back in the car I look across at Liliad strapped into the passenger seat. As I won't be able to attend Lily's funeral I think I might have a little ceremony with my new friend, just so that I can say a proper goodbye. Such traditions are important.

Once back into built-up areas it's surprising how little of the fog still lingers. I park in the municipal car park by the civic centre and walk across to the police station.

Approaching the officer behind the desk I give a small, nervous smile, 'Good afternoon, officer. I need to speak with Detective Chief Inspector Munroe.'

'I'm not sure if he's available, Miss. Can you tell me what it's about?'

'It's about the murder of the tramp, the one that was found in Melsham Park. I know who killed him.' I pick up the biro that's lying on the counter and agitatedly twist it between my fingers. Fixing the young officer with a determined stare, 'It really is imperative I see DCI Munroe, it's very urgent.'

The young officer reaches for the telephone, 'Very well, Miss. Just sit down over there and I'll see what I can do. What's your name?'

'Amelia Thompson.'

I walk to the far wall and slump onto one of the hard plastic chairs. If this is the kind Ben sat on for hours I'm not surprised he was exhausted; I don't think I've ever sat on anything so uncomfortable.

The officer lowers his voice so I can't quite make out what he's saying but there's a controlled, determined urgency to his tone. Putting the receiver down he smiles across at me, 'DCI Munroe is on his way down, Miss.'

'Thank you.' I take a couple of deep breaths and briefly close my eyes. In a few moments I will have to give the performance of my life.

I hear the connecting doors to the rest of the station swing open and stand as Munroe, waiting at the opening, beckons me to follow him. He already looks weary, his shoulders slumped, his head thrust forward, the collar of his shirt slightly large around his neck as though he's lost some weight recently. He reminds me of a tortoise I once had; wrinkled and leathery.

There's a degree of antagonism in Munroe's manner as if he expects I'll be wasting his time once more.

'Miss Thompson.' He holds open the door of an interview room, indicating a chair on the far side of the table as he pulls out the chair closest to him and nods to the WPC standing in the corner. I settle myself, placing my hands in my lap, out of sight under the table.

Munroe leans back in his chair, 'So, all of a sudden you know who killed Edward Howden.'

'There's really no need to take that tone, Inspector.'

'I apologise, Miss Thompson, please, continue; I'm all ears.'

I can't say I'm surprised at his attitude; it's likely DC Wilson did disclose who'd given the leads to Gary Stevenson and Jess Saunders, both of which had come to nothing. Those fruitless lines of investigation, coupled with a lack of real progress with Barry must be leaving the DCI feeling pretty jaded. Also, and I have to control a slight smirk that threatens to curve my lips, the last time he spoke with me he had the embarrassment of being practically ejected from my apartment by a tiny, frail, seventy year old woman. It can't have done his ego much good.

Putting on my best conciliatory look, I speak in a reasonable tone, keeping my voice even, emotion under control.

'Inspector, before I go on I need you to understand that the last thing I've ever wanted to do was hinder your investigation but I've been so very frightened and my fear, I realise now, caused me to make some very bad decisions which I deeply regret.'

I pause to take a breath as I lower my eyes from Munroe's implacable face toward the table, fixing my eyes on a strangely shaped coffee stain on its surface.

'You can't imagine just how much I regret those decisions. I thought, if I did what he said, he'd leave me alone but things have just got worse, much worse. Inspector, I really do need your help.'

Munroe shifts slightly on his chair, eyeing me thoughtfully, trying to balance his scepticism against his desire to solve this case once and for all.

'Go on, Miss Thompson, I'm listening.'

'I'm ashamed to have to admit that I've been very foolish.'

I swallow hard and close my eyes; then, looking up once more at Munroe, moisture glistening behind my lashes, 'To get the job at the college I forged my references.'

I emit a deep sigh as though I find it a relief to come clean at last.

'Don't ask me how he found out, I really don't know but I began to sense I was being followed, that someone was always lurking close by so, by the time he approached me, my nerves were already in shreds.'

I reach down for my handbag, rummaging for a tissue. Dabbing at my eyes I make a show of the effort it takes me to continue. Munroe remains silent, his arms folded across his chest; I can tell that now I have his full attention.

'He said he'd seen me at the park, hiding behind the gate pillars. He knew *I* knew what he'd done but ...'

Munroe cuts across me.

'Wait a moment; are you now telling me that you *did* see who assaulted Barry's father?'

Panic and fear evident on my face I plead with Munroe.

'I'm so sorry but he said if I didn't keep silent he'd let the college know about my false references, get me fired. I couldn't risk that, I need that job and something like that would probably stop me teaching ever again. It was him who told me to suggest to you about Gary Stevenson and Jess Saunders involvement; to keep your attention diverted from him.'

Munroe's look is thunderous as he gives the briefest nod of his head. Ah, as I thought, DC Wilson had squealed; the prick!

'So, what has made you come forward now, after all this time?'

'Because now he's turned to blackmail; it seems your repeated questioning has got him anxious and he wants out. He wants money from me to make it possible but I don't have that kind of money.'

I take my voice up an octave as Munroe remains calmly observing.

'I take it we're talking about Barry Mason.'

'Yes, yes of course; I'm sorry, didn't I say? I meant to, it's just my nerves, I can't think straight anymore.'

'Have you given him any money yet?'

Guiltily I wring my hands and nod, 'Yes, five hundred pounds. He wanted more but I said I couldn't get any more that quickly. He's expecting me to get him the rest by this evening but I can't, I don't have enough and I'm terrified of him. I don't believe he'll just let me walk away; he seems desperate and I've seen what a violent temper he has and I know he has guns!'

Munroe stiffens. 'Guns? What sort of guns?'

'I don't know what *sort*; I don't know anything about guns but I know he's got some; I heard him talking with his mates before class one day. They belong to his landlord. He was claiming he's a crack shot, been taught by his landlord and they often go out shooting together. Inspector, I'm so very scared, I don't know what to do … and I'm also really worried for your daughter.'

'Lily? How do you know Lily? What's she got to do with this?'

'Is that her name? Very pretty; I don't know her, it's just that I happened to see you out together in town one weekend and assumed she was your daughter. Well, it was obvious really, she's so like you.'

'Please, Miss Thompson what has Lily got to do with Barry Mason?'

'Oh dear, I thought you must know. She's been going out with him for a while now, I think. He's not made a secret of it, been boasting in fact. I did think it odd but it was really none of my business.'

Munroe's face contorts in a twisted agony of rage and concern.

I raise my hand to my mouth, feigning horror, 'Oh my God, I've just recalled something I overheard in college yesterday.'

Munroe juts his head forward, exactly like my pet tortoise, 'What, Miss Thompson?'

'I heard Barry on his mobile; he was making arrangements for someone to stay at his home at the weekend. You don't think it could be your daughter, do you? Perhaps they're planning to go away together but … you must know where she is.'

Munroe looks slightly sick, a faint sheen of perspiration coating his forehead. I bet he's starting to doubt Lily's "staying with Shirley" explanations.

He swallows hard, gathering his thoughts, trying to decide priorities, the first of which is to get rid of me.

'Miss Thompson, thank you for coming forward; we'll take it from here and I'll get someone to take down a written statement tomorrow, that'll be time enough.

'Tomorrow! You can't just leave me, I'm scared. If I don't turn up with the rest of the money I don't know what he'll do. I need protection.'

'You'll be perfectly safe, Miss Thompson, I assure you. We'll deal with Barry Mason. The best thing you can do is get yourself home and leave me to do my job.'

'I'm really not happy about being on my own, not until I know he's in custody.'

'Then stay with a friend, Miss Thompson; you'll be fine.'

Pushing my chair back I stand, pausing long enough to compel Munroe to look directly at me. I can sense his impatience for me to be gone so that he can reassure himself of Lily's whereabouts.

'I'm so dreadfully sorry that I didn't mention before about Lily and Barry. As I said, I just assumed you must know. When I'd seen you together at the shops that day your closeness to each other was obvious. It didn't occur to me that such a delightful father/daughter relationship would harbour secrets.'

As I walk past on my way out I place my hand lightly on his arm, 'I wouldn't worry too much; I've probably got it wrong; I seem to keep doing that lately.'

Turning my back on him, I allow myself a satisfied smile.

Emerging from the police station I'm surprised at how the light has faded; I didn't realise I'd been so long. I can't think Munroe will delay, he's likely to check with Lily's friend, Shirley and press her until he gets the truth; once he knows, he'll be over to Barry's cottage.

He'll go prepared; my mention of guns will ensure that.

Settling myself in the car, I take a leisurely drive to my pre-determined vantage point. It'll take Munroe a little time to get organised.

I can't see enough if I remain in the car so, hugging my coat tighter around me, I walk forward about twenty yards. From here I've got a good view, right down into the front yard of the cottage. The fog has lifted, not completely but enough to give better visibility although the evening is drawing in and the natural light fading. I can make out the glow of internal lights that spill from the windows out into the yard, illuminating an area of about four feet in front of the cottage. Smoke is curling seductively up from the chimney indicating that Barry and Lily have created a cosy little country idyll? How sweet.

Turning my gaze away from the cottage I look back along the lane that leads from town. I can see headlights shining intermittently between the trees as the vehicle makes its way around the sharp bends but it's a lone car, someone on their way home.

I stamp my feet and swing my arms around my body in an attempt to keep warm. Where the fuck is Munroe? I thought he'd be here by now. I did convince him, didn't I? I'm aware of what a huge gamble this enterprise is; that's been half the fun; it's a challenge but, at the same time, I can't believe he wouldn't act; his parental instincts will override everything else. No, I refuse to even contemplate failure; he'll come, I'm sure of it.

In any case, I have one further weapon to deploy that, like all the best incendiary devices, is the most seemingly innocuous.

A shaft of light catches my eye as it spills out from the direction of the cottage and, turning my head, I see Lily coming out of the front door. She walks around to the side of the building, carrying two large bowls. 'Hitler. Goering.' As she calls, the two Doberman rush from the wooded area at the back of the property, Lily places the bowls inside a small shed, spends a few minutes fussing the dogs and shuts them inside.

As I watch her return to the cottage I see sets of headlights in the distance; no sirens, no flashing blue lights, just a quiet, stealthy snake of law enforcement heading this way. Good on you, Munroe, no need to announce your arrival until you're absolutely ready. I look back at Lily; she's stopped by the corner of the cottage looking back toward the large barn that houses her car. Please, please get back inside, you stupid bitch; Munroe mustn't see you. She turns and I breathe a sigh of relief as the cottage door closes behind her.

A couple of police vehicles coast up; turning their headlights and engines off as they approach the entrance. Munroe, obviously deciding to play this quietly, steps out of the front vehicle with DC Wilson, leaving two firearms officers to position themselves; one behind a tree, the other toward the back of the cottage, behind one of the animal shelters.

The dogs, sensing intruders and frustrated at being locked up, suddenly start up a ferocious barking, jumping and clawing at the closed door of their shed just as Munroe is cautiously approaching the cottage. He's about six feet away when the front door is flung open and Barry steps out to investigate the noise.

Both he and Munroe freeze; each startled by the sudden, unexpected appearance of the other. Barry recovers first and instinctively makes a dive back into the cottage as Munroe yells, 'Barry Mason, this is the police. Leave the cottage with your hands up.'

I wait just a few moments before lighting the touch paper. Taking out my mobile I press SEND. It's a text message, one that in true Blue Peter fashion, I prepared earlier; informing Barry just who his girlfriend's father is.

The silence seems to go on for ever and I wonder if I've miscalculated but then, I can hear clearly, even at this distance.

'What the FUCK? Tell me, is this true?'

I can hear Lily's distraught sobbing so I'm damn sure Munroe can. I strain to see as he makes a dash towards the cottage door.

'No, Sir! Wait.' DC Wilson rushes forward and grabs at Munroe's arm, speaking urgently as he pulls him backwards towards the yard entrance. They stand for a few moments by the car, deep in conversation, Munroe occasionally nodding in agreement.

From the cottage Barry's angry voice spills out into the yard accompanied by the continual snarls and barks of the dogs. The door to their shed shudders violently; they must be hurling themselves against it in a frenzy to escape. The noise they're creating is preventing me hearing what's being said in the cottage but I can pick out Lily's voice in hysterical response. She must be desperate to convince Barry of her innocence and her faith in him.

How I wish I could see what's happening in there. I'm hoping that Barry's violent temper and Munroe's desperation to protect his daughter will combine and result in Lily becoming collateral damage. I so want Munroe to be an instrument in his daughter's destruction but I know it's a long shot and have already decided that if it doesn't come off this time, I won't give up.

Munroe takes a few tentative steps into the yard, Wilson close at his back.

'Barry, be sensible, let Lily go; she's not involved in this. I just want to talk.'

Nothing but silence from the cottage in stark contrast to the maniacal noise still coming from inside the dogs' shed.

'Barry, you're not helping yourself. I've got two firearms officers out here with their sights trained on the cottage. Just give it up and come out, slowly and quietly.'

Tension fills the air, suspense seeming to prevent natural movement; then, very slowly, the front door opens. Lily stands in the opening, Barry a fraction behind her. With her body effectively shielding Barry and holding onto his hand, she takes a couple of steps into the yard. As they near the centre of the yard Munroe moves towards them.

'Lily, come over here to me, now.'

'No, Dad, I won't. You've got it all wrong; you're the one frightening me, not Barry. Tell your officers to stand down, *please*.'

Munroe hesitates; loathe to do as his daughter begs but finally ….

'OK, Lily.' Munroe puts up a hand. 'Hold your fire.'

I can't believe what I'm seeing; it isn't going to work. What the hell has that cunning bitch said to Barry to quell his temper so effectively; he's behaving like a docile lap dog; now the police will never shoot; they're just going to all quietly walk away. Cold fury soaks into me as I fear I must acknowledge failure.

Everything is happening in slow motion. Munroe and Wilson, walking toward Lily and Barry, are effectively blocking my view. I step to one side, trying to get a better angle when suddenly all hell breaks loose; shock freezing everyone in the moment as the dogs' frantic clawing bursts open the door of their shed and they hurtle into the yard, teeth bared in a frenzy of snarling fury as they race toward the little group.

The first dog, launching itself at Munroe, is dropped by a single shot in mid-flight, its agonised scream of pain ripping through the air as the second dog swerves at break-neck speed between Barry and Lily's legs. Aiming for Wilson's ankles it knocks Lily forward just as a second shot rings out. Wilson tumbles to the ground, kicking in frenzied panic at the dog savaging his leg. Barry's shout is heard above the melee, 'Hitler, stop!' The dog instantly releases its grip and slinks to Barry's side.

'Lily! Oh my God, no!' Munroe pitches himself to the ground, gathering Lily into his arms. 'No, please God, no.'

Barry drops alongside as the firearms officers hurry across.

'Oh Christ, she fell forward just as I fired, I couldn't …' the firearms officer stands in total dejection, his mistake too awful to contemplate.

Looking at the tragic tableau before me I'm elated. It's over; at last it's over. I can't believe my luck, I could hug those dogs. I know I need to leave but can't resist looking, savouring the moment; I want this scene imprinted on my memory for ever.

What? What's happening? Wilson is hobbling toward the car and Lily is being helped up, Munroe on one side and Barry on the other. I can see blood on her dress, her head is hanging limply back as the two men support her but I can see she's making a feeble effort … Not dead? *Not dead!*

The unfairness! How can life be so cruel, to let me think I'd succeeded only to take it away again? Anger engulfs me, submerging any sense of reason. No, no, no!

I hurl myself back toward my car. Turning the ignition, I don't even bother to properly close the driver's door but slam into first, third and fourth gears, my foot pressed hard down on the accelerator as I aim the car toward the temporary opening in the fence. I nearly spin out of control as I make the sharp turn left toward the front of the cottage but straighten just in time to avoid smashing into the post and wire fence now on my left. Keeping my foot flat on the floor I hurtle toward the cosy little group as they make their way slowly toward the police cars. They loom larger and larger; a bit closer, just a bit closer and I'll have them.

A gun is fired, the crack of the explosion slicing through the roar of my engine and the thrumming in my ears. The car veers violently away from the group. Frantically, I turn the steering wheel, desperately trying to regain control and direction but it won't respond; it seems to be skidding and sliding over the mud in the yard, carried on by the force of its own momentum even though I'm now applying the brakes, trying to slow it down.

Desperately I spin the steering wheel to the left, the car screeching in protest as it slithers in the mud. The driver's door swings open as the car veers and, in a split second of weird practicality, I register that I didn't fasten my seat belt.

There's a tree, huge, looming out of the darkness. An avenging demon, its branches reaching down, pulling me toward it until it slams into my body, blackness descending and I know I have nothing left.

CHAPTER 16

It's very dark but I'm not frightened; it feels warm, enveloping, like a soft animal pelt wrapped around me, muffling sounds and scents. I want to stay here; I want this peace, this nothingness.

I feel as though I'm suspended in the blackness, gently swaying backward and forward, forward and backward, like I'm on a swing and Matt is here, I can sense him standing just behind me, his hands lightly pushing on my back, keeping the swing in motion. I feel happy, truly happy for the first time in years. He's here for me, doing my bidding. I have him back.

Something touches my face, something external and I raise my hand to brush it away but my hand is held down. Someone is pulling at my eyelids, forcing my eyes open. I can see a pin prick of harsh, white light in the distance that comes closer and closer as I again try to swipe it away. I don't want it; I don't want it to intrude on my darkness. My limbs lash out as my body convulses; a scream rents the air as it's expulsed from my throat and lungs in an agony of despair and futility.

I'm aware of bodies around me, large hands wrestling me down and voices, firmly insistent, 'Annalee, Annalee, it's alright, you're safe now. You've had a bad accident but you're safe now.' I feel a sharp prick in my arm, 'Just relax and let the medication do its work,' and the outside world once more melts away.

The darkness comes and goes but each time it returns it's slightly less dense and Matt is fading with it. I can no longer feel his hands on my back, his breath on the nape of my neck as he leans forward to push me on my swing. 'Don't go, I won't let you leave me again!' I try to twist my body round to see behind but something prevents my moving; my cries are futile. Inexorably I sense the distance between us lengthening and this time, I know his escape is complete.

A bright, cheerful nurse bustles into the room, all crisp linen efficiency. 'Properly awake at last. You had us worried for a while.' She smooths down the covers on the bed before taking up the chart hanging on the metal foot frame. 'Right, young lady, let's just take your temperature and blood pressure and we'll see about getting you up; it's time you found your feet again.'

'Where am I?'

'In hospital; you had a nasty car accident but you'll be fine.'

'How long have I been here?'

'A couple of months,' the nurse notices the horror on my face, 'but don't you worry about that, you'll be seeing Dr Metcalfe this afternoon, he'll explain everything to you then. Now, I want you to try to swing your legs out of the bed and stand, I'll help you and we'll see if you can walk to the bathroom, shall we dear?'

It's late afternoon before the nurse returns pushing a wheelchair.

'I don't need that,' everything in me rebels at the prospect.

'I'm afraid you do, dearie, you're still very weak, your muscles aren't strong enough after so long lying in bed and you need time to build up your stamina. In any case, Dr Metcalfe's room is a long way down the corridors and on the upper floor so we don't want to keep him waiting, do we?' She turns down my bedclothes and helps me out and into the wheelchair, 'There we go, let me just tuck this blanket round your legs and we'll be off.'

It's the first time I've been outside my room and as we trundle down the corridor I'm puzzled by the line of closed doors on either side, designed with reinforced glass in the upper third, all shut; there appear to be no large multi-occupancy wards. There's a man in pyjamas shuffling toward us, head bowed down onto his chest, his fingers tracing the wall as he moves. As we draw level he looks across at me, 'Pretty lady,' he mumbles and reaching out, tries to touch my hair.

'Now then, Jeremy, no touching; remember?' my nurse gently pushes his hand back and keeps walking. 'Sorry about that, dearie, he's quite harmless really; just doesn't understand what's acceptable and what isn't, that's all.'

'What is this place?' I can hear the anxiety in my voice.

'I told you, dearie, you're in hospital.'

'Yes, but which one?'

'Oh I see, St Joseph's.'

'St Joseph's? That's the psychiatric hospital.'

'Yes, that's right.'

Her affirmation tears through me like a poison dart; my fear a silent shriek in my ears.

'Now, here we are; you'll like Dr Metcalfe, I'm sure,' and with that she propels me through the door into a light, airy room. There are a couple of easy chairs, a mahogany desk with inlaid leather surface and a small coffee table. On a unit to the side, I can smell proper coffee as the machine gurgles away. It reminds me of the all-day breakfast café near the park and I feel my mouth moisten with longing.

The man behind the desk is small and dark; he wears a black suit with deep red silk lining that catches the eye as his jacket falls open. His shirt is a pale grey and at his neck, a bow tie, red to match his jacket lining. He's clean shaven yet has a rugged look, the outdoor type. His eyes are grey but not cold, a seductive warmth to them as he looks directly at me.

'Ah, Nurse Fletcher, who do we have here?'

'Annalee Theakston, Doctor,' the nurse replies handing over a file.

The sound of my true name catches my breath; how do these people know such things about me? Instinctively I try to gather my defences but my weakened state makes me vulnerable; I don't seem to be able to marshal my thoughts properly.

The doctor settles himself in one of the chairs and motions to her to help me into the one opposite.

'Thank you, Nurse, I think Annalee and I can manage by ourselves now.'

'Very well, Doctor.' Nurse Fletcher gives me a reassuring pat on the shoulder and leaves the room, quietly closing the door behind her.

Dr Metcalfe sits thumbing through my notes. Glancing up he notices that my eyes are riveted on the coffee machine. 'How very rude of me, would you like a coffee, Annalee?'

I nod, 'Please.'

Immediately he crosses the room and pours us both a cup; standing before me he holds the cup out but retains it until I look up and meet his eyes. 'Thank you,' my voice is a croaked whisper and I notice my hand shake slightly.

He smiles warmly, 'You're welcome.'

He sits back down opposite me, watching intently as I sip the hot liquid, closing my eyes in appreciation of both scent and taste. Noticing, he comments, 'It's surprising how much the little things matter when they've been missing for a while.'

I nod in agreement, continuing to sip, revelling in the sensations.

'Now, Annalee, may I call you Annalee?' Looking at the notes, 'or would you prefer Amelia, I see you've been using that name more recently.'

I decide there's no point denying it.

'Annalee is fine.'

'Right, Annalee it is then, a very pretty name if I may say so.' He shuffles the papers back into a neat pile, returns them to the file and plops them onto his desk. Looking across at me he asks, 'Tell me what you remember about your accident.'

I close my eyes and, hesitantly, 'I was driving too fast, I skidded, there was a tree.' I feel tears prick my eyes and my breathing quickens. The images that parade before my eyes are frightening. 'How badly was I hurt?' I whisper, 'What have I done to myself?'

Dr Metcalfe speaks calmly, reassuringly. 'You were quite badly hurt, Annalee; a couple of broken ribs, a broken collarbone but more importantly you suffered severe head trauma. You've been in a clinically induced coma for six weeks whilst the surgeons and doctors tried to assess the damage to your brain, but it seems you've been incredibly lucky. We believe, in time, you'll make a full recovery.'

Relief wraps its warmth around me as Dr Metcalfe's words sink in but then I remember, 'But, why am I here?'

'You're not well enough to leave yet, but in time.'

'No, I mean, why am I *here*, in St Joseph's?'

Dr Metcalfe leans forward in his chair, resting his elbows on his thighs and looks directly into my eyes. 'We need to talk about what you've been doing; we need to find out why.'

'I … I don't know what you mean?'

'That's why we need to talk, so that together we can unravel all that's been going on and you can move forward, away from all this confusion and pain. Will you take that journey with me, Annalee?'

I hesitate but I instinctively know that, if I refuse, if I obstruct, I will never get out of here, so I nod my agreement.

'Good.' Dr Metcalfe rises and picks up the internal phone, 'Ask Nurse Fletcher to come up please.' He turns back to me, 'Have some food and try to get some sleep. I'll see you again tomorrow afternoon.'

The door opens and the nurse enters, helping me once more into the wheelchair. Pushing me back along the corridor she chats away, 'There's shepherd's pie and apple crumble on this evening's menu so I hope you've got some appetite back; we've got to start building you up, dearie; you're like a veritable stick insect.'

I let her chat away while my mind tries to make sense of my session with Dr Metcalfe but my brain is sluggish, I can't concentrate on any one thing for more than a couple of minutes. As Nurse Fletcher helps me into bed I lie back onto the pillows and give in to overwhelming exhaustion.

◆

Its morning, the sun's watery, winter brightness reflects back off the sterile whiteness of my room, making me squint as I assess my surroundings. Despite having apparently lain in this room for weeks it's only now that I'm starting to function properly that I'm able to take any notice. There isn't much to see; a bedside cabinet, a hospital radio connection and headphones, alarm pull cord and a small drawer unit on the far wall. Idly, I wonder what it contains; I'd like to get up, have a look into those drawers; perhaps my clothes are in there.

Tentatively, I turn back the covers and cautiously manoeuvre my legs over the side of the bed. I notice my shins are covered in multi-coloured bruises and, when I try to use my arms to lever myself up off the bed the weakness in my limbs frightens me and I feel like I'm going to faint. I try to wriggle myself back onto the pillows but my body simply won't co-operate. Hot tears streak my face as panic at my helplessness surges. In fear and desperation I pull the emergency cord. Within a couple of minutes Nurse Fletcher rushes into the room. 'Oh dearie, what are you trying to do? Do you need the bathroom?'

I shake my head as I fling my arms around her neck and sob.

'There, there, dearie, don't distress yourself so, it just takes time, that's all. You'll get back to being your old self soon enough but you've just got to be patient.'

Very gently, as if dealing with a fragile and frightened child, she helps me back into bed. 'You've another session with Dr Metcalfe at three so I'll be here about two. Then you can have a nice shower and wash your hair; I'll help you and you'll be ready to face the world – at least, our little part of it, OK dearie?'

I nod and give her a grateful smile.

Nurse Fletcher is true to her word, dead on two o'clock she reappears bearing shop bought toiletries, 'I thought you might like to use these, much nicer than the hospital issue.'

As she gently helps me remove my hospital gown I catch sight of my reflection in the full-length mirror. The shock is so intense that my knees buckle causing the nurse to catch me in her arms and help me to a seat.

'Now don't you go getting yourself upset over any of that,' she admonishes, 'the bruises will fade soon enough and your hair will grow back before you know it.'

She tries to block my view but I brush her aside. I want to look at what has been done to me. Section by section, I appraise my reflection; the extensive bruising, my shorn scalp, one side covered with barely a quarter inch of spiky tufts. Munroe, Lily, Barry; it feels like they're all mocking me.

As we trundle down the long corridor once more I cast about, looking for other patients but all is quiet, every door firmly closed.

'Nurse, where are the other patients?'

'A lot of them will be in the day room. Once you're stronger and Dr Metcalfe thinks it's OK then you can join them if you'd like.'

I feel myself bristle at the suggestion. Why would I want to join a load of loonies?

Dr Metcalfe rises from his desk as we enter.

'Annalee, come in. Nurse Fletcher is looking after you well, I hope?'

'Yes, thank you, she is.' I smile my thanks at my nurse as she helps me into the chair and takes her leave.

'Coffee?'

'Please.'

'I thought so, I know a fellow coffee lover when I see one.' He pours out two cups and hands me one, waiting to allow me a couple of uninterrupted sips, before he begins. 'Tell me about Matt, Annalee.'

I stop mid-swallow, my surprise evident. By way of explanation he continues, 'You call out his name in your sleep.'

I pause, gathering my thoughts remain an effort. It isn't all caused by the head trauma; I'm sure it's made worse by the pills they keep giving me.

I look into Dr Metcalfe's calming grey eyes as he waits patiently for my response. According to the certificates displayed on his walls he's been practising his craft for many years; has a wealth of practical experience. I silently acknowledge to myself that these sessions will be a very different challenge to those with Barnaby. I'm going to need my wits about me.

I realise that if he knows my true name he knows who Matt was.

'What is it you want to know?'

Dr Metcalfe settles back more comfortably in his chair.

'Tell me about your relationship with him.'

'We were close; he was my big brother; I miss him.'

Simple statements of fact, nothing the good doctor can pull apart.

'What happened to him?'

I don't want to talk about this; I know I'll probably be compelled to at some point but I need to be more in control of my thoughts first, more coherent. I have to put this off so I change the subject.

'How did you know my true name?'

Dr Metcalfe puts down his pen and eyes me thoughtfully, considering his response.

'As I've told you, you were unconscious after your accident and were kept in a clinically induced coma in intensive care for several weeks which meant the medical staff couldn't communicate with you yet it was important that they found out as much as they could, to ensure they gave you the best treatment.

They asked the police to make enquiries into your background but they weren't getting very far, you seemed to be something of a mystery, so eventually the police had your photograph, from your college application papers, published in all the national newspapers. It was then your parents got in touch.'

'My parents?'

I've had nothing to do with my parents for the past couple of years.

'Yes, they identified you from the newspaper article and photograph and got in touch with the area police who put them in touch with the hospital doctors.'

'And they told the hospital doctors what?'

'They gave us some information about your medical background which was useful; it helped us decide on treatment.'

'Have they been to see me?'

Dr Metcalfe looks slightly uncomfortable, concerned as to how I will take his reply.

'No, they said you'd become estranged from them a few years ago and they didn't think you would want to see them.'

I remain silent; I'm not going to be manipulated into a discussion about my relationship with my parents; that would be a whole new can of worms. If he's been speaking with them, then he probably knows something about my past and about Matt and Addie. I need to put an end to this session now; give myself time to think; get my head clearer.

'I'm feeling really tired, Doctor; I'd like to go back to my room now please.'

Dr Metcalfe doesn't argue,

'Very well, we'll talk again soon.'

He reaches for the intercom to summon Nurse Fletcher.

She arrives in just a few minutes; I wonder if she has little else to do but tend me. I've become aware that she seems to be my sole carer; I imagine she reports on me to Dr Metcalfe so I must not let her too close, despite how friendly she seems.

Back in my room, Nurse Fletcher helps me into bed and starts sorting out my pills. Handing me the small container and a glass of water she watches as I make to swallow. I lean back on the pillows and close my eyes until I hear her quietly leave. As soon as the door closes I spit the pills into my hand and get up, flushing them down the toilet. I've no intention of having my wits dulled any longer.

◆

It's been three days since I saw Dr Metcalfe, three days since I stopped taking their damn pills and my head is much clearer.

Nurse Fletcher is bustling about my room, straightening things that don't need straightening. 'Let's just concentrate on getting you stronger. The weather's improving so I think it'd be a good idea if you took a few strolls in the garden, get some fresh air into your lungs.'

'Oh, yes please; anything to get out of this room for a while.' I can get out of bed unaided now and take a few wobbly steps.

'Come and have a look here.' Nurse Fletcher is standing by the drawer unit and as I approach pulls open one of the drawers. 'You can take your pick of what you'd like to wear. I'm sure you're desperate to get out of that hospital gown.'

'But … those are my clothes. How …?'

'Well, I don't know all the ins and outs but I imagine, because you'd been in an accident and were unconscious, the police would have been involved; trying to trace next of kin, finding out what they could about you to help the medical staff. I expect they went to your home. I heard you'd made it really easy for them; everything was neatly packed into a couple of suitcases. Were you supposed to be going on holiday, dearie?'

I shake my head, 'No, at least, I don't think so.'

'No matter, there'll be plenty of other holidays, I'm sure. Now, what are you going to choose?'

I'm finding it difficult to select, it all seems so removed from my current reality but eventually I settle on a long-sleeved T-shirt and jogging pants. Nurse Fletcher looks at me approvingly, 'There, that's better; makes you feel more human, doesn't it? Now, do you think you can walk down to the garden? I'll help and if it's too much to walk back, you just tell me and I'll get the wheelchair.'

I decide to give the walk a try and although very unsteady, I manage it with my nurse's help even though at the start it feels as though I'm dragging my limbs through treacle.

The gardens are lovely, a riot of spring colour. Nurse Fletcher walks a little way with me and then leaves me to sit on a bench by the fountain. The spring sunshine is warm on my face, the breeze a gentle caress. It's so good to be out of the hospital's sterile environment, to re-connect once more with the world.

Nurse has told me that I've another session with Dr Metcalfe at ten o'clock tomorrow morning. I imagine he'll want to resume his questioning about Matt but I shall be better prepared this time.

◆

Morning comes round incredibly quickly, my sleep has been deep and dream-free for the first time in ages leaving me feeling refreshed and looking forward to my session with Dr Metcalfe. I'm sure that he likes me and now that my bruises are fading and my hair is starting to grow back, my natural beauty is slowly being revealed which can only add to my attraction.

'Good to see you already awake, dearie,' Nurse comes in carrying my breakfast tray, 'do you think you'll be able to manage by yourself this morning or would you like me to stay?'

'No, I'll be fine, I'm sure.'

'OK then, I'll be back in an hour to help you down to Dr Metcalfe.'

I bolt down my breakfast; I want to leave as much time as possible to get ready. I've had a chance to look through the things that came from my apartment and found my make-up bag and hair curlers. There are some new slacks and a pretty blouse amongst my clothes that I think I'll wear.

'My word, look at you, what a transformation!' Nurse Fletcher is genuinely surprised, 'and you've curled your hair too; very pretty I must say.'

'Thank you, it does feel good to do something normal for a change.'

'I'm sure it does. Now, off we go, mustn't keep Dr Metcalfe waiting.'

Dr Metcalfe is already settled in his usual chair, two coffees poured and waiting on the low table. I can't believe he behaves in such a thoughtful manner with his other patients and my hopes rise.

'You're looking much better today, Annalee. Are you feeling better?'

'Oh yes, Doctor, much better. I feel I could go home soon.'

'Maybe, but we have some more talking to do, I think; I'd like to understand you better, you're an interesting young lady.'

I find his expression of interest very encouraging.

'Annalee, would you like to talk about your relationship with your parents?'

'There's nothing much to tell. I moved out when I was twenty-four and I haven't seen them since. They're divorced now, did you know?'

Dr Metcalfe shakes his head.

'No, I didn't.'

'Yes, well, they would keep that quiet; need to keep up the pretence of a successful marriage. It took several years but it was Matt's death that was the catalyst. They hung on, for the sake of appearances, until I'd left home. It destroyed them, you know; Matt's death.'

I shrug my indifference.

'We were never close; they're not important to me.'

Dr Metcalfe simply nods an acknowledgement and lets the subject drop.

'At our last session I was asking you about your brother, Matt. I'd like to continue with that now, if that's alright with you?'

I nod my agreement.

'Do you know why Matt took his own life?'

Indeed I do but I give my standard response.

'His fiancée died; a tragic accident.'

I look back down the years, to the day that changed everyone's lives.

It's hot, so very hot and we're on a picnic, Matt, Addie and me. Addie is always good to me, including me, trying so hard not to make me feel left out but I don't care, I simply don't want her here, coming between Matt and me.

We've finished the picnic and lie out on the blanket. Addie's quite squiffy having drunk most of the bottle of wine Matt brought; she's giggling, cuddling up to Matt as he whispers in her ear. I shuffle further away toward the edge of the blanket. I can't stand all this gooey, lovey-dovey stuff; it's embarrassing.

'I'm thirsty.' I can hear the childish whine in my voice.

'You can't be,' Matt looks exasperated, 'You've just drunk a huge bottle of lemonade.'

'Well, I am. It's hot and I'm bored.' Sulkily I start pulling at a loose thread in the blanket.

'Go and get her some more lemonade, Matt. It is hot and I could do with a cold drink too.'

'OK, I'll drive to the shops; anything to please you ladies.'

Matt always does what Addie asks; he *used* to be like that with me.

As Matt's car pulls away I turn to Addie, a cheeky look on my face. 'Now that Matt's gone shall we strip off and have a swim; I'm so hot.'

Addie looks a little doubtful.

'I thought the river wasn't very safe.'

'Oh no, it's fine here; it's further down, nearer the village that you have to be careful. Matt wouldn't have brought us here for the picnic if he thought there was any danger.'

Addie looks from me to the river and back again, a huge grin across her face.

'OK, you're on. Last one in the river's a sissy!'

So saying, she pulls her dress up over her head and stands before me in her white broderie anglaise shift, looking so beautiful with her pale yellow hair catching in the breeze like gossamer strands … a fairy queen.

'Great, oh but I need to pee first, too much lemonade; you go ahead, I'll be back in a minute.' Turning I walk toward the tall bushes behind us. It's true, I do need a pee and in fact, it seems like I'll never stop; I squat there for ages getting rid of all I'd drunk during the afternoon. I eventually emerge and look toward the river; Addie's already in.

She's drifting on her back into the centre of the river, gently moving her arms, propelling herself further and further out, away from the bank and safety. Her eyes are closed, her hair and shift drifting around her reminding me of the painting of Ophelia by Millais.

Dr Metcalfe's voice breaks into my remembrances, gently asking. 'What happened?'

'It was the river, you see; it's not obvious from the bank but there are large holes in the river bed where the flow of the water can drag you down. One second she was floating free, like the most beautiful water lily; the next the river had swallowed her.'

I fall silent, the consequences of my actions that day playing out across my mind like a Shakespearean tragedy.

Quietly, Dr Metcalfe asks, 'What happened when Matt returned?'

Looking back, I'm amazed at how convincing a liar I could be even at the tender age of nine.

'I told him what had happened; that I could only think she'd gone into the river; that I'd gone for a pee and when I got back, her dress was there on the blanket and she just ... wasn't.'

Dr Metcalfe merely continues making notes on his pad. Looking up he reassures me,

'You were a child, Annalee; it's understandable. Well, we've had a very good session this morning but I think it's enough for now.' He steps across to ring for my nurse.

'Just one more thing; the police would like to talk to you about the accident. Do you feel you can do that?'

For a brief moment my stomach knots in a paroxysm of alarm.

'I ... I'm not sure.'

'Well, I can always tell them that you're not up to it yet but they will need to talk with you at some point.'

I consider, maybe it would be best to see them now for it'll be easier for me, if things get tricky, to close the interview; I can claim weakness from my injuries.

'Yes, alright Doctor.'

'Good, I'll let them know.'

Nurse Fletcher knocks and enters.

'Ah, Nurse, would you help Annalee back to her room please?'

My nurse offers her arm to steady me but I hardly need it now. Once my recovery had begun, strength has been returning to my body each day. I'll soon be able to manage without her assistance.

CHAPTER 17

It's another couple of days before I receive a message from Dr Metcalfe that the police will be coming to speak with me that afternoon.

As the time nears I can feel tension building inside me. I've opted to speak with them in my room, that way I can stay in bed and appear weaker than I truly am; which should give me the advantage.

I hear them approaching down the corridor, a murmur of voices and heavy treads. My scalp crawls with an itchiness from new grown hairs and prickling suspense. I close my eyes, take a couple of slow, deep breaths and shrug my shoulders down into a more relaxed posture.

The door opens; Dr Metcalfe enters followed by DC Wilson, a WPC and Nurse Fletcher.

'Annalee, I believe you know DC Wilson.'

I incline my head in acknowledgement. Wilson's stare is coldly appraising.

'DC Wilson wants to have a few words with you about your accident. I've told him that you're still recovering and he's not to stay too long. Nurse Fletcher will remain to ensure you're alright.'

He turns to Wilson as he leaves. 'Not too long, please.'

'I understand.' Wilson nods acceptance.

Nurse Fletcher moves to stand beside me at the head of my bed whilst Wilson remains at the foot with the WPC by the door.

'Hello, Amelia,' he gives me a cursory smile for formality's sake. With a suggestion of sarcasm he continues.

'Or would you prefer Annalee now?'

I look steadily at him, 'Either will do.'

'Then I'll stick with Amelia as that's the name I know you by. Amelia, why were you near Barry Mason's home the night of the accident?'

I lower my eyes and nervously fidget with the edge of the bed sheet.

'I wasn't convinced your DCI believed me when I'd told him how frightened I was of Barry. He just told me to go home, wouldn't offer me any protection, told me to stay with a friend!'

I look up at Nurse Fletcher who places a reassuring hand on my shoulder, her face an expression of disgust at the police treatment.

'I was scared, I had to be sure that you'd arrest Barry; take him into custody so he couldn't harm me. So I went to the cottage to find out if that's what you'd done.'

I look up into Wilson's impassive face; I can't tell whether he believes me or not.

'But why did you drive your car down into the cottage yard and at such speed?'

I let out a trembling breath, working tears into my eyes as if the memory is still so painful.

'From the distance, I wasn't sure what was happening. All I could hear was that dreadful noise of the dogs, barking and snarling and then I saw them break out of their shed, running to attack you all; it was awful. I didn't really think; I just knew I had to try to do something to help so I got in the car and drove. I suppose I thought I could drive at the dogs, scare them away from you but I lost control.'

I put my head into my hands as if the images before my eyes are too horrible to contemplate. Nurse Fletcher takes charge,

'I think that's enough for today, Officer.'

'Just one more question, Nurse. Amelia, why didn't you just leave everything to our firearms officers?'

I raise my head, dabbing at my eyes with the tissue my nurse has handed me.

'Firearms officers? I didn't see any firearms officers. When I'd arrived you were already there; I only saw you and DCI Munroe.'

Wilson appears sceptical but, at a stern look from Nurse Fletcher, decides to let it go.

'Alright, thanks, Amelia. We will need to speak with you again.'

'Why?'

'Just one or two matters we'd like to clear up so we can close our files but we'll liaise with Dr Metcalfe as to the best time.'

He turns, beckoning to the WPC who follows him out.

I lean back on my pillows, a sense of relief tinged with apprehension that they haven't finished with me yet.

Nurse Fletcher tidies my bed linen, smoothing down the covers and plumping up my pillows.

'You just rest there for a bit, dearie and I'll get you a cup of tea.'

As she leaves, I reflect on my situation. I shall have to tread very carefully if I'm to get out of this madhouse.

◆

Another session with Dr Metcalfe but I'm strong enough to walk there by myself now. With every step I take I feel my control returning, both mentally and physically. The relief is immense.

Dr Metcalfe's welcome is as warm as always, I find his concern for me quite touching.

'Annalee, sit down. How are you feeling? I hope the police interview wasn't too bad.'

I'm sure he'll have been given a first-hand account from Nurse Fletcher; it's why he insisted she was there.

I adopt a slightly anxious expression.

'I didn't like having to talk about the accident.'

'No, I expect not. Hopefully you'll be able to put all that behind you very soon.'

He hands me a coffee without asking if I'd like one; it's nice that he's so attentive.

'Annalee, I'd like to talk a little more about Matt and Addie. I understand from your parents that, for quite a while, the police suspected that Matt was responsible for Addie's death. Do you know why they should have thought that?'

The memory of those days still grates, just as it did all those years ago; the way I was side-lined and ignored during the police questioning; their accusations toward Matt; Matt's utter despair at the loss of Addie, it was quite sickening. I still find it hard to comprehend why it should have affected him so much; after all, he still had me.

I take a large gulp of coffee and look directly at Dr Metcalfe to explain.

'Addie was wearing a heavy, rope effect gold necklace; Matt had bought it as a surprise and given it to her the afternoon of the picnic, no-one else knew anything about it. When the water dragged her down, the necklace must have caught on something on the river bed. If it hadn't she might have been able to get herself back up but the clasp didn't release in time. When Matt came back and she wasn't there he was frantic. He immediately dived in, searching and she just sort of bobbed up out of the hole, like the Lady of the Lake. It was horrible. The necklace had gone but the marks of it round her throat were obvious. The police said Matt had strangled her and put her body in the river, to make it look like she'd just drowned.'

'Was there a particular policeman that you can recall?'

I pretend to consider for a while.

'I seem to remember there was one who came round to the house a lot.'

'Can you remember his name?'

'No; I was only nine. It's such a long time ago.'

'Do you think you'd recognise him if you ever saw him again?'

'I can't think I would.'

I cast my mind back to the day the police first knocked at our door.

'Mrs Theakston, I'm DS Munroe; I need to speak with your son, Matt.'

Mother stands meekly back to allow him in. She looks haggard, like she's aged overnight.

Matt is sitting in the lounge with me beside him. A couple of times I've tried to hold his hand to offer comfort but he pulls away, withdrawing further into himself in his misery.

To my nine year old self Munroe seems huge, filling the room like a dark emissary from Hell, the smell of tobacco smoke clinging to his clothes. Ever since the scent of pipe tobacco makes me physically sick.

He starts to question Matt about the picnic but Matt is muddled by grief, his replies are mumbled, incoherent. I can tell Munroe is suspicious.

'It wasn't his fault; Matt wasn't there.'

Munroe ignores me and continues to question Matt.

'There are ligature marks around Addie's neck. Can you explain how they got there?'

Matt dumbly shakes his head; I don't think Munroe's words have even registered.

I try again, louder this time.

'Matt wasn't there. Addie just went for a swim. It was an accident.'

Munroe turns to my mother with an expression of exasperation.

'Will you get your child out of here, please?'

Mother takes hold of my arm, 'Annalee, OUT NOW!' and tugs me off the sofa toward the door. I'm struggling, pulling back towards Matt but it's no use. As

Mother thrusts me out into the hall, closing the door firmly behind me, I hear Munroe.

'Thank you, Mrs Theakston. This is not the place for little girls with wild imaginations. They're merely an irritation.'

Standing in the subdued lighting of the hallway, I vow that one day Munroe will discover just how much of an irritation I can be.

I can tell from Dr Metcalfe's line of questioning that he's been speaking with Munroe for now that Munroe knows my true identity he's probably been putting two and two together.

'Have you ever believed that the police might be to blame for Matt's suicide, because at one time they accused him of Addie's murder?'

I lower my head as if in shame.

'I did think that for a while but it was just my young self, trying to lessen my feelings of guilt that I hadn't been there to stop Addie going into the river. I guess I just needed to blame someone for Matt's death. As I grew up I came to realise how wrong that was.'

'Why was it wrong?'

Dr Metcalfe looks enquiringly into my eyes. I feel he's willing me to prove I'm not harbouring any misconceived notions of blame; if I can satisfy him on that front it could be a big step toward getting out of here.

'Because it wasn't the police's fault they thought what they did; it was understandable. Eventually, the police divers found the necklace; it had caught around a jagged piece of rock on the river bed. They'd also interviewed the village shop keeper who confirmed that Matt was in the shop buying lemonade at the time of the tragedy. Apparently, they hadn't been able to confirm that earlier because the shop keeper had been away; he'd only just returned.'

Dr Metcalfe is writing feverishly in his notebook so I decide to reinforce my steps into the light.

'I admit I thought differently at first but I came to understand that I was just a child trying to deal with the adult world.'

Dr Metcalfe smiles his acknowledgement of the truth of what I'm saying. I smile too but at the gullibility of the self-congratulatory, self-deceiving profession of therapists.

I decide I've had enough for one day and point to a framed photograph on Dr Metcalfe's desk, 'Who's that?'

He glances across, a smile of pleasure on his lips.

'That's my fiancée, Melissa.'

'She's very pretty.'

Dr Metcalfe nods an acceptance of my compliment.

'Well, I think that's all for now, Annalee. Would you like me to call Nurse Fletcher or would you prefer to make your own way back?'

'I'll be fine on my own, thank you Doctor.'

'Oh, I almost forgot. The police would like to speak with you again; a Detective Chief Inspector Munroe.'

Dr Metcalfe looks at me intently, assessing the impact his words have had. I keep my face expressionless.

'When?'

'Tomorrow, about eleven o'clock.'

I simply nod and leave the room.

◆

The weather next day is fine and relatively warm which is a blessing as I organise my meeting with DCI Munroe to take place in the gardens. Control of the situation is everything.

I watch as he makes his way across the lawn to where I'm sitting at a small round table, two chairs positioned opposite one another. He looks like he's over-burdened with responsibility and worry. I wonder why he doesn't just do the world a favour and retire.

'Miss Theakston.' He extends a hand in greeting which I ignore. Sitting down, he looks uncomfortable, over-large for the metal seat.

'Dr Metcalfe says you are well enough to answer a few more questions, to help us clarify some issues in our recent investigations.'

I remain silent, my face impassive so he launches straight in.

'Why did you claim that Barry Mason had threatened and tried to blackmail you?'

'Because he had; because I'd seen him kill his father.'

Munroe leans back a little on his chair, a look of patronising tolerance on his face.

'I have to advise you that our investigations have concluded that Barry didn't kill his father. He hit him and knocked him out for a while but that's all. His father died from a drug overdose.'

I don't understand this.

'But you kept questioning him.'

'Yes; some leads we had pointed in Barry's direction as the main drug dealer in the area but our further enquiries and the recent arrest of a known dealer has found those leads to be false. Barry did not supply his father with drugs and is innocent of murder. Miss Theakston, do you still contend that Barry tried to blackmail you?'

'Yes, Inspector, Barry *did* threaten me to get money from me and I *was* scared of him.'

'Barry emphatically denies that.'

'Then check my bank account; you'll see I withdrew five hundred pounds recently. What do you think I've done with that money; gone on holiday?'

'We have and yes, you did withdraw £500 but we've no evidence of Barry ever having that money and in view of our recent investigations, we are inclined to believe him. On the contrary, I believe you have wasted a great deal of police time and resources.'

As if I care about that.

'But if you didn't believe me, why did you act?'

Munroe's annoyance at the dilemma he faced is obvious.

'At the time of your statement Barry was still a suspect for the drug dealing. We couldn't take the risk.'

You mean you couldn't risk your precious daughter; you weren't concerned for me at all.

He decides to move on.

'Tell me, Miss Theakston, do you know a man called Peter Everard or maybe, Graham Baxter?'

I try to hide my confusion at Munroe bringing Graham into the conversation.

'I … I think I may do. Why do you ask?'

'We clearly have you on CCTV footage entering his apartment block in Coventry and later, you're caught on camera walking down Wigmore Street and going into Brown's Estate Agents. We've spoken with residents in Cadogan House and with an employee at the estate agents who tell us you were making enquiries about him or his apartment. Care to explain?'

My brain is performing somersaults; I can't see the harm in being open about this, after all, I was surely an innocent victim of Graham's stalking.

'I met the man I knew as Peter Everard quite by chance when I spent a few days in Sheffield and we had a brief relationship but after it had ended, I discovered who he really was.'

'And who was that?'

'The younger sibling of Addie, my brother, Matt's girlfriend; she'd drowned; it was an accident but as I was with her at the time, her brother had always blamed me for her death. When I discovered who he was, I was afraid of what he might be planning to do and then it seemed he started stalking me. I considered reporting it to the police but realised they probably wouldn't do anything. If you recall, I told you when you interviewed me at the police station that my nerves were on edge because I felt I was being followed. By then, I was so screwed up with everything that had been going on; I didn't know whether it was Graham or Barry following me about.'

Munroe's look is one of pity as he sighs.

'Well, Miss Theakston, I have to inform you that you're mistaken; he isn't Addie's brother; her brother's name was *Greg* Baxter; he's living in Australia now. Graham Baxter or Peter Everard as he sometimes calls himself is nothing more than a conman.'

I'm having difficulty taking all this in.

'But ... I don't understand. Why should he just leave me without a word, if it was nothing to do with me?'

'Did he? Well, I don't suppose he ever found the right moment to tell you he was bogus from start to finish; probably just easier to vanish. What we do know is that he received a message from an associate warning him that some people were looking for him. He needed to disappear but before he could do that he needed to collect his gear from his Coventry apartment.'

'How do you know all this?'

'Because he was recently found badly beaten up; he'll recover to spend some time at Her Majesty's pleasure but he squealed like the proverbial pig; I think he found on balance he'd be safer shut away. It seems he conned the wrong people, the sort that don't forgive easily. Having investigated further and seen the CCTV footage we questioned him regarding your connection. We needed to be sure you weren't part of his scams, especially in view of your interference with our investigation into the death of Barry's father; but it seems he just saw a relationship with you as a pleasant interlude.'

Munroe's look is of smug satisfaction.

I can't make sense of this, surely I can't have been that wrong as to his true identity; he'd told me his family had moved to Australia and Mrs Lewis …

'But Mrs Lewis, she told me he'd been hanging about, asking questions about me. It was definitely him; he had a kangaroo logo on his jacket.'

I realise as I say it how pathetic that sounds but I'm clutching at straws.

'Ah yes, dear Mrs Lewis. It seems she's very fond of you and was so worried that you were in some kind of trouble she approached us for help and we made some enquiries. It turns out that the man asking questions was a private investigator employed by your college secretary, Janet Stevenson. She was suspicious of your professed qualifications and, along with her apparent animosity toward you, was basically trying to "dig the dirt" to have you fired.'

Munroe fails to hide his amusement at my distress.

'But the emblem?'

'Mrs Lewis' eyesight really isn't very good. It wasn't a kangaroo, it was a rampant lion. The private investigator plays rugby for the local team; it's their emblem.'

I stare at Munroe in disbelief. I can hardly credit it; it's almost funny. I think back to the fateful evening when I recklessly drove my car at that sickening little group. I'd acted on impulse; I'd tossed the coin without planning, unable to resist a momentary urge, compelled by anger and frustration and it had cost me dear. No matter. I'm a great believer in learning from one's mistakes and I haven't lost the main pieces in this game; they're all on the board so I still have everything to play for.

Munroe, oblivious, begins again.

'Do you remember me, Miss Theakston?'

'What?'

'From several years ago; I was the investigating officer into the death of your brother's girlfriend.'

'Were you? No, I hadn't recognised you. It was a long time ago.'

He looks slightly deflated but doesn't argue, instead he asks,

'Why did you befriend my daughter, Lily?'

I knew this would come at some point.

'I didn't know she was your daughter, not for a long time. I met her by chance at an art class and we simply got friendly. How is she now? I don't think I'll ever forgive myself for the accident.'

'She's doing well, thank you.' I hear the slight break of emotion in his voice and can tell he's suspicious but he's aware it's merely a gut instinct, no basis in fact. After all, what harm had I deliberately caused Lily; none that anyone can prove. I want him gone; I want to plan the future.

'If that's all, Inspector I really need to get back inside, it's time for my medication.'

I push my chair back as Munroe stands, stretching his back to relieve the aches the metal seat has caused.

'Yes, I think that's all, Miss Theakston. Thank you for your time.'

His manner toward me is patronising; that of an adult dealing with a difficult child. I watch as he walks toward his car. He may think he's walking out of my life but no-one walks away from me – just ask Matt.

As I stroll back into the hospital, my mind replays that last afternoon with Matt. I was getting fed up with his depression since Addie's death. His misery was way beyond the pale and instead of gravitating back toward me he seemed to be pulling further away.

I was angry that Addie still had such a hold, even in death, so I told him.

'Addie didn't really love you; I've seen her out with someone else. When you went to get the lemonade she was so drunk from all the wine she'd had that she let slip she had no intention of being with you; she even scoffed at the ring you'd bought her. She's been playing you for a fool the whole time!'

Matt places his hands over his ears, crying out that he doesn't believe me but I keep on, yelling now, insisting,

'Why would I lie? I knew all along she didn't love you; it was just a game to her; she thought you were pathetic, moaning after her like you did. I'm glad she went in the river.'

Matt takes his hands away from his ears and looks directly at me, all colour drained from his face like a bloodless corpse, horror etched on his features as sick realisation dawns; his voice a strained whisper.

'No-one swims in that part of the river, you know that. Why didn't you warn her?'

My hands clenched into fists, I glare back.

'Why didn't *you*? I'm not her keeper. Why should I tell her? I never wanted her here. I'm glad she's dead; it's what she deserved. You don't need *her*; you never did; you need *me*!'

Matt looks at me with undisguised revulsion, as if he's seeing me properly for the first time, then walks out into the winter night without another word.

Next day, his body was found at the bottom of the cliff; he'd gone over the edge at our favourite spot.

Everyone assumed that he'd either missed his footing in the dark or that he simply couldn't deal with his grief; that the intense initial police investigation and suspicion of him had upset the balance of his mind.

I didn't bother to disillusion anyone.

◆

It's taken another month of the best performance I could muster but it was worth it – I'm out! I stand at the gates, looking back at the imposing façade of St Joseph's; waiting for my taxi. I have, at my feet, my two suitcases, first packed it seems, a lifetime ago, and in my arms I hold Liliad. I'm told she was found strapped into the passenger seat of my car, although I can't recall putting her there, and had been damaged in the accident. Apparently, when she learnt of everything I'd been through; my estrangement

BIOGRAPHY

Born and brought up in Norfolk (an area still very much in her heart) Lynne Fox moved to Hertfordshire in the 1970's. Having home educated her son for a number of years she worked in a variety of administration roles, eventually becoming a PA and Practice Administrator in the construction industry.

Now happily divorced, retired and living in Welwyn Garden City, this is her debut novel.

from my parents and the loss of my beloved brother, Lily had felt sorry for me and taken Liliad to a doll's hospital to be mended. So sweet and thoughtful; I've written Lily a thank you card, suggesting we have coffee together once I'm settled. She was hesitant at first but I've managed to persuade her that I'm completely well now and she's agreed. So the game can continue.

Looking up at the building I can just make out Dr Metcalfe in his room, standing by the window. He's told me he's very pleased with my recovery, at how well I've adapted, that I've been a model patient and he's proud of me, the way I'm planning to rebuild my life.

I understand from Nurse Fletcher that he's conducting research into psychopathic tendencies in the young; whether nature or nurture has the most influence on how the child develops into adulthood. Like most in his profession he takes himself and his subject seriously; he can't see that it's just a game, of no more significance than a game of chess.

I'm sure he's looking down at where I stand. He says he'll miss me but he needn't worry, I won't be far away. I understand he lives in the new apartment blocks that have been built close to the hospital and I've managed to rent a flat just one street away. That way I'll be close by to give him comfort, to help him over the tragic loss of his fiancée. I know this will happen; I've talked it over with Liliad; we haven't decided on a timescale yet but there's no hurry.